A SKY-Ł

A SKY-BLUE LIFE

MAURICE MOISEIWITSCH

COLDSPRING

First published in Great Britain in 1956
by William Heinemann Ltd

This edition published in 2006
by Coldspring
122 High Street, Burford, Oxfordshire OX18 4QJ

ISBN-10: 0-9553931-0-8
ISBN-13: 978-0-9553931-0-5

Cover design by Cox Design Partnership, Witney
Printed and bound by Alden Group Ltd, Witney
Oxfordshire

PREFACE

This novel was first published fifty years ago, in 1956. It features "an imaginary post-Hutton England test team" taking on Australia in Melbourne. At that time, the distinction between professional and amateur was still made, if less rigidly than before. The last Gentlemen v Players match at Lord's took place as late as 1962. In addition to the tensions that any international sporting event imposes on its participants, A SKY-BLUE LIFE illustrates the cross-currents inherent in a team obliged to unite across a social divide.

The game of cricket has itself moved on. In 1956, only 24 years had passed since the infamous bodyline series, less time than now separates us from the "Botham's Ashes" series of 1981. The laws have changed too, notably, in this case, to limit the number of fielders who can be placed behind square on the leg side. Fast bowlers can no longer pitch short balls to a packed leg trap; nor could the Laker of Manchester 1956 nowadays spin his off-breaks into a field with the likes of Lock and Oakman lurking round the corner. Tactics and expectations were different then. The reader will notice, for example, that an out-swinger, for Moiseiwitsch, is any ball pitched on the stumps and veering away from them, whether to the off or on side, whereas we now talk about away-swing and in-swing (and reverse swing). And these batsmen have no qualms about coming forward to short-pitched deliveries and driving them over cover "on the up".

What can never change is the battle of will and wits between bowler and batsman, the personal demons that drive or destroy each player, and the sheer excitement of a marathon run-chase. However much conventions evolve with the times, the game is still the thing.

CONTENTS

PART ONE

Batting Order

By late afternoon the Australians, having pulled away to a lead of four hundred and seventy-three runs, declared their second innings with two wickets still standing, challenging the English team to beat the total in some eight hours' play.

Wilson, the England team's wicket-keeper, was drinking salt water in the pavilion. "Couldn't even get up a sweat any more out there." He nodded, returning the glare of the Melbourne sun. Jeffers, opening bat, sprawled in an armchair, his water and lemon untouched at his side. Wilson peeled off his pads, nursing a welt at the back of his leg where it had been rubbed raw by the friction of the padstrap. "It's the right leg. Always the right leg. Guess it gets the action all right. You think you use both legs equally? Supposed to be equal partners. You're dead wrong." He put embrocation on the raw place, then began to strip off his shirt, steamed dry in the afternoon heat.

Noel Erskine, number four, splashed a large soda into his liberal measure of Scotch and drank it off in a couple of gulps. "Well, looks an interesting situation. A day and a quarter to make four seventy odd, and the wicket won't help. Nor the damned heat. It's ninety-two in the shade. Hate to think what it is out there."

Wilson looked pale and peaked as he said, "That oven has baked me down to the bones. I've even lost my nut brown complexion. I feel bleached."

He got on the table for a massage and the therapist worked him over with supple sensitive fingers that soothed the tensions and eased the aches of his rigid muscles. He fondled the joints until the pain began to flow out of the limbs. The welt looked angry and red, was obviously agonisingly painful; it would get worse before healing.

Skipper Driffield sat at the writing table studying the list of the batting order:

DRIFFIELD, Sydney
JEFFERS, Robert Owen
STAVENDEN, Don ('Steve')
ERSKINE, Noel St. John
SINCLAIR, Richard Wayne
HALLIDAY, Samuel
HALLIDAY, Harry
WILSON, Benjamin
TOWNSEND, William Francis
MACREADY, Alexander ('Mac')
GOGARTY, Daniel

He liked the challenge of this game; the declaration was a gauntlet which he was determined to pick up. The batting order was the orthodox one for the usual offensive-defensive opening innings. Jeffers and Driffield, the solid players, wearing down the bowling for the principal stroke players, Stavenden, Erskine and Sinclair. Back to the stalwarts, the all-rounders, Sam and Harry Halliday, then Wilson, the hitter, erratic, but when he had his eye in, first rate. The rest were bowlers, pure and simple, but Townsend was a useful stone-waller. Very strong down to number five, with the possible exception of Jeffers, who was the weak spot this series; and the middle order, the Halliday twins, Wilson and Townsend . . . plenty left there to make a fight of it if mere survival was in the balance.

But if Jeffers failed again and young Stavenden was called upon to wear the edge off the fast stuff it would impose a burden on an attacking player and handicap the offensive strategy necessary to win. Stavenden, Erskine and Sinclair was the three-pronged attack he relied on to break through and conquer in the time necessary; they would have to score at the rate of seventy or eighty runs an hour to make up for the lower rate of scoring by the others; if Stavenden was frustrated in his normally aggressive impulse from the start the best they could hope for was a draw. Therefore, it was vital for the openers to wear down the attack. He could not risk Jeffers failing again.

The logical thing was to promote Sam or Harry Halliday to number two, but if separated the twins lacked heart; they leaned too much on each other, and to make them open was too revolutionary a tactic for a Test. Townsend, the stone-waller, was not good enough, either; good enough to make the tail wag when the bowling had passed its peak, but not to face the first furious assault of Ryder and Sterndale, the Aussie fast bowlers.

Driffield's pencil passed down the list several times and then stopped at Wilson. Driffield felt his pulse quicken. Wilson, as wicket-keeper, had been snapping the ball up for more than four hours; he had his eye in; the ball would be the size of a football. When he was seeing the ball big Wilson was a magnificent attacking player.

Of course, he was dog-tired at the moment, but there was a quarter of an hour to rub the numb ache from his limbs and Driffield could hang on to the bowling by avoiding singles until the end of the overs. An hour's rest and Wilson would be a giant in action. Jeffers, at number six after Sinclair—no, number eight in Wilson's place—no need to upset the order for the twins, who were used to partnering Sinclair—yes, Jeffers at number eight might redeem himself. With the bowling worn down he might flower into the dour powerful batting force of his prime.

The longer he thought about it the better the idea appealed to him. Driffield drank his tea and rose.

"How are you feeling, Ben?"

Wilson twisted round on the table and dropped his thumb. Grinning, he said, "Why?"

3

"You've got your eye in. How do you feel about opening?"

Jeffers looked up and exchanged glances with Erskine.

"Me?" Wilson looked startled.

"I know you're tired, Ben, but I think you can see the ball after all those hours behind the stumps. If I collar most of the bowling, think you can make it?"

"If I have to."

"Don't say you can if you're at all doubtful."

"I can make it," said Wilson slowly.

"Good. Then get under a hot shower and put your feet up for as long as you can."

"He's got a nasty bruise here, Mr. Driffield," said the masseur. "Any more rubbing by the padstrap and it's liable to burst and start festering."

"Don't make a thing of it," grumbled Wilson, who was not anxious to miss the honour of opening for England.

Driffield examined the leg. "Can we bandage it?"

"That might not be a good idea in this weather. It's the heat as much as anything that's liable to aggravate it. Bandage will make it comfortable against friction but not against heat."

"I'll play without one pad. It's my right leg, skipper. I'm facing the bowling with my left."

"I know which leg faces the bowling," said Driffield. "No, you can't face that fast stuff without a pad. Besides, you'll feel unbalanced. Can we adjust that padstrap to prevent it rubbing? Cut it free and resew it lower?"

"We'll need twine; thread won't stand it."

"All this fuss. I can manage," said Wilson.

"Anyone here know how to use a needle? Is there an ex-sailor in the house?"

"Anyone can use a needle," said Jeffers.

"Bob," said Driffield to Jeffers. "You'll go in number eight. We'll need a strong player in case the attack breaks down and there's no one who can strengthen the tail as you can."

"I see," said Jeffers. He said quietly, "'Number eight?"

4

"I know it sounds a long way from opener but you'll be a tower of strength there."

Driffield turned from Jeffers. He said to the others, conversationally. "Four seventy-three sounds an awful lot to make in a fourth innings. It works out at about a run a minute. We can do it, I think. It has been done. The Aussies did it way back some years."

"Yes," said Erskine. "But they had Bradman."

There was a laugh.

"Well," said Driffield, "we've got Erskine."

"That's what I mean," said Erskine, and they laughed once more.

"See how it goes," said Driffield. "No need to break our necks. Let's have a go and see how it shapes. We can stone-wall them to death later if we have to."

"You don't want me to stone-wall them, skipper," said Wilson pathetically.

"You just play your usual game. Only more so."

Driffield said, after a pause: "Any comments?"

"Yes," said Jeffers.

"Well, Bob?"

"The Aussies have declared with two wickets in hand. If we go after the runs—which I think is what they're hoping we'll do—we stand a far bigger chance of losing than winning. Sixty runs an hour is all right for an hour or so. But not for eight hours, and not on a crumbling wicket. Why not play it out safe? We're one up in the series. We don't need to take a chance, do we? *Such* a chance. This isn't the game."

"Anyone else feel that way?" said Driffield.

"Don't look at me," muttered Gogarty. They all laughed because Gogarty, who had averaged three runs per innings, was a complete rabbit whose main talent was for turning the ball sharply either right or left at some eighty miles an hour.

"Never mind you," said Driffield. "How about you, Steve?" he asked Stavenden.

5

Stavenden shrugged. "No comment." Stavenden would play an aggressive game under any circumstances; the state of the wicket, the reputation of the bowler, the circumstances of the struggle for victory were of no concern to him; he thrived under opposition, words like caution were not in his vocabulary.

"How about you, Noel?"

Noel St. John Erskine ducked it. He liked Bob Jeffers and his opinion coincided with his; you couldn't divide a policy of play into two: attack to win and, if you couldn't, play for a draw. But he would not let down the skipper.

"Include me out," he said.

"Dick?" Driffield turned to Sinclair, the youngest member of the team, with a soaring reputation.

"I don't know. I guess we can make the runs if we have to."

"Let's be fair to Bob," said Driffield. "It's no good deciding on a policy if our heart isn't in it. I know what the odds are against making such a total in the time. I know that we stand a much better chance of a draw if we don't go after the runs. But . . ." His dark, rather saturnine features, broke into a melancholy smile: "But . . . if we *do* pull it off . . ."

They were visibly impressed. If it did come off, it would be a victory that would never be forgotten.

"I'd like to have a go," said Wilson.

There were no other comments. Driffield nodded. "It's agreed then. We play to win. We're going after the runs. Ben and I will try to open out from the start. It's our only hope in the time. If I'm lucky enough to stay in I'll try to get the field scattered. Once we can get them running in this heat we've got a real chance. They'll be half-dead in an hour. If they start sweating they start dropping catches. If the chance is there get the prima donnas chasing the ball." (The 'prima donnas' were the fast bowlers, Ryder and Sterndale.) He turned to Stavenden. "That new kid, the googly; he's good, he might prove a menace in later games. You've hit peak form, Steve. Can you make him your special target? Go after him. Hammer him.

6

Knock him off his length. Knock him out of Test cricket. Nip him in the bud. Special assignment."

Stavenden nodded; he passed his tongue over his dry lips.

"Well, I guess that's all. Good luck."

Driffield went to have his shower.

"Gentlemen," said Erskine, with a mock flourish guying his brother amateur, the captain: "We play to win. Ours not to reason why."

"Yes," said Jeffers, mirthlessly, "Mr. Driffield and the Duke of Wellington both." He was more alarmed by the effect of the words on his team mates than by the captain's policy. Anybody with common sense would know that the chances of victory were so remote as to be excluded; the Tests with Australia were not light-hearted contests, but big-money commercial propositions; it was the skipper's job to see that England retained its unsurpassed reputation and that could only be assured by wresting every point, every honour. To sacrifice the opportunity of an honourable draw for the sake of something spectacular which was doomed to failure from the start was clearly irresponsible. Jeffers knew it. He was certain that Townsend, the Hallidays, and, for all his stellar reputation, Stavenden, the tried and youthful veteran pro, all knew it, too. They had let him down. For all his amateur aloofness, Driffield was a just man; he had given them every opportunity to voice an opinion, and they had kept quiet. They all knew Jeffers was right, yet one pretty speech full of backs-to-the-wall platitudes had dissolved their common sense.

Driffield rubbed himself down with a rough towel as Erskine entered the shower, humming under his breath.

"Good speech, captain," said Erskine whimsically.

Driffield regarded him sardonically.

"After all," ventured Erskine, "cricket's only a game."

"I take it," said Driffield, "from that remark, that you don't think much of my policy to play to win."

"On the contrary, I think it's absolutely the only thing to do.

7

They've declared, given us a chance of victory. We've got to show them we're men. If a chap with a tommy-gun tosses you a pen-knife it's your duty to attack him with it."

"If that's what you think, why the hell didn't you say so when we were out there?"

"Because," said Erskine, "I have a morbid prejudice about contradicting my skipper. And also," he added, cheerfully, "because of class solidarity."

Driffield shook his head. He was too well accustomed to Erskine's sense of humour to fall a victim to it. "What you mean is that if you were the captain of this team you would do exactly the same," he said. He put on a fresh shirt and new immaculate flannels.

Erskine said, "My, what a figure of a man. No wonder Cynthia repelled all my advances. By the way, while we're on the subject of Marquess of Queensberry Rules, do you think it was quite in order to make that double gaffe about Ben Wilson and Jeffers. You were wrong on both counts."

"Was I?"

Erskine continued amiably: "Ben's out on his feet. He's even lost his tan. He couldn't even get up a sweat after lunch. He was drinking salt water for tea."

"He's got a tongue in his head."

"Damn it, you might have noticed what *I* noticed."

"What about Jeffers?" said Driffield, after a pause. "You mentioned him."

"Bob Jeffers at number eight! Really, Sydney, you might demote a man to second lieutenant, but not to lance-corporal."

Driffield eyed his friend quizzically. "Number eight is a rallying point. I've got to consider the team as a whole, not the vanities of individuals."

Erskine shrugged: "The skipper hath spoke."

"You don't agree?"

"With the policy, yes. But you're wrong about Jeffers. His trouble is confidence. He's off form and if you play him you

8

should play him in his usual batting order. Encourage him to think you have faith in him. Or don't play him at all."

"It's something to think about, Noel. You may be right."

Driffield picked up his bat.

He swung it in his hand. "Do you notice," he said, "how heavy it is at first? When you first face the bowler it seems to weigh a ton. But when you've got your eye in it's like a wand, a baton."

"The brush of Van Gogh, painting pure sunlight," said Erskine, trying to keep a straight face.

Driffield coughed faintly, made a slightly deprecating gesture and went to the door.

"Luck, skipper."

The words were echoed throughout the pavilion as Driffield, joining Wilson, walked out into the glare of the sun once more. Although only a quarter of an hour had elapsed since they had left the field there was a new sense of reality about it; there was a new feeling about the crowd, a sea of white-shirted figures beyond the vast green cameo of the arena, something altogether more ominous yet inspiring about them. Driffield knew it was illusion, and yet surely the only reality was in the relationship between the mind's eye and the object; now the crowd was more ominous and inspiring because its attention was on him . . . and on Ben, of course. When he was the target, when he was the attention of how many thousands of pairs of eyes, wasn't there a form of magnetic impulse directed against him from all these multitudinous telepathic charges communicating their messages? There was no doubt of the difference between this crowd when it was supine, indifferent, like a lazy animal basking in the sun, and the beast it now was, lurking, ready to spring.

Driffield put these feelings away into some secret compartment of his mind with resolution; even the thought of the broadcast commentators who were describing minutely his every action as though he were some fabulous oddity, a freak of nature (he wondered if the others felt the same way about it—

B

Noel, Stavenden, Jeffers), ceased to have a dreamlike absurdity. When he was a boy (and not very good at games) he envied the attention received by the glittering schoolboy personalities of the athletics field, and yet he thought it rather absurd. After all, you played games out of sheer pleasure in being alive, and the contests were merely devices to find fresh expression for it; the solemnities and the pomp, the national fervours that were involved in sport surely reached their final lunacy in these Tests. Here he was in Melbourne, twelve thousand miles away from home, wife and children, for the express purpose of playing a game with a bat and ball, just like any boy on a village green on a Sunday afternoon; and here were these tens of thousands looking on and finding it all perfectly reasonable and proper, as did the millions who listened in every hour or so for days on end, or read the accounts in their papers as religiously as though the fate of nations was involved.

Driffield took stock of the fielders and became aware as always of the easing of tension in himself as soon as he was involved in play. He thoroughly enjoyed cricket and was only uneasy about the preliminaries. Ryder, a tall, good-looking, dark-haired youngster who had been taught to adopt a ferocious scowl when facing new batsmen, gave Driffield a friendly grin; there was no change to be got out of Driffield, who had become inured to crude forms of psychological warfare on the cricket field many years ago. Ryder was the faster of the two fast bowlers, Sterndale the more accurate. Ryder bowled at the rate of ninety miles an hour, Sterndale at the rate of eighty-seven miles an hour. Ryder bowled leg trap, bumpers, yorkers and full tosses aimed at nothing in particular with equal impartiality; on the iron-hard sun-baked pitch the ball was calculated to do odd things. Not that Ryder calculated on anything much. Things just had a habit of happening when Ryder bowled, even the ball hitting the wicket.

It had been a long-standing argument as to whether Ryder had any real skill with the ball, that is, whether the things

Ryder did with it he intended to happen. Nobody had a really conclusive answer to that. The only safe assumption was that Ryder could hit the wicket with the ball occasionally, that is to say, once in every four or five balls; but whatever he did with the ball he probably did faster than anybody in the world.

Driffield assumed from the fact that there were five fielders crouching behind his leg stump that Ryder intended the ball to swing out to leg. In order to do that he would have to use the seam of the ball to turn the eight or nine inches necessary to find the edge of the bat. If it turned, its speed would be such that few batsmen in the world, amongst whom there were only three in the English side, could play it with the middle of the bat. If it did not turn, then nine times out of ten a good batsman could hit it solidly—provided it was within reach of a reasonable stroke.

The first ball bowled by Ryder, which was done in dead silence, and followed a tremendously extended run up to the crease, bounced in the middle of the pitch, soared over Driffield's and the wicket-keeper's head (he was standing about thirty yards behind the stumps) and went for four byes.

Ryder stared disconsolately at the wicket-keeper, who kept a completely expressionless face; he did not wish to discourage the erratic genius or he would have retorted crudely. The next ball, pitched short on the leg, swung unaccountably inwards instead of outwards and buzzed past Driffield's shoulder, missing his ear by a hair, and leaving him somewhat alarmed by the narrowness of his escape. Ryder mouthed something apologetically and Driffield sternly stopped the progress of the game whilst, at his leisure, he examined a rough spot on the leg side. He patted it down.

The next ball seemed to be aimed at Driffield's feet. If he was really quick about it he could half-volley it. Murder to try to play one of Ryder's yorkers off the back foot; the ball was liable to bounce up under his chin and knock him cold. He drove forward. He felt the ball contact easily and speed away. There was a little applause for the first runs of the innings, a comfortable two.

Ryder tried another short-pitched ball, and Driffield guessed that this one would turn a little. It would be necessary to half-volley ruthlessly. His bat flashed in a tremendous off-drive; he caught the ball before it had a chance to play tricks, and it went away faster than it had arrived, beautifully fielded on the boundary after Driffield had taken another two runs.

Usually, either a batsman or a bowler feels himself master of a situation; in this case, neither Ryder nor Driffield quite understood who was mastering whom. Driffield had no knowledge what would happen next, and he was alarmed by the speed and suddenness with which the ball was rising. He could not see the ball all the way. It was out of focus after pitching. This was dangerous, too dangerous with a fast bowler. He would not be lucky again, half-volleying blind.

Then Driffield had a bit of luck. The next ball had gone for another two byes, and Ryder, irritated, had sent down a full toss which Driffield saw clearly. He shifted and then gave it the long handle with a tremendous hook, one of the greatest boundaries seen that day. The crowd were in uproar.

When he faced Ryder again it was with new confidence. There is no one as expensive as a fast bowler off his length and the badly shaken bowler was being quickly out-generalled by a player who had long graduated from face-pulling tactics of intimidation.

He had seized the initiative at the first opportunity and gave every indication of a confidence which he was not altogether feeling. Driffield understood the brittle nature of Ryder's temperament; when he was confident he was a controlled fury, but when shaken and off his length, highly vulnerable to a cool, accurate batsman.

Driffield was no stylist in the superlative sense of the word; he lacked mastery of delicate wristwork which is the hallmark of the truly great. That dazzling late cut, the leg glance judged

12

to an inch and taken at great speed with absolute precision, were not in his repertoire. He was a dour, off the back foot player, easing himself in gradually to mastery over a bowler and then making his runs forcefully in front of the wicket. A slow starter, and then a powerful dominating hitter.

These tactics were useless against an erratic fast bowler on a crumbling wicket. Erskine, Stavenden and Sinclair, once they could see the ball, were fast and agile enough with a variety of strokes to get on top of such a bowler; the danger to them would be in the preliminary phase before their eye was well and truly focused. It was Driffield's task to dampen such a bowler's spirit before he could do damage to the break-through boys; and he had to do it by bluff, by a show of confidence which he was far from feeling. That early boundary was a black eye to Ryder's self-esteem.

If he could follow up his advantage in later overs Driffield knew he had great opportunity of taming the most dangerous opponent his team-mates had to face.

At the end of the over there was a tremendous burst of applause. The crowd were not yet sure, but hopeful, that the English team were out to play for a victory; it seemed incredible that they would have the nerve to attempt anything except a draw. The boundary might well have been a desperate counter-stroke to Ryder's aggressiveness, nothing more. Wilson's tactics with Sterndale would be a clearer indication of intention, because Sterndale's accuracy was proverbial. He was a lanky, bony, wiry figure; Erskine's description of him was an 'animated pair of scissors'. His run up was stiff-legged, with a curious deceptive hop, skip and jump before the bowling crease that confounded inexperienced players, who never quite knew when the ball was intended to leave his hand. He bowled a perfect classical length to a far closer leg field than Ryder, and there was no hope of taking liberties with him; any lapse of concentration was sudden death.

Driffield watched Wilson's stocky figure, powerful and for his bulk surprisingly agile, and prayed that he had been right in his decision to open the innings with him. He heard the bowler's sharp exhalation of breath, the hard stamp of the foot at the moment of propulsion, watched the ball whip up waist-high off the pitch, dead on the leg stump. Wilson shaped up for an easy stroke as though he had all the time in the world, and drove the ball back to the bowler, safe as you please. Driffield blew with relief; there was no doubt about it, Wilson had his eye in; those hours behind the stumps were reaping their reward; Wilson had the chance of the innings of his life. Driffield turned to the precise, almost prim, figure of Sterndale (he looked clerical even in flannels), and said, "How's Margery?" Sterndale pretended he did not hear; it was possible he failed to hear the words at all, his concentration was all-absorbing. The next ball, breaking away to the off, shoulder-high and very dangerous, was left severely alone by Wilson, who shouldered his bat.

"How's Margery?" repeated Driffield as Sterndale passed him back to the run-up point, and once more Sterndale failed to reply. The ball was lower this time, knee-high, swinging to leg, and Wilson moved across its path, drove it to mid-field; they ran twice.

Sterndale caught the ball and was almost out of earshot when the question, tantalising, amiable, like a nagging twinge of tooth-ache, was repeated.

"Shut up, Sydney," Sterndale muttered under his breath.

Driffield was unperturbed. When the ball was bowled and safely patted into the ground he said, "Only trying to be sociable."

Sterndale shook his head in irritation.

Driffield spun the bat and then gently began to toss it by the handle from hand to hand. He timed it that it would be in flight at the moment the ball was bowled.

The ball went wide off the wicket. Wilson stepped across it once more and this time he opened out to it. They ran three times. Driffield, facing Sterndale, gave him a wintry smile; Sterndale returned it venomously. He bowled his ace, a tremendous in-swinger, shooting towards the leg stump; Driffield got on top of it and drove it inches off the ground past mid-on for two runs. There was a roar of appreciation.

The next ball no longer had quite the fire of the earlier balls and was lacking in length; Sterndale was over-compensating his sense of annoyance and had now gone to the other extreme, sent down a slack ball. Driffield seized his chance. He stepped right into it, stepped right down the pitch, with all the leaping grace of Erskine himself; the ball flashed across the boundary with a speed that rooted the fielders.

The crowd was on its feet; the cheering, which lasted for more than a minute, was not for the boundary but for the *decision,* the acceptance of the Australian challenge to make a fight of it. The gauntlet had been picked up. Twice Sterndale was about to make his run and each time the cheering swelled up and he stood, waiting. He looked at Driffield, who stared up at the sky innocently.

The next ball Driffield tapped for a single and Sterndale said to him, "Next time you do that I'll make a sound like a snick."

Driffield pretended not to understand.

As Sterndale turned away to commence his run, Driffield could not resist it. He said: "You never *did* tell me how Margery is."

Sterndale's sense of humour was equal to the strain. "Knock it off, Sydney, or I'll brain you with a bumper."

Driffield pulled the peak of his cap down and waited to face Ryder, momentarily relaxing as the field began to change for the new over. He noted for the hundredth time that the grass was parched, yellowing in the dry heat, and could not be compared with English turf. His focal point of concentration, the red sphere against the aching blue of the sky, the immediate calculation and instinctive co-ordination of movement, the tension, the satisfying contact, how many thousand thousand times . . . The

15

oddity of the situation, the kindly interest of all these multitudes in the personal outcome of his duel with Sterndale or Ryder over a game of ball, was a recurring source of mild astonishment to him. Here, in this green field, under the blue dome of the sky, with the perfume of grass in his nostrils, the relaxed attention of his friendly audience, he felt calm and at peace, a million miles from the world from which any sensible man would want to escape, the world once centred in his father, the northern industrialist who had inspired such fear and respect for all the virtues. What would he say now were he here? A sombre, melancholy man, an upright, forthright citizen, a stiff-necked, church-proud public benefactor, a financial force with a sense of charity, but unloving, aloof, rather frightening. A shadow passed over Driffield's face as the memory of his father came to him unaccountably. What on earth did he have to do with a cricket match in Australia? How he would have lectured his son about too much laxity and self-indulgence; schools were for learning; games were for children, not for men in their prime. It was quite true, of course. It was different for pros, Stavenden and Jeffers, who had made a handsome living, young Sinclair, who was being taken up in a big way, too. But for himself, for Erskine . . .

Noel Erskine had told him not to rely on him for next year; he would not be available for the Tests. This had been a shock to Driffield. Erskine and he had been friends for a number of years, they had been to school together. They had both fallen for the same girl, Cynthia, daughter of the Hon. Vanessa Hannay, and it had looked as though Noel, with his fatal charm for women, would get her; but being Noel he had played with it, refused to be serious, let her slip from his fingers. Sydney had got her, not on the rebound exactly, because Sydney had always been in the picture, a sort of background figure, vigilant, haunting the place like the ghost of Hamlet's father. In the end she turned to him and he promptly married her. She had said to him: "You know I was keen on Noel, darling. In fact, I

16

think I still am. But you're the chap for me. I can respect you. I've been brought up to think that I must respect the man I marry, and I always do what I've been brought up to do." Of course, he knew he hadn't Noel's sparkle, his wit, his worldly manner; he was a bit of a slow starter, rather a dry stick, but he thought he could make her happy; secretly he thought he would make her a darn sight better husband than Noel and, as it happened, he was absolutely right.

They were very happy together, and it got better with the years, too; the children, a boy and a girl, absolutely ideal. Cynthia was County, of course, but she was not one of your hockey-playing, overgrown schoolgirl types who crash into things, clump about the drawing-room in riding boots or snore at the first strains of Chopin. Cynthia enjoyed country life and did all the things she was expected to with spirit and style; she looked well on a horse, was a born diplomat at local functions, and was positively the guiding spirit at the tennis club; but there was something more. She was kindness itself with the children, and Sydney, remembering his frightened, pallid mother, remarked proudly at the easy-going, affectionate relationship between Cynthia and her children. When they were alone they even called her by her Christian name, which he found somehow at once rather shocking and nice. Kindness itself, was the way he thought about her. And so she was. She was the most amiable person. She was warm and affectionate and their physical life was particularly satisfactory. She had a sunny disposition; no one had ever seen her out of sorts or in an ill-humour, and he often complimented her on it. She said: "That's the reward of having a good husband and eating plenty of green salads."

Of course, Noel came to stay with them. They kept open house and Noel, after all, was Sydney's oldest friend, his best friend, perhaps, after poor Roger had been killed in the war; and although Sydney had qualms about their meeting again— Cynthia and Noel, that is—they were soon dispelled. Noel, of course, was the soul of propriety in his friend's home and Cynthia laughed about their former attachment as though it had been some schoolgirl crush; it was obviously all over for her.

Driffield watched them together and decided that the ghost was well and truly laid. He complimented himself on his perspicacity in bringing them together; it was by far the best way of dispelling any lingering memory, however faint, of their former attachment.

Then the West Indies tour cropped up and Noel was not available. Driffield was not happy about leaving Cynthia alone for all those months; it was the first time they had been separated for any length of time. He would have asked her to come with him, but the children were too young and it would be untactful, he felt, as far as his team-mates were concerned, if she were the only wife on the trip; this business of separation from wives was a damned nuisance. "What will you do whilst I'm away?" "Press on regardless," she said. "Seriously, darling." "Well, I have a large house and garden to look after, two children, the tennis club, and there's the charity bazaar the vicar's running next month. The prospect is so exciting I can hardly wait to see you off." "Will you be frightfully bored?" "Darling, I shall be thoroughly bored and there will be moments when I'll miss you so much that I'll feel like breaking things. Don't you know that? But if you think I'm going to deny young John the chance of telling his school friends in later years that his dad captained the England team on the West Indies tour, you're mistaken. No mum has a right to deny that to her schoolboy son."

Driffield was touched. He tried to persuade her to keep open house just as though he was there, too; but she refused. "It won't be much fun unless you're here. And I can't ask single chaps because the situation will be, as they say, somewhat dodgy." Then she turned on him roundly: "But see here, who's worrying about me? What about you and your manly comforts? Who's going to look after them? What are the native girls like? Don't they wear grass skirts? I think that gives them a very unfair advantage, darling." "I'll try and resist the local talent," he promised. "From you," she said, "that's as good as Prudential."

He said: "Wouldn't you care to see Noel whilst I'm away?" She started, then laughed heartily. She kissed him warmly. "So that's what's worrying you!" She looked at him with fond amusement. "You know, I think Noel must represent something rather special in your life. Was he a sort of school-boy hero, the captain of the sixth, who could run a mile in under forty minutes?" "Four minutes," he corrected absent-mindedly. "There, I thought it was something like that." He said: "But doesn't he mean anything to you any more? You were very keen on him at one time." She shook her head won-deringly. "And have the years we've known meant nothing to me? Haven't I grown up and filled out a bit . . . in what I am? Don't you feel how happy we've been together? If you think I'm going to risk any nonsense that might upset us you're eligible for the loony bin." All he could say then was that she must not be too lonely and that he had no objection to her seeing any of their friends, including Noel. "Noel!" she said in contempt. "If it weren't the middle of the morning I'd show you right now how much I love you. And," she added, "for two pins I will anyway."

On the eve of his departure something of his old jealousies and fears were reasserted in spite of her obvious tenderness and sincerity; it was a weakness in himself, he felt, this unworthy suspicion, this lack of faith in her love for him, and, as she recognised, it had something to do with Noel's odd mental ascendancy over him, as though his friend, the golden youth of his schooldays, was the eternal challenge of which he was un-worthy. Driffield shook his head; this sort of self-analysis seemed fanciful stuff to him. The hard fact could not be faced with equanimity: Noel would remain in England whilst he was away at the other end of the world for some months. If

Noel took her out and began to prey on her loneliness, started spinning his masculine charm . . .

Driffield felt gloomy about the whole business; he was particularly annoyed with himself for what he believed to be his unworthy suspicions about Cynthia's sincerity. He felt however that the main danger lay in Noel himself. Now, if Driffield were away in the Army, Noel would never . . . The thought gave Driffield an idea.

He arranged to dine with his friend at his club and for the greater part of the meal they discussed the prospects for the forthcoming tour. Once again Driffield expressed his regret that Erskine would not be with them to strengthen the team and his friend assured him that his commitments were such it was impossible for him to devote any time to an extended trip, but his thoughts would be with his old comrades, and so on. Over the brandy whilst they were exchanging final regrets and good wishes Driffield leaned towards him and said, "By the way, Noel. Do me a favour, will you?" His friend gave him every assurance that he would do everything in his power. "Whilst I'm away . . . Cynthia will be lonely. I hate to think of her by herself and—forgive me if it sounds rather old-fashioned—unprotected. I would appreciate it if you kept an eye on her for me. Saw that she was all right."

He nearly choked over his brandy at the expression on Erskine's face: the glow of conviviality was gone and was replaced by a look of such dejection that Driffield nearly collapsed.

Noel gulped down his brandy and said, "I don't know whether you're really a sitting bird or a crafty old serpent, Sydney."

Driffield kept a blank look of bafflement on his face. Noel nodded: "All right, I'll see she's all right," he promised.

And here came Ryder, more determined than ever. Funny how much can flash through your mind in the moments a field changes, even in the run up for a delivery; no one knew why Driffield smiled just at that moment.

Ryder more determined now. He was used to far more respect in the first fine rapture of his onslaught. The ball hissed off the leaden pitch, almost imperceptibly slowing. It was not ideal for fast bowling by any means. Still he got every ounce of speed off the turgid surface.

"Skipper's in form," said Townsend to Halliday (S.) in the pavilion.

"Skipper arrange anything about a 'night watchman' in case a wicket falls late?" asked Jeffers.

"I reckon he must mean I should go in as usual, in case," said Townsend.

"Did he say so?"

"It's understood."

Jeffers murmured and Stavenden said a trifle irritably: "What does it matter? I don't care if I go in tonight or next day. What difference does it really make?"

"We can't have you exposed to double risk."

Stavenden said under his breath, "What the hell."

"What did you say?" asked Jeffers.

"I said to stop clucking over me like a hen, Bob. I don't care whether I go in tonight or not."

"You don't understand tactics," said Halliday (S.). "Cricket is a contest consisting of tactics. That's something to do with holding back your main force till the most effective use can be made of it."

"You must have read that. Listen to Sam—or is it Harry? (Which one of you is it?) Anyway, he's suddenly become interested in strategy. But I find myself in the embarrassing position of interrupting the genius. Carry on, son. What else?"

Halliday (S.) said with a show of great patience, "Another thing about tactics. It's not so important how the ball is thrown, it's where it finishes up that counts." He paused for his effect. "I made that one up myself," he announced.

"Somebody knock those twins' heads together," grumbled Jeffers. "Listen. If a wicket falls late—say half an hour before close of play—Townsend goes in."

"That's understood," said Townsend, anxious to conceal the skipper's oversight.

"It's understood *now*," said Jeffers. He made a private unprintable observation on captains of amateur status.

Erskine said: "It doesn't matter how the ball is thrown, it's where it lands that counts. You know, that has a swing to it."

"I'm glad," said Jeffers.

"Bob," said Sinclair, "you're the old man of the mountains. How would you sum up cricket in a word?"

Jeffers said it.

"Frightful cynic," said Sinclair, grinning.

"What's eating you, Bob?" asked Halliday (H.).

"It's playing to win. The Battle of Waterloo and the Eton Wall Game. Both," said his twin.

"No, it's not that," said Halliday (H.).

Gogarty, fresh from a shower, came in looking a curious colour in spite of his tan, a tinge of green in it, or so it seemed to Sinclair, who remarked on it; Gogarty brushed the observation aside and sank slowly into a deck-chair, closing his eyes. "You haven't pulled another shoulder muscle?" asked Sinclair.

"No," said Jeffers, "but how would you like a two-hour fast bowling spell in this heat? It's over a hundred out there in the sun."

"Why didn't you cry off?" asked Sinclair.

Jeffers said, "Why did the skipper keep him on?"

Sinclair looked at Halliday (S.) and coughed dryly.

Jeffers said, as though to himself, "It sounds all right putting Wilson in first because he's got his eye in. As an experiment it might come off, once in ten. Not in a Test. They're after blood. They really mean it. A new ball, and going all out in the opening overs. . . . Has Wilson ever faced Ryder when he's taking his thirty-yard run? Not at number eight. The tempo's a bit different then. . . . The edge has gone off the fast stuff. . . ."

"Shut up, Bob," said Stavenden. "There's no one faster behind or in front of the wicket than Wilson with his eye in. I've seen him catch a fly with his left hand. Didn't believe he did it, it was so quick, till he held his fist to my ear and I heard it buzzing." He added: "I wish you and Driffield would get together, Bob. It would be a relief to everyone."

"Sixty runs an hour for an eight-hour spell in the fourth innings. It's ridiculous, isn't it? We all know it is. It's only been done once before in four hundred tests. What sort of odds are those? We've got to play out time. Sam Halliday has a bat as broad as a horse's rump. With me opening with Driffield, Sam going in next, then, with the bowling worn down, Noel and Steve and Dick Sinclair, the cut-and-thrust boys, could have a go if there's a hope of pulling it off. But the edge of the bowling must go, and the heat must take its toll of the field before we can set it up for the kill. Round about three tomorrow we might have broken their backs, and then . . ."

Stavenden was silent.

Halliday (S.) nodded. "There's something in that."

"Wilson would be good then, with the bowling in rags. *That's* the time for a hitter."

"Never mind, son," said Stavenden. "It's only a game."

"Now who told you that?"

They were bringing in Harkness to silly mid-on. Ryder's logic seemed to Driffield quite impenetrable as usual. Twice he had driven past mid-on, an unstoppable ball each time; Ryder was issuing a flamboyant challenge. Wilson, too, was a great puller. This would mean danger to life and limb to Harkness, either way.

Ryder's foot dragged yards past the bowling crease in his follow-through, roughing up the worn patch. Driffield waited till the ball was returned and said, friendly, "Complaints, please."

"Well, what?" said Ryder.

"You're raising a lot of dust with that foot drag. Why don't you let the thing break up naturally?"

"I'm taking my normal follow-through," said Ryder, with dignity. He was about to carry on when Driffield stepped across the wicket. The umpire strolled over.

"Anything wrong?"

"No, not much. This boy drags his foot well in front of the wicket. Look at those skid marks."

"I'm a fast bowler, I can't stop dead in my tracks."

Driffield and the umpire looked hurriedly at the press box. The journalists were watching them through field-glasses; Driffield went through a pantomime demonstrating a churned up pitch. He knew the boys would understand.

"Watch it, Tony," said the umpire to Ryder.

Whilst all this was going on Wilson was taking a quick half minute on the grass. The flannel was sticking to his leg where the strap had rubbed. He wished to heaven the blister would burst; the pain was excruciating. Driffield, knowing Wilson's predicament, went on talking.

"Does that mean you won't do it?" he said to Ryder.

"I'll try not to."

"I want a promise."

"Come on. You heard him say he'll try."

Driffield, watching Wilson out of the corner of his eye, saw him nurse his leg; Wilson was trying to make the blister burst.

"I don't want ifs and maybes. We've had a ruling from the umpire, Tony. How about it?" said Driffield.

"I can only try."

"You can do better than that. I want agreement."

"Come on, Mr. Driffield, let's get on with the game."

"It was your own ruling that he stopped roughing up the pitch. That's how I understood it. Am I wrong?"

"It's my ruling now that we get on with the game."

"When the point is quite clear."

"Oh, come on, Tony. Promise him."

"I promise. Let's get on with it."

"Thank you."

Driffield went over to the *place* and began to pat it down elaborately. Wilson suddenly stretched convulsively, shook his head, and then signalled to Driffield, who looked at him encouragingly. Wilson got up, a little shaky.

Driffield dropped his bat and began to fumble with his gloves.

"What's the matter now?" called the umpire.

Driffield indicated the tape of his gloves. He began to re-tie it carefully. Harkness strolled over, grinning, and helped him.

At last Wilson, catching Driffield's eye, nodded.

"Bit of an old fox, the skipper," said Stavenden appreciatively.

"Reckon it must have been Wilson's blister. Nerving himself up to try and break it," said Jeffers, approvingly. "Don't think much of that glove business, though. Too obvious."

"What would you have done, Bob?" asked Sinclair.

Jeffers said calmly, "Appealed against the light."

"What! With five billion watts of blazing sunshine?"

"That's right. My objection would be that there was too *much* light. Sun dazzle. There's nothing in the rules that specifies what constitutes a legitimate appeal against the light. You look it up. It's taken to mean deficiency of light, but the book doesn't say so. Could be the other way."

"I'm not sure that you're right," said Gogarty, in the long pause that followed.

"Does it matter? By the time the umpire looked it up the job's done."

"I like that," said Halliday (S.) appreciatively. "Yes, I like it."

Jeffers chewed a long straw as he watched Wilson shaping up to Ryder's express special. Without much prospect of rain, and very little dew to bind up the grass, the ground would be a battlefield tomorrow. Fast or slow, the bowling would perform odd tricks. He mentally wrote off the match as a loss; with Driffield's determination to make a fight of it, the possibility of a draw was remote. He wondered how much of the feeling between the skipper and himself was due to his own sense of insecurity. He had nothing against Driffield personally; he often wondered at the bitterness which he felt towards him. Many of the things he said about him in criticism surprised himself. Odd, too, to think that there was no man he personally respected more than the skipper; there was a touch of real character there, a bit of the old hickory; no man could mean more with less words than Driffield, and he stuck to a decision like a leech. There was the time during the second Test when one of Ryder's bumpers chipped a bit off his elbow, and he carried on for more than two hours, and nobody knew a thing about it till later. Jeffers had a retentive memory about things like that, memory going back over the continuing pattern of cricket events for many years now.

He had seen them come and go. Twenty-two years and sixty-six Tests ago he had started as a lad at Lord's, apprenticed to the ground staff. Four years later he was playing for the County; six years, and he was opening for England. He would never forget that match. Not a single face on this field of play, not even Noel, a lanky youngster of eighteen at the time, was there. Driffield was at school, and all these others hero-worshipping him from the stand, Stavenden, the ace of trumps, century-maker, giant and veteran, was a kid with an autograph book. "Oh, Mr. Jeffers—won't you please write something, too? Yours sincerely, I mean, or something like that. I got Wally Hammond, Hutton and Denis Compton, too." And Stavenden was the master now, the spearhead of the assault, the brilliant star burning with an intense light that eclipsed its satellites. And Sinclair, the newcomer, a rising star, waiting to eclipse Stavenden in his turn—he had been in knee trousers. Jeffers shook his head. He came to with a start as the ball thundered from Wilson's bat to the boundary from what looked like a scorcher of matchless length from Sterndale. A shadow passed over Jeffers's face. What did it matter to Wilson? Who would blame him if, uprooted from his customary number eight position to the dizzy eminence and responsibility of opener, he flopped after a few slashes at the ball. It was a four all the way, and the crowd were applauding vigorously. The crowd of course just wanted to see action; they cared little for the finer points of the game, the real subterranean contest of skill when the opening batsman plays for mastery over the preliminary shattering attack, gets the measure of the bowling, learns to get the ball clean in his vision, 'outlined', as Jeffers privately put it to himself, or 'silhouetted', as Erskine in his more fancy jargon expressed it; when a batsman has his tussle of wits and battle of nerves for survival, that period of intense calm with all the real struggle going on under the surface as it were, as when two wrestlers deadlock each other in parallel holds in the ring. There are no fireworks then; the bowling is beaten back and back with a dead bat until the fire is dampened; it's not much to look at to the untrained eye, but to the man who understands cricket such a contest can often speak more eloquently than all the slogging and haymaking in the world; a contest when every trick of the bowler's wrist is studied, every inch of ground before the wicket is tested.

What did Wilson know of such play? Lucky Wilson, Hit-or-Miss Wilson. What did he know of batting as a fine art, as an intellectual problem?

Whilst these thoughts were nibbling at the corner of his mind, he was watching Driffield preparing to remove the menace of Harkness from silly mid-on.

Harkness was the most agile fielder in the world; he could pick them off the ground or out of the air like a conjurer; and he hadn't a nerve in his body. If he wasn't such a useful spin bowler he would have developed into a great wicket-keeper. He usually played first slip, but Ryder was trying his crowding tactics on the leg side, and Harkness was hardly more than ten feet from the batsman, and moving in foot by foot with predatory purpose as Driffield stone-walled a few into the ground. Ryder was beginning to get a good length, and the crowding in movement on the leg side was increasing. If the ball bumped and found the shoulder of the bat or flicked off the edge, there would be a chance. Driffield seemed unconscious of what was going on; he played them back or cautiously dropped them near his feet. He appeared unwilling to attack Ryder bowling an accurate length.

Jeffers knew what would happen. Had he not taught Driffield the art of simulation? Another couple of balls and this one would be a maiden—the first of the new innings.

Sinclair said: "The skipper's beginning to show a bit of respect at last. Ryder's swinging them well now."

Jeffers grinned; the next ball was played with a dead bat cautiously, dropping to within a few feet of the sprawling figure of Harkness. Driffield studied the ground, oblivious of the exchange of glances between Ryder and his favourite fieldsman.

Ryder's run up was a little shorter now, his action more studied; he was sacrificing pace to accuracy and swing. What followed happened with such suddenness that for a few seconds no one on the field moved, unable to understand the situation. Then the umpires hurried across to the prone figure of Harkness. Driffield dropped his bat and joined them, then Ryder and Fallon, the wicket-keeper.

There was some doubt whether Harkness would be able to resume play; after a minute or two he decided to carry on. He then stood a clear thirty yards from the bat at square leg.

"Did you see that? What happened?" They instinctively turned to Jeffers.

"Skipper pulled the ball smack into Harkness from about six feet. Nobody in the world could have fielded it, not the rate it was travelling. Chest-high. Just enough to wind him and discourage him a little. Harkness would have been a real menace there. What we openers have to do for you lot!"

We openers!

It hit him at that moment of speech, but it was too late. The others exchanged glances.

"Sorry, old man," said Driffield. Harkness was rubbing his congested chest, trying to draw breath. "My own darn fault, crowding you." He tried to grin. "Should have known better." Ryder helped his stricken fielder to his feet.

There was a little parleying about whether the twelfth man should be called on, but Harkness waved it all aside. "Square leg for you, Jack." Harkness nodded. Nothing would have persuaded him to return to that. Although he pretended to feel better, he was in fact still suffering acutely. The ball had been driven into his body with such speed that he could not get his hands to obey his instincts in time. That had been the uppermost thought, survival. He knew he was in danger; suddenly it had ceased to become a game. The ball had caught him hard, low on the chest and on the left side.

He crouched down on the turf in his new position and as the bowling continued he felt a wave of nausea, dizziness, and the congestion under his heart was agonisingly painful. Did Driffield really intend to hit him? How near to real antagonism were these contests? The over had started now and he couldn't break off in the middle of it. He should have let twelfth man field in his place. God, he had never felt so sick in all his life. For a moment he knew real fear. It had caught him under the heart, that ball. A ball? A bullet was a ball, too. It could maim . . . and kill. If ony he could vomit, but it wasn't really that sort of pain. More as though someone had found a nerve and banged it hard with a blunt instrument. Just the thought of it brought on a dizziness and there was a redness in front of his eyes.

"Hallo, we're in business again." Townsend rubbed his hands as the ball left Wilson's beefy bat with a crisp acknowledgment. He was not anxious to follow on as 'night watchman', and the way the opening pair were getting control of the game his chances were good. Driffield had scored thirty-two and Wilson twenty-seven in less than an hour. After a very bright and forceful opening, the bowlers, temporarily gaining assurance, had forced them on the defensive, and then, as the sharpness of the pace became dulled a trifle, Driffield began to force the ball away again. Wilson's hitting was still erratic and his placing of the ball bore no relation to the field; such elements of tactics eluded him. Driffield, not nearly so aggressive, got runs the easier way; time and again he found an opening between fieldsmen with strokes that had little of Wilson's savagery behind them.

Wilson had given a difficult chance when he was seventeen, and for a moment it had looked like a running catch at fine leg, but it was missed; such chances had no sobering effect on Wilson, who hooked the next ball in exactly the same way and this time caught it squarely for three runs. Thus in the first hour the rate of scoring was maintained without a wicket fallen, and Driffield, playing a fine innings on a poor pitch that helped Ryder's bumpers, was beginning to bend the field to his will.

Both Jeffers and Stavenden were keenly appreciative of Driffield's intentions. Every stroke, whether a scoring shot or not, was a teaser to get one or two men running, and he continually forced Ryder and Sterndale to field the ball, placing it within their natural orbit but just out of range. On that blazing afternoon every extra exertion was a sore trial. Running or even starting to run, stooping or straining, in addition to the ferocious bursts of energy when bowling, rapidly reduced their effectiveness.

Harkness was replaced by twelfth man almost as an afterthought; he appeared to have been more hurt than was at first

30

realised (Driffield watched his departure with a certain anxiety, not that he felt himself particularly responsible), and Ryder was rested for a few overs by a medium-paced left-hander, Foreman, not a front-line bowler, but extremely accurate, who began to feel for the rough spots raked up by Ryder's foot drag. He found them soon enough, but Driffield knew all about them; and he indicated them to his partner opposite by going over to pat them down with some deliberation. He got a couple of shots off the back foot a little later, and an odd switch was made: Sterndale taken off, a spin bowler, Carmichael, put on for one maiden over, and then Ryder at Sterndale's end. The point of this appeared obscure. Stavenden's opinion in the pavilion was that Ryder could get more bumpers off that end of the pitch, but Erskine and Jeffers offered no comment.

With the third one of his over Ryder got a ball to lift and Driffield staggered back with a badly bruised shoulder; the speed of the ball was such that it sailed high over the wicket-keeper and fine leg and went (as with the first ball of the innings) for four byes. Driffield's shoulder was numb with the shocking impact, and he felt a little cold in the pit of his stomach with the thought that three inches higher it would have caught him on the ear, most certainly have knocked him senseless and possibly burst his ear-drum.

"You're right," said Jeffers to Stavenden. "He can get it to lift that end. It was the old foot drag."

"Does he actually intend to bowl body stuff?" demanded Sinclair.

"Did the skipper intend to hit Harkness?" countered Jeffers.

They contemplated the problem. "This business of body line bowling and hitting out to free a congested field," said Sam Halliday, "it's a bit like the Irish, slip in a whisky when I'm not looking."

Driffield nodded to Ryder, who mouthed his apology dutifully.

31

Of course, this business with Ryder was exactly the same thing as the Harkness incident. You played the normal game, and if in the follow-through your action might endanger someone, the responsibility was not really yours. Harkness had crowded him, Ryder had urged him to play the stroke towards the fielder; Driffield had met the threat with the natural response, but made it retaliation. There was a difference between this and a deliberate policy to injure an opponent. Had he consciously sought to hurt Harkness? He intended the ball to force Harkness from that position in the field regardless of the consequence, and in this sense, in the strictly technical sense, he was guilty, just as the fight to the finish pugilists in pre-glove days would be guilty of manslaughter in the event of a fatality. And similarly Ryder, whose intention in making the ball rise sharply was to catch the shoulder of the bat or the handle, regardless of possible consequence to the batsman, was equally culpable. In this way, at least, the game was no longer a game in the pure sense of athletic contest.

Driffield was one of the very few players who genuinely regretted the unwritten code of permissible practice, but he had long become inured to it, and he accepted the rule stoically and the risks loyally.

His main objection personally was that it ran counter to his other professional loyalty, to the medical profession, of which he was an almost retired member; here of course the code was to subject all other considerations to preserving human life and limb.

He braced himself not to flinch from the next ball; that was another consequence of this type of bowling, the intimidation of it, a very real danger from which not even the most experienced players were immune. It was a little shorter pitched than the others. He hesitated just at the psychological moment, then stepped forward, felt the thud against his pad.

"How's that?"

The decision was poised on the knife edge of judgment; the

ball was swinging out, Driffield knew. . . . The umpire turned his back to the batsman, shaking his head to the bowler.

Gogarty got up and went inside the pavilion. Harry Halliday, catching his twin's eye, followed him. Jeffers rose, too.

"Are you all right?" Jeffers asked the bowler, who had lain down.

"Just a fainting spell. I'll be all right. It's the sun, I think."

"Nothing wrong with the sun," said Jeffers to Harry Halliday. "We all had that."

"What is it then?"

"Exhaustion. Plain and simple. He was in trouble long before tea. A two-hour bowling spell in this weather . . . What do you reckon's the matter with the skipper, letting him carry on? Couldn't he see?"

"Maybe you're exaggerating," said Harry.

"Am I?" He turned to the unconscious figure. "See if you can wake him."

"He's asleep. Why should I?"

"Unconscious, you mean. He'd go on like a sick actor. It riles me to see Driffield so lacking in instinct."

"Good grief, man. There's nothing we can do about it," said Harry. "If we could vote, we'd elect you skipper. Now forget it."

"That's not what I meant, Harry. I don't care who's skipper as long as he confers with the experienced players. It's the team I'm thinking of."

"All right, so he likes to make his own decisions. That's not a bad thing in a captain, Bob, knowing his mind. Even if he does make mistakes occasionally. He didn't ask to be captain. He gets nothing for this tour, except the honour. And his medical practice must suffer like hell as a result."

"You're barmy. Apart from having a fortune of his own he need only whistle and the B.M.A. will give him a sinnycure."

"How do you figure that 'sinnycure' stuff, Bob? Being a

33

doctor isn't like being in a commercial firm. Besides, he's a thundering good bat."

"Nothing wrong with him by County standards. About a dozen pros as good or better. If we had to have an amateur for captain, why not Erskine? He's worth his place in the side as a player, anyway."

"Noel? He's not a solid citizen the way Driffield is."

"I reckon," said Jeffers, easing up a little and grinning sourly, "that what really annoys me about Driffield is that he thinks he's W. G. Grace." He pointed an accusing finger at Harry. "Why do you reckon the Aussies declared? Did they think we have a hope in hell of making the runs? They hoped and prayed we'd fall for this trap; they were counting on the Battle of Waterloo and the Playing Fields of Eton——"

"Maybe they're right, maybe not. Bob, you must get this straight. Driffield isn't skipper simply because he's an amateur and a gentleman. All that stuff was exploded after Hutton. Not only is he worth a place in the side, he's intelligent, got guts, and used to responsibility. I'm for him; maybe he's wrong about going after the runs, but it might come off."

"There's no need to take such a gamble. We're one up in the Tests. Play this one out to a draw and we've still got the advantage. If we lose we'll have a tough road. And you know what a successful English Test team means to cricket. I'm thinking of the game as a popular draw at home."

"That's the way you look at it. Now look, Bob, I hope you don't mind me saying this, but it's the pro's outlook."

"And I'm proud of it."

"I'm not saying anything against it. Maybe you're right; we must play to win the series, that's number one. But here's another point of view. Every Test has its own problems, its own challenge. Look at the odds against us winning this one. Which of the experts would give us a chance in hell? Then . . . what if we do? I reckon we've done something bigger than winning a series. A victory like that doesn't figure any bigger in the record books, but we know it's bigger, you and I and the team and the Aussies, we all know. It's like meeting a challenge which even if it's bigger than the reward itself, after it's over we know something about ourselves we didn't before, and feel good about it. It was a real test." He pulled out his pipe.

Jeffers, unimpressed, sank into a deck-chair; it was no good talking to them while they were under Driffield's spell. Logic and reality made no appeal and was no answer to sentiment.

Harry said, "How many years you been in cricket, Bob?"

"Joined the staff at Lord's when I was fourteen."

"How many Tests?"

"Sixty-six. Thirty-five against the Aussies. Average forty-three, thirty-nine against the Aussies. You should read your Wisden, son. I know yours and Sam's to a decimal point, every player on this field." He nodded. "This will be my last series."

"You're good for years yet. Hobbs played for England in his forty-sixth year, didn't he?"

Jeffers said: "I'm slipping, Harry."

"Balls. A bad patch maybe. Everyone has it. Even the great Walter once made seven ducks in a row."

"In the old days, somehow, there seemed to be a lot more charity in cricket, a lot more heart. They didn't pick and drop players right and left. You should read the papers. It's an education, Harry. A player is just as good as his last game. Headline: *Is Bob Jeffers Finished?* What a thing to wake up to in the morning. . . . And then he puts me in number eight. For twelve years I've opened for England."

Harry was uncomfortable. "It doesn't mean a thing. It's strategy. We need a strong player if the scheme goes wrong and we have to play out time."

It was a distinct relief when Ryder was taken off; Driffield for the first time felt really relaxed, noticed small things like his shirt sticking to his back, things that were driven out of his mind when the tall, good-looking youngster was sending down those erratic expresses. Foreman was back, and Sterndale also relieved by ace off-spinner, Goodger. Wilson faced Goodger with serene self-assurance which the first ball, swerving like a motor out of control, did little to dispel. As it swung out he shouldered his bat and clubbed the ball happily past first slip, who nearly twisted an ankle diving for it. Driffield, as they ran twice, wondered how long Wilson would keep it up; if he hadn't been seeing the ball really well, one of these flailing strokes would have seen it off the edge of the bat without any doubt. Wilson paid little heed to the new disposition of the field, five men within twenty yards of the bat at slip, one at cover, the leg side almost denuded. Goodger made one bounce mid-field, a long hop, and Wilson greeted it agricultural style, with all his strength behind it.

It seemed a loose one, but that was possibly deceptive the way Goodger could make them turn or hang; Wilson connected but not squarely, and the ball began its enervating parabola as Wilcox, on the boundary, began to run; but Driffield was grinning. There was too much beef behind it even with the slice shot of Wilson not to cross the boundary. It fell well into the stands, Goodger shaking his head. Wilson didn't deserve that one.

It was the last big hit of the day. From that moment onwards, with five men on the off side, Goodger began to tie down the batsmen, varying flight and spin, dropping the ball at an unplayable length, forcing one maiden after another. Twice Driffield tried to walk out to it; twice he fell back, his bat upraised, refusing to make a stroke. It was a great compliment. Foreman's stuff was easier; the medium bowler could get nothing like Goodger's turn off the pitch. Even the well-paced length—and in first-class cricket, medium is almost synonymous with fast—proved no obstacle to the batsmen. Driffield had never felt more comfortable. He saw the ball clearly and began to settle down to that hard forcing stuff off the back foot for which he was famous. Even with four men on the boundary—he had managed to scatter the field in this last half-hour of the game—his powerful driving time and again found an opening. Driffield was in his element. The ball, a red comet, flashed along the green, remorselessly impelled by the lunging, graceful figure.

Bob Jeffers said, "You know what I think? I think he doesn't want me to open with him because he feels the atmosphere between us."

"No, Bob."

"He could have asked me, at least, how I felt about going in at the tail end. I mean, not with everybody there, but man to man."

"Sixty-six Tests. . . . That's pretty wonderful. Just a few of the really great. . . . You should at least be thankful for that."

"And then what? What happens to me now, Harry? I needed something to finish it off in style. What have I got to look forward to? A few more years in county cricket, and then . . . coaching in some school, umpiring maybe. Once you know the sort of sound this crowd makes. . . ."

Both men, however, were thinking of more practical matters than their popularity with crowds.

Jeffers said, "If Wilson really comes off he'll open again. And if I fail at number eight, I'm through. Out of the last Test. And then there's no talk that I retired at my peak. I'm out because I'm washed up." He paused; both men understood one another. On retirement, the plum jobs in coaching were given to the really successful pros. "No, I need to make that hundred more than I ever needed it in my life."

Halliday felt uncomfortable. He said: "You'll make it. You can when you want to; you've got the nerve, the experience, what they call the big game temperament."

37

"When you don't need it, that's when you make the runs," Jeffers said.

Sinclair came into the pavilion, complaining about the heat and helping himself to a drink of iced lemon squash.

"How are we doing, Bob? Skipper seems happy."

"It's bumping a lot."

"Better get ready to duck," said Harry Halliday.

Sinclair said, "Duck hell. I'll hook them out of the ground. You heard what the skipper said? We play to win."

Jeffers and Halliday exchanged glances. Harry said, "What do you reckon to make this time, Dick?"

"A hundred. I feel it in the air."

"That'll be three in a row, eh?"

"Will it? If you say so."

"You know darn well it would be," said Bob Jeffers.

"They're bringing back Sterndale and Ryder for the final curtain. Grand finale," said Sinclair happily. "Leg field and bumpers. . . . What they call an attacking field, isn't it, Bob?"

"Driffield doesn't seem to think so."

"He's attacking, too," said Sinclair. "What happens now, Bob? Both sides are attacking each other, nobody defending."

"Doesn't make sense, does it?" said Jeffers.

"No," said the youngster happily, "but it's lots of fun."

The grand finale. Ryder and Sterndale, refreshed, keyed up for the last overs of the day. A tight ring of fielders; seven men on the leg side again. Almost two hours of uninterrupted concentration, and now the batsmen were to face the toughest ordeal of the day.

But after the first few balls had been played successfully and Driffield, refusing to yield to the artificial tension of the time factor, began to push the ball away through the field once more, he had a fleeting moment's thought for the other side. It was an oddity of his, to see the game from either side of the fence at will; he felt that there was a certain amount of desperation

38

about the bowling in the last phase, and wondered if any advantage could be gained by going over fully to meet attack with attack. A psychological point for the next day's play. It was risky, and not very profitable, to try to carry over the memory of supreme confidence. On the other hand, there was little doubt that the fast bowlers would open the attack the next day and any break in their confidence might carry over. Wilson, too, would try anything in his present mood.

At the end of the over he ran a single and faced Sterndale. His leg field was as packed as Ryder's, and Driffield signalled to the umpire and, to the surprise of the bowler, asked for off stump. The umpire, expressionless in spite of his mystification, gave him the new guard. Although this new view of the ball gave Driffield no real advantage he felt that the request might suggest some finesse on his part.

He planned to clear the field with a couple of hooking shots; off stump gave him just a little more room to manœuvre. The mere request at this stage in his innings created a certain mental discomfort on the bowler's part. Sterndale began to have second thoughts about the form of his attack. He had planned a series of outswingers, pitched fairly short, varied with a yorker for the middle stump. Driffield's new stance gave him a moment's doubt; he rather oddly obscured the wicket and gave the feeling that Sterndale would be bowling at the man. Sterndale was more a thinker about these things than Ryder, on whom such finesse would have been wasted.

Driffield's reputation for subtlety was such that the bowler, as he walked off to the mark for his run, had a moment's panic about his field. If he wasn't convinced that Driffield hadn't the supreme timing to try hook shots through a packed defence, he would have spread his field there and then.

The views expressed in the pavilion were mainly sceptical of Driffield's intention.

"Sydney's no hooker," said Erskine, studying the new guard through binoculars. "What's he up to?"

"Get them worried," said Stavenden.

"About what?"

"Does it matter? The artful bugger's kidding them."

At first it seemed as though Stavenden was right, but when the third ball, a good two feet wide of the leg stump, shot past, Driffield, conscious that it wasn't his style, let fly with a round swing that hit the bat *twice* in the hurried follow-through, at the neck and the base of the bat, and sent it past four fieldsmen to fine leg on the boundary. Although only one run was made there was a lot of applause for goodwill to keep the game really lively right up to the last moment.

Wilson, facing the bowler, raised his hand to catch the umpire's attention, and asked, with a straight face, for leg stump.

There was an ironical shout from the leg side field, but the request was repeated and duly granted. Sterndale sent down a snorter spot-on, moving from off to leg stump with the suddenness of a whip, and only by a supreme effort of judgment was the ball blocked. Sterndale walked back to his mark, polishing the ball against his right buttock with every stride.

"They've got him annoyed," said Erskine appreciatively.

Townsend hurriedly took the binoculars as Erskine put them down.

Jeffers said to young Dick Sinclair, "What do you hear from home?"

"She's in Switzerland." He broke off to applaud Driffield's roundhouse swing. "It's fun this time of the year, ski-ing. Sun and snow together. She sent me a picture." He pulled out a snap from his wallet and passed it to Jeffers and Harry Halliday.

Harry grinned, Jeffers looked startled.

"She's only wearing . . ." began Jeffers.

"What the hell! Never seen a girl in a bikini?"

"But she's only wearing the trunks."

40

"Well, it's only a snap." He took the picture back. "We're practically engaged, you know. Don't be so stuffy, Bob."

Jeffers considered it a breach of gallantry to show a private photograph of that sort, but he said nothing.

"Well played, sir!" shouted Sinclair suddenly.

"What's that for? He didn't make a stroke."

"It just came out. I can't help it. Why don't they hurry up? Hit the ball or go out. What a dull game cricket is to watch."

Jeffers said, "That one turned a bit."

Sinclair snorted. "Turned nothing. How on earth can you see from here? It staggers me to hear the commentators make remarks like that. Turned a bit! It looked like a perfectly honest up-and-downer and why Ben pussyfoots around behaving as though it's a hand grenade, I don't know."

"Cricket is a mighty sudden game, Dick. You may feel you're there for the rest of the day and suddenly you're caught with your stumps down." He added quietly, "I knew it turned by the way Wilson covered up. He always does that when the ball plays sudden like."

Sinclair wasn't listening. He mouthed the words, "Hit out or get out."

"Are you really going to marry Barbara?" asked Harry Halliday, who was more than a little envious of Sinclair's facile charm.

"Or Connie. Maybe Stella. I don't know. I haven't decided."

"Just play the field, maybe?"

"No," said Sinclair, a little shortly, not liking Harry's manner.

"Stella is the one you met in Sydney, isn't she?"

"No. You're thinking of Stephanie. She's the one in Sydney."

"My mistake," said Harry.

"Not that I'm sure I want to get married at all," said Sinclair carefully. "I mean, you have to be serious about it. Marriage is a responsibility, you know."

"Of course."

"Some fellows," Sinclair enlarged on his thesis, "they just get married to the first pretty girl they fall for, but a chap has to weigh the pros and cons."

"Such as?"

"I mean, if the girl's the right type."

"Compatibility is important," said Harry Halliday. "What sort of girl are you looking for?"

"Well, that's just the point. I'm not even sure. When I fall for a blonde I think that's what I've been looking for. But then I think, how do I know I wouldn't rather have a red-head?"

"I see what you mean."

Sinclair warmed up to his argument; it was one to which he had obviously given more thought than most topics. "You mentioned compatibility. After all, a girl must share your interests, mustn't she?"

"Yes, that's important, too."

"I should say. For instance, a girl I met once; she was interested in tennis and ice hockey. My interests are cricket and motor racing. Wouldn't do at all. It's important you should find out those things before marriage."

"Very."

"That's what I mean when I say it's a serious problem. That girl I mentioned, Liza, the one who liked ice hockey—you know, she actually offered to give it up for my sake. Well, it was very sweet of her, but I knew it wouldn't work out. I mean, one has to have a sense of proportion about such things. I couldn't really expect her to make such a sacrifice for my sake."

"I see what you mean."

Jeffers said, "Sterndale can be tricky. He can move the ball to leg pretty sharp."

"If you clout it on the hop—any spinner—you're home," said Sinclair. "Clout it before it has a chance to play tricks."

"With slow stuff, yes. How would you deal with the fast?"

"You don't need to hit them. Guide them and they'll go to the boundary on their own steam."

Harry chuckled. "That's my boy."

Jeffers shook his head ruefully.

Noel Erskine entered the pavilion to telephone. "Everybody happy? Still asleep?" He looked at Gogarty's prostrate form questioningly; Jeffers warned him not to touch him with a look. "He'll be all right when he wakes up. Just exhaustion."

Erskine picked up the phone; they half listened, pretending not to. Erskine's telephone conversations, which were made anywhere in the world he found himself, including mid-Pacific, were fascinating.

"Hullo. This is Noel St. John Erskine. May I put a call through to England? Private. I'll pay for it personally. I see . . . that's very gracious of you. I want to speak with Mr. Hillary Forsyth in London. It's a Grosvenor number. . . . Well, what time is it out there? Well, we'll wake him then, won't we? Thank you." He put his hand on the receiver. "I've got a horse in the 'Stakes called Phœnix. I thought you boys might want to avail yourself of a little inside gen."

"Good enough for me," said Jeffers. "Put a fiver on."

"I don't bet," said Sinclair, "Still, seeing it's you, I'll risk a couple of quid."

Erskine made a note.

"What are the odds?' asked Harry Halliday.

"Twenty-eight to one."

"What's wrong with it? I mean the horse."

"Nothing."

"How can you be sure it's going to win?"

"I'm not."

"Then, Noel, for Pete's sake, why?"

"Where's your sense of sportsmanship, Harry? The horse is

called Phœnix." There was no response to this and he was forced to explain. "Beauty rising from the ashes."

"Ah, I didn't know."

Erskine replaced the receiver whilst the call was being put through to England. He slumped down, rubbing his long fingers, and looking hard at Dick Sinclair as though he had seen him for the first time. Sinclair responded with caution; he was a customary target for Erskine's humour.

Harry Halliday got up and strolled out on to the veranda; he had a feeling about his twin brother, who, as he expected, was looking over his shoulder to catch his eye.

"She's there," said Sam. He nodded towards the stands and handed him some binoculars. Harry looked in the direction his brother indicated.

"You taking her out tonight?" asked Harry.

"Well, strictly speaking, it's your turn."

Stavenden was saying to Townsend, who was sitting padded up, watching the last overs, "You can relax. They'll see it through to the finish."

"Don't say that," said Townsend, tapping wood.

"I was holding a bat," said Stavenden, grinning. He added, with good-humoured irony, "What's the idea, tapping wood? I thought it would be a thing of the past, seeing the way you feel about things these days." In recent weeks Townsend had felt the call of religion and was talking about giving up cricket and taking the cloth.

Townsend smiled. "Yes. These old habits die hard. Still, I'm sure He understands."

Stavenden said, "You know, I don't understand it. How does one suddenly see the Light? What happens, Bill? You heard voices?"

"If I'd heard voices," said Townsend, "I'd cut down on the liquor."

"Then how do you get it? I mean, it's not guilty conscience,

44

anything like that. You're no playboy. Now, if it was Noel, or Dick Sinclair, I could understand it, seeing the sort of life they lead. A bit of religion wouldn't hurt them. But you don't have to slow down; you're a quiet type. Peter will be standing with a large key in one hand and a tankard of foaming Bass in the other. You can bet on it."

Townsend smiled at his friend's levity.

"I'm sure He doesn't mind if I haven't been guilty of a cardinal sin."

Stavenden was surprised. "How do you mean? Doesn't mind you *not* being guilty of a cardinal sin?"

Townsend didn't explain and Stavenden shook his head. He tried again. "The way I see it, you don't need to take to religion like that. You're all right. You've got credit in heaven." He was trying to persuade him not to be too serious about his new enthusiasm because of his threat to leave cricket. All Townsend's friends had, in turn, tried to persuade him to give up his idea of becoming a priest. They were concerned about the possible loss of England's greatest fast bowler to the game. Townsend had doggedly persisted in his threat of resignation and had told the selectors about his new vocation, for which he proposed to take tuition on his return to England.

Apart from his simple announcement he did not discuss it at all, made no effort to convert anyone to his beliefs, although there was more than one agnostic in the team, and resisted quite passively all arguments to dissuade him.

"After all there are hundreds and hundreds of good parsons up and down the country. One more or less wouldn't make any difference, but there's no one can bowl fast seam stuff like you." This argument, which Stavenden had repeated almost parrot-like on instructions from Driffield, had no more effect than the others which were on similar lines. Townsend appeared not to hear. This was impressive because Stavenden was not noted for efforts to dissuade anyone from his chosen course of action, spoke rarely at any time, and invariably held the ear of his

45

audience when he did. Townsend had hero-worshipped
Stavenden and had till recently treated his pronouncements as
oracular.

Stavenden shrugged good-humouredly at the lack of response,
and said, "Looks better now, doesn't it? A hundred and eight
for no wickets. If we start the innings tomorrow with all
wickets intact and three hundred and sixty runs to get, we've
got a real chance. Not like four seventy. A *real* chance now,"
he repeated, and added, "Who'd have thought it?"

Driffield, praying inwardly, swept the ball to leg for the fourth
time in the long over, and connected squarely. They ran twice.
The fieldsmen began their general move for the end of the over
as the ball was tossed back to the wicket-keeper. He looked at
the clock. Two more overs, possibly three. It looked as though
the first squall had been weathered safely. He was thinking, as
Stavenden and thousands of others were thinking, three
hundred and sixty with all wickets intact was vitally different
from four seventy. They still had an immensely difficult, almost
superhuman problem, but the chance had ceased to be
theoretical; it was now a practical possibility. He wondered
with a quick prick of humour what the others thought about
it now. And then, for the first time, he thought of Jeffers.
Jeffers, the master tactician, the long-headed planner, the veteran
whose advice was to be his mainstay. He frowned a little; he
would have to watch his antipathy towards Jeffers. It sometimes seemed to Driffield that the fellow had a bee in his bonnet.
He must try harder to understand the man, and more than ever
to master his own feelings about him, which were suspect.

And then, as Sterndale began his run to bowl to Wilson, he
tried to concentrate on the play and dismiss Jeffers from his
mind. Wilson was as confident now as any time during his
innings; even the mistakes he had made did not detract from
it. Of course, he had given one chance, but it was not an easy
one, and during a long innings how few batsmen give no

chances? There it was, Wilson's opening innings justified, his plan of campaign to force the play justified; Jeffers wrong on both counts. . . . *Jeffers*. . . . Was he anxious to make the right decisions for the sake of the game or to score over Jeffers? *Watch it.* A captain was supposed to be beyond ordinary human weaknesses, free from prejudices and personal feelings, and yet he felt more strongly over his triumph over the veteran cricketer's opinions on the method of play than about the success for the team's sake. No, it was not possible. He was hypersensitive in his feelings about Jeffers; he felt guilty before trial. There was no rule in cricket that a captain had to be sympathetic towards every team-mate. He had even argued with the selectors and the manager of the team for the inclusion of Jeffers for the fourth Test; majority opinion was against his inclusion. He had failed in two of three previous Tests and it was strongly believed that if a youngster were to be broken in it would require both of the remaining Tests to acclimatise him to conditions of Australian Test cricket. In spite of this, Driffield had advocated Jeffers's inclusion with a fervour that surprised himself. Did he really feel so guilty about the old-time cricketer that he veered to the other extreme to compensate for it? His arguments, a captain's advocacy, had exerted a tremendous influence on the ultimate decision, he knew, and now he had swung round to the opposite view and demoted him to number eight. Was he entirely sincere in his purpose? Did he really think Wilson was the best opener in the circumstances, or was he rationalising his feelings about partnering a player during the most vulnerable atmosphere of the game? He had never been altogether happy with Jeffers at the opposite end, he had to admit to himself. He did not like his running tactics. Jeffers was a run stealer, in Driffield's opinion; of course, it could be suggested that Jeffers was usually so accurate in his placing of the ball that he had the edge on the field and always took advantage of it. . . . No, to be honest, it had nothing to do with the running between wickets, this aversion of his for opening with Jeffers; it was the older man's dominating control of the game that annoyed him. Jeffers could size up the opposition with a speed and accuracy that was a bit uncanny, and Driffield had to fall in with the programme devised to deal with it by Jeffers, often against his own estimations and in spite of himself. Driffield did not like to be dominated by a player whom he considered his inferior these days in the purely technical sense as a batsman. It was a bit too much to expect that. His other team-mates, on the occasions he partnered them later in an innings—Stavenden, Erskine, Sinclair—usually dominated the game by sheer virtuosity. Stavenden, the scoring machine, Erskine, the stylist, Sinclair, who could hit a cricket stump with a ball from fifty yards—he was content to play second fiddle then; but with Jeffers, who was a shadow of his former glory, it was irritating.

And then this question about the captaincy itself. There was some talk of Jeffers as captain in view of his proverbial knowledge and shrewdness, although, if a professional were to lead the side, why not break in Stavenden, who, although only twenty-eight, already had over thirty Tests behind him, and was a natural choice for an ultimate captaincy of the English team? But the selectors felt it fitting to choose an amateur, provided he had the experience and could support his place as a player, and there was some purpose in their view, which had nothing to do with their own class prejudice. With someone like Erskine in the team who was quite incapable of being kept in order by an old pro like Jeffers, and because of the snobbishness of some of the professionals themselves, it was preferable to have a gentleman lead the team; these class distinctions were good enough for the greatest testing ground, the Army, and they were good enough for a cricket team. (Driffield's own class prejudice, in his opinion, had nothing to do with it.)

And, the captaincy once established with Driffield, it was the duty of the players to support his decisions; argue as much as one liked whilst the discussion was in the open, but once a decision was reached, loyalty to the execution of the plan and the captain was imperative. Driffield was aware that the arguments continued long after a decision was made; the trouble spot was Jeffers, and he felt and suspected that the rest of such over-ripe arguments was Jeffers's conscious or unconscious resentment at Driffield's appointment.

A complicated situation, and regrettable because both men were honest by the ordinary standards of conventional behaviour, and both corrupted by the underground conflict; both were men of stature whose size was diminished by the relationship: a situation full of mischief, yet there was no real villain in the drama.

And now, in spite of himself, Driffield was aware that he was even more pleased with having scored over Jeffers than with the success of his tactics.

As he sent the first ball of the over to Wilson, Sterndale's thoughts automatically shifted to a different set of factors. This was probably the last over he would bowl and, apart from the damage the new innings had done to his average, he was goaded by the confident strength of Wilson's defence. He had never known him so sure of himself. These last balls would carry with them everything Sterndale knew: speed, accuracy and movement. He was determined to clean bowl Wilson if it cost him all his strength. He was aiming to pitch on the off and swing to the leg stump, bowling short of a length, and finally a couple of yorkers.

"Who's the girl?" Macready said to Harry staring through his binoculars.

"Susan."

"We met her at the do the other night. Harkness's sister."

"The willowy one with the superstructure?"

"Quiet, Mac," said Sam. "Harry's serious about her."

"And how about you? Tell me, do you and Sam share the same tooth-brush?"

49

Sam said, "I don't think that's very funny."

"I think you boys are a perfect scream. How much older are you than Sam?"

"About forty minutes."

"A photo finish. What happens when you boys have had a few drinks and look over each other's shoulder into a mirror? It has interesting possibilities," said Macready amiably.

There was no reply.

"If Sam's out and Harry has to go in to bat who can tell that it's not Sam coming back for a second innings, with his eye in? We could tease the Aussies to death with it."

"Jokes about twins are getting a bit thin, Mac. Knock it off," said Townsend.

"They're sitting birds. I can't help it," said Macready.

In the pavilion, Erskine was saying to Sinclair, "And how many runs do you intend to make this time?"

"Bob asked me the same question. I guess I'll make a hundred."

"That would be your third this series?"

"Fourth. I made a hundred in the second innings of the first Test."

"A hundred and twenty-three in the second innings of the second Test," Jeffers corrected absently.

"That's right. It was the second Test. I made sixty-odd the other time."

"And you're going to knock up another century tomorrow?"

"That's it."

"Well," said Erskine, "I'll make a straight bet with you. Even money. A fiver."

"No," said Sinclair, "that would make me a bit anxious."

Erskine caught Jeffers's reaction out of the corner of his eye and felt a twinge of real sympathy for the older man.

"All right, then, I'll bet you that Sam gets Susan. A fiver."

"I don't mind betting you that."

"When Noel gets to the cross-roads he'll toss for Hades or the pearly gates," said Jeffers.

Erskine shook his head, tossing a cigarette over to Jeffers. "I won't have to toss. I'll know."

He turned to Sinclair, who declined the cigarette.

"Still don't smoke?"

"No, sir."

"Don't call me sir. It makes me feel an old man. When will you be twenty-one, Dick?"

"Couple of months."

"What are you going to do to declare your independence?"

"Celebrate, I reckon."

"Wine and women?"

"Up to a point. Got to look after myself, you know."

"Yes, that's the important thing. But, if you don't smoke, it's going to be a frightful handicap to you when the advertisers start signing you up."

"How do you mean?"

"Well, after you've won the series for us all the advertisers will be after you to promote their products, you know."

"You think so?"

Erskine appeared surprised. "Naturally. They do it with all the top stars of sport, films, TV. You'll have to pretend to smoke, perhaps."

"Oh, no," said Sinclair, shocked. "I wouldn't let my fans down. Besides, I couldn't honestly advertise a product if I didn't believe in it."

"Do you really mean that?"

Jeffers said, "Leave the kid alone, Noel."

At this point the telephone rang and Erskine went to answer it. It was his call from England. "Hallo, Hillary. I'm sorry to wake you. Thank you, that's appreciated. Oh, yes, I think we must. We have youth on our side. A hundred and twelve for no wickets. Thanks, Hillary, I heard about the stock. Any chance of the market changing?—What a bore.—About six weeks. There's one more Test and the bits and pieces. I intend to fly back. You'll keep me posted by wire? Good.—Before you go back to bed, my horse Phœnix is running tomorrow your time—the change of time confuses me. I'd like to put some money on for some friends. Five and two. And a thousand for me.—Yes. Thanks. All the best. Love to Claire. Good-night to you. Bless you."

He hung up. Sinclair tried to catch Jeffers's eye when Erskine announced his own bet; Jeffers shook his head.

"Noel," said Jeffers reproachfully.

"Don't say it, Bob."

"You really think that horse will win?" asked Sinclair.

"You really think you'll make a century?"

"Cripes, if I had a thousand on a horse I'd not sleep all night."

Erskine said, "Do you think I will?" He said it lightly, but Jeffers stared hard at him.

"Noel . . ." he began, but Erskine deliberately turned to Sinclair. His voice had the same calm innocence he had used before with the youngster. "Now, Dick . . . who's the latest?"

"No one special. You know what they say about numbers."

"No recent snaps?"

"Well . . . seeing it's you. I got this from Barbara." He extracted the well thumbed photograph much to Jeffers's disapproval.

"I say, she's a pip," said Erskine, and whistled dutifully. "These lean-breasted ones are very passionate, aren't they? It's a form of compensation. They're trying to prove it."

"Prove what?" said Sinclair, fascinated.

"Well, you're a little young to understand. . . ."

"I'm not that young."

"When did you lose your virginity, Dick?"

Jeffers said, "Turn it up, Noel."

"Nonsense. The boy wants to tell me. You want to tell Uncle Noel, don't you?"

52

"I don't like to be kidded all the time, Noel," said Sinclair.

"But I'm not. I'm very interested. Don't you know, Dick, you're a modern phenomenon; the things you do are practically of historical interest?"

"Oh, rot."

"You think not? What made the Greeks famous? A few pieces of sculpture and the fact that they originated the Olympic Games. Who remembers their politicians, their generals? Nobody. But everyone knows Olympiad, marathon. Why, in a popularity contest, who do you think would get more votes, Dick or the Minister of Labour? Who remembers the name of the man who discovered penicillin? But everybody knows Stanley Matthews. What you do or say, Dick, what you eat for breakfast, your sleeping habits, are matters of public importance. Aren't they, Bob?"

"Stop trying to take the michael," said Jeffers.

"I don't mind," said Sinclair.

"You see, he really believes it. You do, don't you, Dick? Tell me," he said, in the manner of an eager interviewer, "what proportion of your fan letters are from beddable young women? Good heavens, if I had your opportunities I would never, never sleep alone."

Sinclair said, grinning, "Oh, go to hell."

"Richard Wayne Sinclair, the golden boy of cricket! Mind you, you've got to have more than a talent for late cutting, you've also got to have dimples."

"That's about enough," said Jeffers.

"He doesn't mind. He said so. As a matter of fact, it will do him good. He doesn't get enough kidding outside this club."

"He's right, Bob. All this fancy publicity I get is enough to turn a chap's head. I have to watch it," said Sinclair, calmly.

Jeffers said, "Enjoy it while you can, son. Don't take any notice of Noel. You're only young once."

Sam Halliday came in and announced, "Lord Longstop's out front. He wants a word with Master Richard."

"Lord Longstop?"

"That's D'Arcy of the *Gazette,* the daddy of them all," said Noel. ."He wants to interview you for his column."

"Right ho," said Sinclair.

Erskine said, dryly, "Dick . . . seriously, watch what you say. He's tricky. Don't overdo your small boy stuff."

"This isn't my first newspaper interview, Noel," said Sinclair.

Sam left with Sinclair, and Bob Jeffers and Erskine watched the cricket. After a while Jeffers said, "You go a bit too far, Noel. I like the boy. He's simple, but he's not really spoiled."

"He will be. Twenty. . . . It shouldn't happen to a kid like that. It's not fair, he doesn't know a thing about life. When he finds out he won't know what's hit him."

Jeffers said, "When the average chap in the average job is forty he reckons he's at his best. All Dick will have is the memory of what he has now."

Erskine said, after a pause, "There's something in that." He added, "By the way, Bob, what did you do in your first series? Didn't you make three centuries?"

Driffield felt Sterndale's shadow, heard the savage exhalation of breath, the thud of the boot as he heeled the turf for the swing that propelled the ball, watched the sure response from Wilson, heard the dry sound of bat meeting leather squarely. Four more this over and Wilson would be out of trouble. The silence on the stadium was complete; even when Wilson scored during the over there was no sound; the thousands of spectators were wrapped up in the drama of final curtain. A hundred and fourteen and an unbroken stand for the opening partnership. Something had to be done in these last couple of overs to transform the picture. The English team had scored at a crisp tempo, a run a minute almost to the minute; from almost certain defeat they had fought back and created a chance of victory. Wilson was playing out the last balls easily

54

and well. Even the presence of a close field did nothing either to tempt him or intimidate him.

How many crises are there in a game of cricket? There are the well marked stages of the game itself, the opening overs, the first overs with a new ball, the last overs before lunch, the last overs before tea, and before close of play; the stage when the batsman needs three runs for his fifty, four runs for his century; the introduction of a new bowler; the first over to a new batsman; crisis and tempo, a series of peaks on the temperature chart of the game. And there was never a moment when one was really secure. It only needed one ball.

Driffield counted the running strides, felt the shadow. This one pitched short, was so fast that Wilson did not shoulder his bat as usual; he stabbed forward, missed, the wicket-keeper gathered the ball twenty yards back. Another inch or two and the leg stump would have been plucked out of the ground. Again, another yorker, dead on the off stump, with slightly less swing; Wilson crouched, felt for it. The previous ball had unsettled him. He connected awkwardly. Two more. Two more, and Sterndale was on top, Wilson feeling the strain, harassed by the aggressiveness of the fast bowler who was putting his final effort into this stuff. Where did he get the energy? A fire flares up momentarily before it dies.

Sterndale running up, the sobbing hiss of breath between teeth, the stamp of the boot, the vicious swing, Wilson no longer shaping naturally for the stroke, the field crouching within a few yards of the bat, the lesson of Harkness ignored or forgotten.

"Three centuries." Jeffers nodded. "Including a double. Two hundred and eighteen not out in the last Test at the Oval."

"Yes, I remember that," said Noel. "I was down from school for the hols. I saw you play on the second day. Yes, Bob, the grass was greener in those days. When you passed your second hundred you straight-drove one clean over the roof. It was one of the best strokes I ever saw in my life. I shall never forget it."

"Well, it was a long time ago."

"Ever thought of retiring, Bob?"

"Did you read the papers this morning?"

"No, no. That's nonsense."

"I was thinking of retiring next year. I was hoping to see the series through . . . finish on a high note. It would mean a lot to me."

"You will, of course."

"I don't know. I've been dropped to number eight. If I don't do something spectacular this time, I've had it for the last Test."

"Think so?"

"What do you think? I've averaged eighteen in this series."

"You made a hundred against Tasmania."

"That doesn't count."

"Maybe you try too hard."

"Maybe. But it's not the Jeffers you remember when the grass was a little greener, is it, Noel?"

"It means so much to you to finish the series?"

"It would make a big difference if I'm not dropped. There are good jobs going—you know the way things are. People only remember what you did last time."

"Don't worry. There's no one who can really take your place as an opener."

Jeffers said, "Noel, I sit here hating myself. Do you know why?" Jeffers pulled at his pipe a moment. "For the first time in my life I've wanted a player to flop. I've been glued here watching Wilson, hoping and praying he'd fail, and feeling sick at the thought of myself."

Erskine said, "It's not that important. Who remembers what Sutcliffe or Washbrook or Hutton made in the last Test?"

"Because they retired. They weren't sacked. If you hang on a little longer than you're wanted it turns sour."

56

"Think of your record, Bob!"

"I keep thinking of the pros who were in the limelight and who finished up as umpires in minor counties or even drunks in the poor-house. What trade will I know when I'm forty-two or three? This has been my life."

"Cut it out, Bob. Go and hit the ball over the roof. You've still got it. You're not as young as you were, but you've a hundred times more experience."

Jeffers said, "Do you really want to help me, Noel?"

"Any way I can."

"You're a friend of the skipper. He listens to you. . . . I think you were at school together?"

"I'll speak to him."

"Not if you think I'm through. Only if you believe in me."

"Listen, Bob, I think we need you and what's more I reckon we owe it to you. After what you've done for cricket, cricket ought to do this much for you. Now forget it. I'll certainly talk to Sydney about this."

"I'm most grateful. . . ."

"Shut up."

Jeffers returned to watching the game. Driffield was no doubt pleased with himself over the success of his tactics; he was playing a sound innings, one of his best, and Wilson might soon top his highest score in a Test; a fighting chance for tomorrow, after all. But Jeffers was still very sceptical. He had seen too many promising situations—and during the course of a game a situation always *looks* promising at some stage or other—to be lured into optimism. There was the new ball tomorrow, a fresh field, refreshed bowlers, and, if there was any dew or other moisture during the night, the possibilities of a pretty fast wicket in the early stages, which, when dried off, would be sufficiently worn to prove a happy hunting ground for the spin bowlers. The Aussies were keeping their ace up their sleeve, the youngster who moved like a cat and could get more turn on a crumbling wicket than anyone since O'Reilly.

57   E

Wilson would no longer have his eye in. Whether he survived the night's play or not wasn't important. He'd be shattered by Ryder or Sterndale within a few minutes in their opening spell. No, Jeffers remained sceptical.

"Why do you never watch play, Noel?"

"It's a ridiculous game to watch. The ball's far too small."

Sinclair said to Harry Halliday, "They want me to write for the press!"

"Well, you can spell your name."

"What do you know? I'm an author. I used to be almost bottom at English composition."

"How much are they offering you?"

"Oh, I didn't discuss terms. I wouldn't do that till I found out how much it's worth."

Harry nodded. "Good boy. You keep your head screwed on."

Wilson snicked the last ball and it was deflected wide of third man, an easy single. Driffield, seeing the almost exaggerated relief in the exhausted face, waved him back. He would face Ryder's last over.

Sterndale went off, frowning, an angry man, genuinely bad-tempered with the batsman's obstinacy. He had been encouraged to allow his more child-like passions to flow whilst bowling. He grimaced at Driffield and this time he meant it. Driffield grinned his slightly sinister grin. As Ryder was about to bowl there was a movement in the crowd. The last minutes of the day's play always carried with them a slight exodus to the gates; some shadows fell on the sight screen, more than an annoyance at this tense stage. But there was nothing to be done about it. Driffield was distracted for the odd fraction of a second, his concentration flagged. When he was focusing his attention, the ball was travelling; it came up high, struck the handle of his bat, shot off like a projectile towards the wicket-keeper, hard to his left hand. Fallon sprawled, the corner of

58

his thumb touched the ball, it was checked and trickled to the ground; there was a groan.

Ryder was fighting mad. The next ball came up even higher, chin-high, and Driffield ducked like a boxer, dropping his bat and going down on one knee; he was breathless. Then Ryder bowled a full toss which normally would be sent contemptuously over the boundary; Driffield played back and let it fall from his bat. There was a moment's relief and then an express, over-pitched again, tempting him to hit out. Matching the bowler's passion Driffield drove it back to him along the ground, a clean powerful stroke and Ryder instinctively went down to field it. The impact of the ball against his naked hand almost split the skin. He sucked the tingling palm. Out of sheer exasperated exhaustion with this immovable object he sent down an ordinary slow one, out of the blue, a chinaman; he had the odd one up his sleeve in certain circumstances. Driffield instinctively stepped out to it, changed his mind in mid-stroke, was carried on by the impetus in spite of himself, and saw the ball move away quickly and safely to mid-on, who missed it and hardly bothered to run for it. Neither batsman moved. Driffield looked towards Wilson, who simply shook his head, continuing to sit on his bat; Wilson had nothing left.

The last balls of the over were almost token deliveries. Driffield was about to move off the field when the umpire signalled a last over. The preceding one had passed so quickly that there was time for one more. There was a hurried consultation as Sterndale came to fetch the ball, then it was tossed to Goodger.

The anti-climax exasperated Wilson. He stared at Driffield, his face stiff with fatigue. Driffield had a moment's panic. Wilson had shot his bolt in that last over, believing it to be the final one; he hadn't the energy or the will to readjust himself. The strain behind the wicket, the even greater strain in front of it, continuing in the grilling heat for six hours, was reaching breaking point.

Goodger began to re-orientate the field, bringing in three extra men to slip and cover. Fallon, the wicket-keeper, came and almost sat on the stumps.

"A long day," he said chattily.

"Christ, I thought it was the last one," muttered Wilson.

Goodger found Driffield beside him. As he commenced his run, Driffield trotted up parallel with him. As he quickened his pace, Driffield increased his. They were running neck and neck. Goodger bowled, Driffield continued to run to mid-field. Wilson took the broad hint, tensed, found the ball well in focus and slammed it with his last mustered strength. It went straight to second slip, fielding deep. Wilson began to run, Driffield sprinted, there was a mixture of cheering, laughing and ironic booing. Driffield flashed home as the middle stump was hefted out of the ground by the indignant Fallon.

Driffield did not wait for any appeal. He wheeled on the umpire pointing to Fallon's gloves which had broken the wicket in anticipation of fielding the ball.

Fallon made no appeal.

There was applause from the pavilion.

"That was a chance," said Townsend.

"I guess the skipper knew Wilson's got nothing left," said Stavenden. He had marked the sad display of the wicket-keeper over Sterndale's last over.

Jeffers had noted it, too. "That was a plucky move," he said to Erskine. "I guess Wilson is played out."

Erskine was quick to appreciate it. "Good for Sydney. Still, it's what I'd have expected of him."

"And he's played a grand innings," said Jeffers.

"Great."

Jeffers looked at Erskine defiantly. "A real captain's innings," he said firmly, and Erskine, knowing what an effort it must have cost him to say it, had a moment's profound wonder about his fellow man.

Conversation Piece

"IT's not exactly like a provincial town," said Stavenden, trying to describe Johannesburg to Sinclair. "There's a bigness about it that has nothing to do with the size of buildings. Noel can explain it better."

They were discussing their favourite touring countries. The veterans were agreed that South African hospitality and friendliness had no equal.

"I wouldn't mind going there when I'm sent out to grass," said Macready. "I'd like to settle down on a farm in a country that has space and opportunity."

They were sitting in the private dining-room in the hotel, eating and drinking. Noel was playing the piano. He had asked for *tournedos* in the French manner and had tried to explain to the head-waiter how it should be prepared. A few evenings back he had dined at a small, well recommended restaurant and was presented with a steak that must have weighed two pounds. When he cut it, blood spilled off his knife. "How can I eat this?" he complained to the waiter. "Call the chef." The waiter went into the kitchen, put on a small apron and returned, carrying a knife and fork. He tossed these down on the table in front of Erskine and said, "With these."

"And their drinking habits," complained Erskine, with a shudder, referring to the peculiar licensing hour (in the singular), when an evening's carousing had to be telescoped into sixty dramatic minutes.

"Never mind," said Harry Halliday, "women are women the world over."

They immediately passed to the main topic of the dining-room.

Erskine played a modern study with a flourish, relaxed, drank a glass of wine, saying, "With a girl faith, with a woman hope, with an old maid charity."

Harry Halliday told a story, Sam capped it. Driffield, noticing Wilson's rather hectic flush, checked his hand reaching for the wine bottle. "Ease up on that stuff, Ben. You know you're allergic to it."

Wilson complained good-humouredly; he was, justifiably, in excellent spirits. He said, proudly, "I'd like to thank you for bringing out my unsuspected talent, skipper. It was a stroke of genius on your part to figure I had my eye in."

The remark was greeted with silence; post-mortems or discussions about the cricket were taboo at the dinner table.

"I'd like to have a word with you, skipper, if you're not tied up later," said Stavenden.

Driffield nodded.

All of them enjoyed the conviviality of the masculine conversation; it was the best club in the world. Townsend toyed with a glass of lager, pushed it away, and went to sit on the balcony. He was still keyed up, a reaction from his anticipated duties as 'night watchman'.

Macready, the googly bowler, said to his colleague, fast-medium Gogarty, "I had a funny proposition put to me by some chaps. They want me to go to Moscow after this series and teach them cricket. They reckon they would like to learn the game."

"Can't see it," said Dick Sinclair. "Erskine, bowled Spinski, Ten. Surrey versus Dynamos. Doesn't make sense to me."

"Certain way of starting a war. We nearly went to war with Australia over Larwood, remember? Not like soccer, you know. Cricket's a pretty gory kind of struggle. Excites lots of passion." This from Erskine.

"Might be a wonderful thing," said Townsend, simply.

"What do you mean, Bill?"

Townsend offered no explanation.

Driffield said, "I think I know what Bill means. I think I agree with it, too." But he offered no explanation either.

After a moment's contemplation of the odd phenomenon of the Muscovites learning to play cricket, Macready said, "We discussed one or two aspects of the game. Bowling, for instance. Seems they've been watching us play over here. They wanted to know my opinion about whether humidity affects the flight of the ball. I told them that it certainly did. Know what they said? Had the gall to tell me it made no difference. Said that they had tested it with a ballistics expert who claimed it didn't. Ballistics expert! See what I mean? What sort of game would they turn cricket into with that sort of outlook!"

Erskine laughed, but the others considered Macready's point had been well taken.

"Discuss anything else with them?" asked Jeffers.

"Money, of course!" said Macready.

The pros laughed.

"Offered me a very handsome retainer and all expenses." He added, "Told me I could bring my wife, if I had one."

Jeffers looked up sharply. The question of the lack of travelling arrangements for wives had been a sore point with some of the players.

"Yes, they certainly do it in style," said Jeffers. "I reckon Russia might have its points. Gave the soccer players a hundred quid gift each, and they were only casual visitors."

"Another thing they wanted to know—and this will make you laugh, Noel—why do we call certain positions on the field *silly* mid-on and *silly* mid-off? They reckoned that if we knew the positions were silly in the first place, why put the men there?"

This was greeted with delight by all the players.

"I reckon if they ever learn to understand that, there won't be much danger of war," said Bill Townsend.

The telephone rang and Driffield, answering it, handed the receiver to Stavenden, who took it into a corner of the room and quietly reproached the feminine voice for calling him at the 'club'.

Driffield exchanged glances with Jeffers.

He tapped with his spoon on the table. "Now, chaps, we've got a big day tomorrow. The time's after eight. I sincerely hope . . ." He looked significantly towards Stavenden, and calmly waited for him to replace the receiver. Stavenden finished his conversation quickly.

"I hope," said Driffield, "that none of you have any strenuous plans for this evening." He looked at Dick Sinclair, at Erskine, at Macready (the confirmed bachelor), finally at Stavenden, who was staring at his plate, lost in thought.

"Yes. . . ." said Driffield. "Anything on your mind, Steve?"

"Not now, skipper. I'll tell you later."

The others looked away, a trifle embarrassed. Stavenden, a married man, had been carrying on a tempestuous affair with a show-girl recently, and looked moody and out of sorts.

"All right, Steve. . . . Now. . . . Dick? What are your plans for tonight?"

Dick Sinclair went a little red at the roar that greeted this question.

"Tell us, Dick," yelled Macready.

Driffield rapped a little impatiently. "Shut up, Mac. Don't encourage him. Dick," said the skipper solemnly, "you're young enough to be *ordered* to go to bed. You know that, don't you?"

"Oh, knock it off, skipper. I promise I'll have an early night."

"Good. Noel. . . ?"

"*Cricket* balls," said Noel, "will weigh half an ounce heavier this season."

"But not an all-night session this time, I trust," said Driffield, who had been with Noel to Melbourne on a previous occasion.

"Sydney, I promise you you shall be the first to try on my glass slipper in the morning," said Erskine.

"Good. Now . . . Mac?"

"May I turn into a broomstick if I don't make it," said Macready, who, although not a playboy, enjoyed the bright lights and found living in a suitcase and the exploration of a new city to his taste.

The 'club' began to break up as Driffield got up from the table. At the door Bill Townsend drew him aside. "Just a word before you go." Driffield turned to the others. "I'll be in the coffee-room if anyone wants me, afterwards in my rooms."

When they were settled in the hotel lounge, Bill Townsend said, "Skipper, a lot of the chaps have been on at me to change my mind about giving up the game next season. They can't understand a man wishing to change his vocation. Well, to save a lot of unnecessary agitation, I would appreciate if it you'd hear my point of view in this. I haven't decided to go into the Church lightly, on the spur of the moment. I've always had it in the back of my mind. But when my parents were younger—I was about fourteen at the time—dad lost his leg in a rail accident and I wanted to earn a living as soon as possible. I've saved some money now—enough, anyway, to help out at home and to see me through my tuition period. So I'm all set."

"Either of your parents religious, Bill?"

"Not specially."

"Mine were. Particularly my father."

"Yes . . . ?"

"Religion," said Driffield, "isn't a matter of churches and pulpits, Bill. You can worship God and be a good Christian in your own home, in Piccadilly Circus, or on the playing fields."

"I'm aware of that."

"You've got a great gift. I know it's only a game. But it makes a lot of people happy, and giving happiness to people—

65

the gift you have for doing just that—is a rare and wonderful thing in itself. It's a pity to waste such a gift."

"I've thought of that. I don't think that my leaving the game is going to make any difference to people's happiness."

"You're a young man. Twenty-five. You've got a dozen great years ahead of you in your profession, of which any man can be proud. Even at forty you'll have plenty of time to start a new vocation if you still wish to by then. But think of the tragedy if you find you have a change of heart about it afterwards."

Townsend said slowly, "Don't you see? I've got to do it. It's the way I feel, skipper. What is convenient, what I might regret later, that doesn't enter into it."

"Mine was a religious home," said Driffield. "I wish I could say it was happier for that reason."

They were interrupted by the appearance of a tall and very beautiful girl who looked questioningly at Bill Townsend.

"Yes, we're through in the dining-room. I think you'll find Steve up in his room now."

She stared about the lounge as though she was not sure whether or not to believe him, but as Stavenden was obviously not there she left without exchanging a word with them.

"That's one who'll give him a close haircut," said Driffield.

Bill Townsend grinned. "You do know your Bible, skipper."

The 'Boys'

THE boys were in the small private lounge, reserved exclusively for them during their stay, by courtesy of the management. Some were writing letters or reading or listening to the radio; Bob Jeffers and Macready were chewing the rag. Ben Wilson sat a little away from them, trying to summon up enough energy to go to bed. Mac's suggestion was that he and Ben should go out—Bob, too, was invited rather dutifully (Bob was somewhat too closely linked to family obligations to let himself go on a night out)—and do the town. Ben declined emphatically. He was thoroughly exhausted and he had to resume play first thing in the morning.

"Come on, you blokes. These long hot evenings aren't made for sleep," said Mac, the confirmed bachelor.

"Draw the curtains and take a cold water-bottle with you," said Ben. Mac looked around the room: the Halliday twins were out to see friends; Bill Townsend had gone to visit Harkness in hospital—a chore that he offered to do on their behalf automatically, and which relieved Driffield, to whom this extra burden would have been something of a strain with all his other responsibilities. Noel was out, of course, on some colourful escapade of his own private device—it was rumoured that a Colonel Summers who had lost a lot of money at poker to him on a previous trip had been trying to get in touch with him for a return match. (Driffield hoped that Noel would be back before midnight as he had promised.) Danny Gogarty was examining the entertainment section of the daily paper— he was a ballet fan and would go to the ends of the town for a glimpse of *Sylphides* or *Boutique* or *Lac,* and hop on a plane to see the *Rites of Spring.* As far as Mac was concerned, Danny, on a night out, would be a dead loss. ("What do you see in that stuff?" Wilson had demanded of Danny one day when the youngster was waxing enthusiastic about a particular performance. Danny said simply, "They make us look like bulls in a china shop," a remark that was greeted with resentment. Danny insisted, "That's real physical discipline, if you must know. Why, some of those fellows put in a daily grind that would kill you lot in a week." Derision! Danny did his training according to some ballet technique and was, in addition, a first-rate tap dancer, much to the envy of Dick Sinclair, who regarded it a great social asset.)

Dick was on the phone to a lady friend, explaining why he

could not see her that evening. He had taken the skipper's instructions to heart. The 'explanation' had now lasted some twenty minutes.

Mac scratched his head in perplexity. It was going to be one of *those* evenings. It looked as though he would either have to go out solo or put his feet up like the rest of them.

Not that he minded going out on his own particularly; plenty of fun that way, with a new town to explore, the freedom of the streets, his wallet well lined. It was fun to be fancy free, take what came, knowing that you had to answer to no one. He enjoyed his bachelor life and these trips had their special attraction. Mac, a pure extrovert, lived contentedly for the moment. He liked the sport which was his work, enjoyed the easy opportunities of popularity and a certain measure of fame. Life had a sharp taste of adventure. He was a raconteur, with a salty wit, and like the really good story-spinners he didn't mind telling the one against himself.

"Any new ones?" asked Ben.

Mac allowed the significant pause of tried technique to whet their interest. Dick Sinclair finished his phone call and sat down to join their circle. Danny Gogarty put down his paper.

"This one," said Mac, "happened in Adelaide, a few days before a Test." He was out on the town one evening, feeling foot loose, when he saw a beautiful creature step out from a fashionable restaurant into a low-slung sports car; both vehicle and owner were built on the most modern and stylish lines.

The sight was so ravishing that a low whistle escaped him. The vision turned with a quick cold look, preparatory to scorn; when she saw him a lovely smile curved the corners of her mouth.

"Why . . . hallo," she said.

Mac almost felt himself blush. This was too good to be true. He approached her, stammering a little. At close quarters she was even more devastating than he first thought. "Hallo," he said, "I'm sure we've met . . ."

68

She laughed. "No, Mr. Macready, we haven't, but I have seen you play."

Supreme luck: a fan!

This was the dream realised. A fan—and simply breathtaking in her looks, and from her style, her car, the cape that she was wearing that must be chinchilla, he saw that she must be rolling in it. What a combination! Mac looked about him instinctively as though there was danger of some of the other players cutting in.

Mac said, "Where are you off to? I am at a loose end, if you'd care to join me for a drink?"

"Why not?" she said.

Better and better.

"Hop in," she said. "I know a quiet little place that's fairly amusing."

The quiet little place was without doubt the most exclusive supper-room in the city; all the waiters and wine stewards knew her.

They had a cocktail which she recommended and insisted on paying for. They talked sport. She was very knowledgeable for a woman. Mac warmed, expanded; he was glowing with well-being.

"It must be very quiet for you . . . on your travels so far from home, Mr. Macready."

"Call me Mac."

"Thank you."

"Yes," he admitted, "it is quiet." A martyred expression was skilfully assumed. "A chap doesn't know what to do with himself of an evening sometimes. Of course, one gets tired of writing letters home to the folks—my parents, that is. I'm not married."

"Of course. I understand. You must miss them."

"Oh, yes." Mac missed them. In England Mac spent two days a year with his parents: Christmas and his mother's birthday. Still, when he thought about it he agreed he missed them.

69

"The worst is the let down," he said.

"The let down?"

"Yes, after the roar of the crowd, you still feel on edge, wanting some sort of follow-through. And," he said dramatically, "all there is is to go back to a quiet anonymous hotel room amongst strangers. So much contact on the field, so much loneliness off."

She nodded. "I see that. Mac . . . would you find it very dull to come over for a while?"

"Your place?"

"My home. It is a *home*, anyway. It's not a hotel room. Nor a restaurant. I'd be honoured to have you."

"Do you mean it?"

"I should be very pleased if you would come. I have a special reason."

"Well . . . if you really feel that way."

They were ushered out by the *maître d'hôtel*. The commissionaire opened the door of the suave sports model, which smoothly ate up the miles. She turned on the radio and they listened to music, an orchestra to accompany them on their way. And when they arrived Mac was pretty bowled over. It was no modest homestead. It was a veritable mansion, with Ionic columns, a marble hall, and a lounge so vast that he was reminded of the banqueting arrangements for a city reception for the team.

"Make yourself at home," she said. She walked off for a while, bringing a tray with brandy glasses and a decanter. She pulled a bell-cord and a liveried servant appeared with discreet quietness; she tried to tempt Mac with some *hors d'œuvres,* but Mac was in no mood to eat anything. She whispered something to the servant, who bowed and disappeared.

She patted her divan. "Come and sit beside me, Mac."

Mac got up, stretching his long legs, and sank down beside her.

"I'm Nora St. Kitts," she said. "Perhaps you've heard the name?"

He had. "The fashion woman?"

"Yes, I have a fairly well known *couturier* and cosmetics firm which my late father founded and which I run."

Mac was a little intimidated; she was quite famous in her line of business; a woman executive in a big way.

"I should have guessed something like that," said Mac. "It gives you quite an air, you know, being independent like that. Unusual for a woman."

She nodded. "Oh, yes, I can't be bothered too much with convention."

"Quite."

"Now, some people would say it is indiscreet to take you home with me, that a woman shouldn't do that sort of thing. Frankly, I don't see it. You either like a person and want to make friends or you don't. If you do, why all the hypocrisy?"

Why, indeed? Mac could not agree more and said so. His heart was beating a little faster. He turned to look at her closely; her matchless complexion, possibly a product of her own manufacture, was as fine as porcelain, as tender as the bloom of a petal; her clear grey eyes stared at him with serene thoughtfulness. Dare he . . . just yet. . . ? He leaned towards her a little.

She said, "I'm so glad you were able to come here. I told you I had a special reason for asking." She suddenly smiled. She called, "Here we are, Timothy darling. This is Mr. Macready."

Mac suddenly became conscious of someone else in the room who had approached noiselessly on the deep pile carpet. He looked round with a start. He saw a young boy of about eight dressed in a perfectly tailored dressing-gown, standing and staring at him with grave eyes. He was a very handsome little boy and he reminded him of Nora.

"Yes," she said. "This is my son, Timothy. We went to see Mr. Macready play yesterday. You remember, don't you?"

"Oh, yes! Hallo, Mr. Macready!"

"He's a great fan, of course," said Nora proudly. "So are all

71

the other little chaps at his school. It will be a great triumph for him to go back to school tomorrow and tell them all that he met the great Macready of England."

"Is that why you asked me over?"

"You will forgive a mother's selfishness, Mac. But you did say you had nothing to do. I'll arrange for you to be driven back whenever you wish to go. Now shake hands with Mr. Macready, Timmy darling."

"Hallo, Mr. Macready."

Mac said, feebly, "Hallo, son."

"One of the chaps has Bradman's autograph," said Timothy. He shook hands solemnly with Mac.

"There!" said his mother. "And now you can go back to bed and tell them all in the morning!"

This latest yarn was greeted with delight by Mac's listeners, who particularly liked the rueful manner in which the anticlimax was related. Even Bob Jeffers, lost in some private thoughts, was temporarily distracted.

A little later the circle began to break up, leaving Bob Jeffers and Ben Wilson together.

"He certainly has fun, old Mac," said Ben with a reminiscent twinkle.

"Reckon he can afford to," said Jeffers, frowning.

Ben looked at his friend. "Anything new from home?"

"Same old stuff. Nothing much new. Kids go back to school in a week or two."

Jeffers had two youngsters in a minor public school, one in a prep school. He said, "I've got to try and decide what to do about young Ian." He was referring to his youngest son. "He'll be eleven in a few weeks."

"You mean—school?"

"Yes. The two elder boys are at Westchester. I can't see how I can let young Ian go anywhere else." Jeffers looked thoughtfully at Ben. "I know there's nothing wrong with a good day school. I was quite happy myself in one. But if his brothers are at public school, is it fair?"

"Nothing special about a public school, Bob. Just a boy farm. Listen to Noel on the subject. I wouldn't let it worry you."

"Nice for Noel to talk like that. Where would *he* send his son?"

"What's worrying you, Bob? It's not the fees, is it? You've got money saved."

"Sure. But next year my income's not going to be what it was in the past. And from then on it will get progressively smaller. With three boys at public school . . ."

"Your eldest will be leaving in a year or two."

"Roger's been promised a chance to go to University. He's really clever. I can't deny that to the youngster. He wants to study law. It's a long business, very expensive."

"Oh, come, Bob, you don't have to kill yourself over this. Most families much better off than you are have to make sacrifices. Not all the kids can have an equal chance."

"I promised Roger, if he was in the first five in class, I'd let him go to University." He added proudly, "Came second. Top in maths and history. Can't deny a boy his chance if he works like that. How can I, Ben?"

"Well, it'll have to be young Ian. He must understand. That's what happens to families. The younger child is usually unlucky."

"Playing one son against another? How can I do that? You're a father, Ben. How does one tell a younger son that he can't have the same chances as his brothers?"

('Oh, hell!' thought Ben.)

"You've got to understand the way children feel about these things. It's what happens when you're young that counts. It can hurt a lot, a thing like that. Thank goodness the last one was a girl. Not the same problem there. Sometimes I wish Liz and I weren't so fond of kids, stopped at a smaller family. (But the first two were boys, and we both wanted a

73   F

daughter. . . .) I was on top of the world then. What did it matter? A child was a blessed event. Another only meant more happiness. Who was to think of ten years' time? They raise you up until you think these things are your natural right, your right for all time. You don't imagine you've only got it on lease."

Steve

'STEVE' STAVENDEN was finishing his letter to his young son, Harry, when the phone rang for the third time. He waited; he thought, 'I'll give it seven more rings . . . if it doesn't stop by then, I'll answer it.'

The phone went on ringing.

He picked up the receiver but said nothing into the mouthpiece. "Steve," said the girl, "Steve . . . what the hell's the matter with you? Why don't you answer?"

"You should have known not to phone me when I was with the team."

"Darling, don't be cross. I forgot what you told me."

"You never forget anything. You do it deliberately. See what you can get away with. Just because you know it's not the thing you have to do it. Embarrassing me. You couldn't care less, could you?"

There was a laugh. "Did it embarrass you?"

"Even the wives wouldn't phone. You know that. That's why you've got to do it, isn't it?"

"Oh, wives . . . this is me. A mistress has more rights. That's why she's called your mistress. Don't you see?"

"Shut up. I hate you talking like that."

There was a faint pause. "I'm coming up, Steve. Don't go. Don't you dare go before I get there. Do you understand?"

He hung up without answering.

74

His pen was shaking so much that he blotted the letter to Harry. He was angry with her, but more angry with himself. He knew it was no good, but he had to stay and wait for her. It was poison, this nonsense he was having. It had always been bad with her, since the first time he had known her, years back. . . .

At twenty 'Steve' Stavenden had been one of those rare phenomena, an athlete so gifted that he combined soccer stardom with cricket; the brief summer season yielded to a long winter when he played for a famous London first division team; he could do anything with his hands or feet, anything with a ball, and even if he played only half so well, the colour of his personality, so unassuming in private life, was arresting on a field of play. His popularity was a watchword, his gate-pulling powers ranking him amongst the elect of sport; he earned more money than a Cabinet Minister (almost as much as a music-hall or television star) from the by-products of his athletic fame, and even a living wage from his soccer earnings.

And then he met Nesta at the early peak of his fame; he was riding the crest of the wave and the normal affection of a young woman could do little to carry over the excitement, the conflict and the applause of the arena; he needed and craved the drama of a grand passion, and Nesta was just the sort of girl to provide it.

From their very first meeting there was a cleaving and clashing like a high-powered voltage spark bridging a terminal gap.

"Who the devil's that?" said Nesta. She appeared to be addressing a friend, but she was staring directly and challengingly at Steve.

"That's 'Steve' Stavenden, the cricketer."

"Oh," said Nesta with pointed indifference, "I thought he might be *somebody*."

Steve accepted the challenge with clear understanding of elementary feminine tactics.

75

A brief glance absorbed her personality and left him with a feeling that he had come to the end of a journey and reached a milestone. ('That's the girl I was looking for.')

The world of sport fringes and overlaps the bohemian world of show business; the roar of the stadium is no less significant and rewarding than the gentle applause of a sophisticated cabaret audience. A young man, vitalised by fame, is drawn to any form of limelight. Steve let his feelings sweep him away with the uninhibited onslaught that only the very young and strong are capable of, disregarding any conventional warnings, contemptuous of caution, indifferent to reputations.

He was determined from the first to capture this prize, bind her firmly to his chariot. There was simply no other woman for him in the world. He published the information amongst his friends:

"I'm going to get her."

"You'll have your work cut out, even you. She's got them all on a string."

He shrugged; the opposition was of no consequence.

From the beginning he thought of marriage.

For the first time in his life the idea of marriage crossed his mind as applying to himself; till then it had been a trap and a pitfall that had befallen other and weaker people.

"To marry a girl like Nesta," Gene Carreras, the clarinet player once said to him, "is like trying to trap moonlight."

Steve said, "Every woman needs the domestic things. Even Nesta with her glamour queen razzamataz."

"If she did, would you love her?"

It took three years for Steve to answer that question, during which time he was tangling with a personality as complicated as a score by Ravel; the high notes and the colour obscured the subtlety of the orchestration.

To have an affair with a glamour girl of the show world is a trial of patience, a test of humour, a challenge to fortitude. To be married to her can be a little worse occupational risk than,

76

say, a test pilot: you put your courage in your hands and trust your life to the other chap.

Nesta was a coloratura soprano; she also had a figure. She also did revue sketches for the private delectation of her friends which were masterpieces of pointed dagger-like satire; she could mimic, speak in seven dialects, swear in eight languages; she was as crafty as a diplomat, as ignorant as a peasant wench, completely unreliable, utterly without any conventional standards of behaviour, or scruples, or morals; beautiful, captivatingly charming or seductive or anything else she wanted to be. She led a slothfully self-indulgent life, wasteful of her talents, prodigal of the goodwill of her friends.

The lights went down on the restaurant, a small spot picked out a woman standing by a microphone in evening dress, a piano tinkled an intro to the band, who fluttered their strings; an expert clarinet, sweetest of instruments, sang the accompaniment; the woman began her solo. She had style, there was no doubt about that. She told a story or two in a droll voice, crooned a couple of numbers in the continental ballad manner, went to the bar and pretended to make an elderly roué the object of her regard, and retired to some moderately warm applause from the tolerant cabaret audience.

This was Nesta. And that was how Steve first met her. Somebody from the band recognised him one evening and urged him to take the sticks for the Drum Roll Blues. Steve agreed. There were only two other instruments beating out the refrain, the trumpet and the piano, and he tapped the soft pigskin, worked up the rhythm until the swing of it entranced the listeners. Nesta came out for a moment and sat down by the pianist; they were introduced.

She led him a dance before their marriage; it was on and off like a series of traffic lights; truth was, Nesta wanted very little of what came easily to her, and Steve came too easily, although she knew his worth. He was a better bet than any of

77

her male acquaintances. She could have married for money easily enough, but she was not interested in money, saying it wasn't important. Only the things money could get were. (That was one of her faults, Steve recognised even before marriage. There were others almost as bad.)

Nesta did not exactly like to have a lot of men on a string; she claimed it was the excitement she wanted, and the variety of entertainment. It was no good arguing with her, because she was easily bored by a discussion. A lot of things had to be happening all the time for Nesta to be amused.

And it wasn't that she was cold-hearted or unkind; she claimed she was merely philosophical about other people's misfortunes, which could hardly be of any concern of hers; she could not help the way other people felt about her.

"Marriage doesn't suit me," she complained when he asked her the first time. They had been living together for some weeks and as he was about to go on tour, he thought it would be a bond between them whilst he was away. She would have a brand new home to keep her amused, and a ring on her finger to remind her of him, and she could make friends with the younger members of his family. Nesta was fairly keen on the idea, the way he put it. A few days before the wedding she got into a panic and wanted to postpone it till he came back from his tour. "What's the use of marrying now if you have to go right away?" He reminded her of her enthusiasm for decorating the new home, meeting his friends and cousins, going down to the country to stay with his parents for a while, things like that, which of course showed how wide of the mark he really was.

Nesta was not really interested in the clan spirit or domestic virtues; marriage would be a novelty, a new relationship, a different social status, and for these reasons she had half a mind to experiment with it; but her real problems were so much beneath the surface that neither Steve nor she could learn to understand them in a lifetime.

She reminded him of her 'career', the sacrifice it would mean to her to settle down to a life of domesticity, and he countered by telling her that domesticity hadn't prevented her from becoming an opera singer, but sheer lack of discipline. (So much simpler to earn money by crooning with the help of a microphone, and so much less effort to rely on the low cut and close fit of a satin evening gown for audience appeal than to study histrionics and learn Wagner by heart.)

She flew into a passion, they had a fight, and he left her. He was away from her for three days, and then returned to her, desperate, contrite, humiliated by his infatuation. He found the flat in total darkness, all the curtains drawn in daylight. She was in bed with a sick headache.

They flew into each other's arms; the curtains continued to remain drawn for some forty-eight hours.

As soon as she realised he had given up the struggle to marry her she became keen on the idea at once. She bought a cookery book containing two thousand recipes of continental dishes, illustrated in eight-colour lithographic opulence, works ranging from knitting to mothercraft in massive bindings, and an entirely new wardrobe of matronly sobriety.

Vaguely Steve realised that for her the whole of life was a sort of pageant, a play of which she was the central figure. He was uneasy when he married her, which was a very swell affair, with Nesta the star performer, the champagne flowing by the bucket, and Nesta's friends scandalising his family and leaving them speechless with shock. But the honeymoon was an enchanted journey; Nesta made it so. She really meant Steve to know just what he would be missing when he went on tour.

With chameleon-like adaptability she became transformed from a radiant bride to a pale, dark-suited grass widow, waving to him with a tiny lace handkerchief from the dockyard when his ship sailed. But then, after the clinging farewells, the cloudbursts of tears, the swooning and the waving, he did not hear a word from her for the first four weeks of the trip, and then only brief notes or cards.

Steve could not remember the first year of their marriage, which some merciful mental censorship cast from his memory; the process of adapting himself to Nesta's headlong progress through all human relationships was like tackling a runaway horse intent on nothing but a dash for freedom. It left them both bleeding from a hundred wounds; with Steve it was a pyrrhic victory. He had frustrated all her efforts for extra-marital associations in the bohemian manner by the startlingly original method of punching every aspiring candidate promptly at the moment of aspiration; Nesta was not altogether displeased with his reaction.

"Steve doesn't say much," she said to a young man who was clutching a handkerchief to a bloody nose, with the manner of a hostess apologising for a shortage of the correct wine glasses. "But please don't go. He won't do it again if you don't put your arm round me."

Her acceptance of a continental cabaret tour started an unforgettable row.

"You can go away on one of your tours whenever you like, but I'm nothing but a domestic slave," she said.

"That's nonsense. It's because I have to go away from time to time that I want you to be here with me when we have the chance. If we're both away it will lead to disaster."

He rang the agent and told him to cancel the tour. When she tried to leave the house he locked her in her room. She went to the windows and broke every pane of glass with her bare fists; then she began to throw everything she could lift out of the window.

In the end he had to give way. When he yielded she agreed that she didn't want to go away on tour whilst he was in England. "I see little enough of you. Why are you willing to have me leave you?" she demanded.

There were, of course, heavenly interludes. Nesta could be a dozen women all rolled into one, a Moslem paradise of contending feminine virtues and qualities. When she pulled the stops out and played her full range of tenderness it was like bursting through the emotional sound barrier, the ascent of K2. Steve would wander for days in a semi-coma, his heart would flutter at the sound of her voice; the vision of her in some specially tricked-out bit of domestic attire, for his eyes alone, was unfailingly spell-binding. Physically, with her long bob of chestnut hair, her tall, slender and superbly handled body, eyes that were like violets in a sensitive fine-boned face, and a mouth that was a miracle of expressiveness, she completely captivated him.

But there were the 'unaccountable' tantrums, the moods of darkness which assailed her like a sickness. It was as though there was a hint of disaster: an invisible black raven sat on her back, a bird of evil goading her with its hard beak. At such times she was capable of anything, any piece of violence to his feelings; and yet she could stand away from herself, regard herself calmly and objectively, with such brisk observations as: "It will soon pass. It's the black bird sitting on my back. It'll be all right when it's flown away."

Their social life was a series of mishaps; often, in the early part of their marriage, Steve would set out with her to visit friends or relatives, and he got quite a kick when she was charming; when she wanted to make an impression she could surround herself with admirers softly whistling under their breath; a lovely wife is a great social asset to any young man. But as soon as Nesta became bored, which was very soon at the homes of his friends, it was another story, and he had to beat a hasty retreat long before the party was over. The odd thing was that Nesta often forgot how bored she had been on any particular occasion, and demanded to know why his stand-offish friends did not invite them again.

"Nesta, you're overdrawn on the account. I put a hundred

and fifty in last week and I've just had a letter that we've had it. How much did *you* spend?"

"Steve, why do we never do anything? I mean travel together, go somewhere. I don't mean the South of France. Everybody goes to the South of France in the season, and Lucerne in the other season. I mean somewhere interesting like Egypt. The desert. The mysterious desert, darling, where we're close to the universe. Just you and me and the Sphinx. Lawrence of Arabia. The Sheikh. Things like that. Or on safari. Why can't we go on safari to Africa? Hunt big game. You in a white topee, a big-bore elephant-gun cradled in your arm. The Great White Hunter. Clark Gable. Ernest Hemingway. Or something. Why don't we?"

"Darling, sometimes I think you have a mind of incredible vulgarity. And what's more it's like a grasshopper. You start to say something, and by the time you've finished, you've forgotten where you intended to go."

There was some talk of a film contract which Steve, remembering the continental tour, also nipped in the bud. He had a premonition of disaster to their marriage in any of these ventures which would absorb too much of her attention and put too much temptation in her way. This time, it appeared, she was really angry with him, and he had to put up with a dozen feminine outbursts beyond his comprehension, vagaries, moods of dejection and frustration, outrageous scenes of jealousy and aggressiveness; he simply didn't understand the score.

On the eve of his second departure on tour, she said to him, "How long do you think you'll be gone? Four months?"

"Yes."

"What are you going to do about sex?"

Steve was not sure that he heard her correctly, so she repeated the flagrant question.

"What do you expect me to do about it? I'm married to you, aren't I?"

"Don't lie to me. I know what men are. I know what you are."

82

Steve tried to maintain an air of dignified reproof; he was shocked to hear such a remark from his wife.

"Well, why don't you tell me?"

"I refuse to discuss such things with you."

"Why?"

"It's horrible to hear such things from your lips. It's indelicate."

"What in heaven's name do you mean? I ask you an honest question. As your wife, it's of interest to me."

"I refuse to discuss it."

She watched him leave the flat in astonishment. When he returned an hour or two later, after having expressed his disapproval so emphatically, he expected the subject to be dropped, but she returned to it without delay.

"What made you go out? Where have you been?"

"You made me very angry. Surely you knew that."

"I think you're being childish. Tell me, were you faithful to me on your first trip?"

He made no answer.

"You would tell me if you were."

"Nesta," he said, appalled, "how can you possibly believe a thing like that could happen when I'd just married you."

"Yes, I was forgetting that."

"*Forgetting* it?"

"Oh," she said, "don't make a thing of it. Still, you've worn the gilt off by now. You'll want your bit of nonsense if you're going to be away for four months. Don't be idiotic about it, of course you will. Well, that's all right with me." She looked at him with a profound mixture of realism and slightly amused tolerance. "Promise me one thing."

"What's that?" He was quite fascinated by her outspokenness by now.

"Don't go with mercenaries. You never know what might happen."

He blushed.

But the ship had hardly docked when there were cables and long-distance phone calls from her.

"If you as much as look at another woman," she raved across six thousand miles of Pacific, "I'll murder you both! I swear I will!"

And then, in a panic that he might have taken her at her word she wrote daily long letters of protest of her love, her agony of mind that he was away from her for so long, exhorting him to patience to resist all temptation, threatening him with dire consequences if he should go with another woman, assuring him of her trust in him, at the same time warning him that she had spies everywhere. This female farrago of genuine affection and malice, deep concern and aggressiveness, tenderness and frustrated sensuality, bombarded him daily for three weeks in the form of ten-page letters written with such intensity of feeling that he could hardly decipher the sprawling handwriting.

The first letter began, 'Darling', by the third day she commenced without any preliminary, 'Why haven't you written? Why haven't you replied? What are you hiding?' the last word being underlined three times with such passion that the notepaper was slashed.

The storm, of course, subsided, like all Nesta's outbursts, as suddenly as it commenced.

It was odd, to look back on it now, that it was, after all, he who divorced her in the end. He discovered that even whilst she wrote him with such white-hot passion about his anticipated infidelity, she was being unfaithful to him. When he accused her of it with all the bitterness in his heart, she looked at him in surprise and said, 'But, silly, it meant nothing. It was only a bit of nonsense whilst you were away.'

She left him with memories that were black and terrible, relieved by patches of dazzling light, like sunshine piercing a dark tunnel. And even years after they were separated the look of a woman from the back which reminded him of her, the

84

sound of a feminine laugh that had the quick hoarse chuckle in it, was enough to make his heart beat more quickly and a tremor of excitement flicker through him.

No woman had the power to move him as she did, not even his second wife, Lucienne, the French girl to whom he was so deeply devoted. Lucienne was rational, mature, deeply attached to him and their boy, and he could not wish for a better wife, but Steve had always known it was not the same thing.

He remembered a significant episode of his engagement period with Lucienne. They were to be married the next day; the invitations had been sent out, elaborate preparations made, the families had met and approved of each other, the bridal gown had been made and fitted and pronounced exquisite.

About ten in the evening, just as she was about to go to bed, he telephoned her and, sounding urgent and mysterious, told her he must see her at once, it was highly important.

She protested; it was bad luck to see him on the wedding eve; she was tired, the excitement had overcome her; she did not wish to be disturbed by anything on the night before the ceremony. It was of no avail, he was determined to speak with her.

In the end she agreed to see him for a few minutes, but he was not to come to the house, which might disturb her family, who were superstitious; she would meet him at their old rendez-vous in the garden, behind the summer-house.

It was a lovely summer evening, soft, fragrant, and with the sickle moon casting a spell over her as she seemed to float towards him. She embraced him, trembling, a little frightened, tenderly amused ("What on earth is so important *now*?"), and with all her pulses fluttering as they always did when he had his arms about her.

When he remained silent, she had a premonition of something terrifying, something ominous, which he no longer intended to conceal from her.

"Steve darling, what is it you wish to say to me?"

"I want to tell you . . . I must tell you now . . . that I don't really love you, Lucienne. That doesn't mean that I won't marry you. That side of it is up to you. I can't let you down. If . . . if you want it to go on, I'll see it through. I've given my word. I won't go back on it. I want you to know how I feel. I am in your hands. The decision is entirely up to you."

She knew that this wasn't a last-minute panic, a bout of nerves; she knew that he meant what he said.

She broke away from him and collapsed on the garden seat. He lit a cigarette. Neither of them spoke for some three minutes, until the silence between them was a torment.

"What do you wish to do, Lucienne?"

She tried to speak once or twice but failed.

"What do you wish to do?" he repeated at last. "Do you want to go on with it?"

At last she spoke. With a short dry laugh she said, "Oh, yes." That was all. She refused to say another word.

He was shattered, but nothing of his feelings was revealed as he nodded. That was that; but her determination fixed him to his promised word like a butterfly pierced by the naturalist's needle. The next day, at the wedding ceremony, she was as serene and gay as though the episode had been some dream, a nightmare dispelled by the morning light.

And they were happy together. She was a good wife, an efficient housekeeper, a splendid cook, a gracious and charming hostess. Steve and she settled down in a handsome house in Wimbledon. For the first time he was able to receive all his friends, rely on his wife's decorum and presence for any of the increasingly important social occasions to which he was now regularly invited. To all appearance it was a perfectly happy marriage.

In a sense, Steve could not have been happier. He had been emotionally exhausted by his relationship with Nesta, which was less a marriage than a contest of arms; he carried scars and unhealing wounds from the encounter, and Lucienne provided the comfort and contentment he needed to become whole again.

Happiness, yes: if you can call an emotional temperature of sixty-six degrees Fahrenheit happiness. But he behaved with unswerving loyalty, and when, after a couple of years, their son was born, a new passion was invoked in him, a new happiness that went into the depths of his nature. He was fond of his wife; he doted on his son, the man child who promised to perpetuate the greatness of his youth, in whom in the years to come he would renew his legendary fame.

And not once in the years of their marriage did Lucienne hint or breathe a word about the eve-of-wedding meeting at the summer-house.

Steve was finding difficulty in adjusting himself to solitude on this latest trip. The jokes the other fellows made about their adventures had found an unusual response in him. He missed Lucienne badly on this trip. He had had some eighteen months of uninterrupted routine of domestic life before the tour—an unusual length of time—and he was no longer in his first flush of youth. Routine in his personal habits had become important to him. The quiet evenings at home with her and the boy, the peaceful but somehow vital Thursdays and Sundays—his at-homes to a small circle of intimate friends—and the regularity of his marital habits had answered a need in this particular stage of his life. Lucienne had ripened, grown more attractive to him with the years. He had expected too little from his marriage at first and had found himself surprised by an unexpected development of his relationship with her. The child, of course, had made her more precious to him, but beyond that, he was becoming increasingly fond of her. He remembered Noel once chiding Dick Sinclair for the multiplicity and general chaos of the youngster's attachments. "With women, Dick, it's like wine —it's the quality that counts."

And the wine was improving with the years.

Their marriage had begun with tension, after that incident at the summer-house, but when he proved to her that he was as good as his word and gave all his efforts to make their life together a success, she had mellowed, responded with warmth and conscientiousness. Her genuine devotion to his interests began to dim the sharp tantalising image that had, in early days, stood between them: the image of the sleek-haired, slant-eyed Nesta.

He had begun to forget Nesta. It was Lucienne whom he thought about when he was away for any length of time. When he was playing in away matches she would often put a trunk call through of an evening about the time they normally retired to bed, and the chats they had were particularly comforting.

On this present tour he was beginning to long for her companionship, missed her in a dozen different ways. And the effect was a curious one. It seemed to make other women more attractive. Steve had never known a time when there were so many pretty and amiable feminine creatures falling over themselves for his attention, and the reputation that he had that he was indifferent to all blandishments seemed to inspire a special regard in them.

"Don't bother," he heard Sam Halliday once say to a young actress, a veritable Calypso, pouting at Steve's taciturn refusal to sit out at a dance with her at one of Raeburn's parties. "Forget Steve. He has to beat them off with clubs." Sam led her out into the garden.

But that night her image had become disconcertingly mixed up with Lucienne's. He dreamed of a girl with a cool poise that was Lucienne's; but when he had manœuvred her into a position of compromise, she unaccountably began to have the young actress's hair and eyes.

Steve woke up in the witching hours of the morning with a start, staggered into the bathroom, and stood under a cold shower. His head was throbbing. In the morning he slept late. A young chambermaid who came briskly into his room whilst he was still in his dressing-gown, rosy-cheeked, clear-eyed, and with the reddest lips he had seen, apologised for disturbing him.

"Sorry. I thought you'd be gone down to breakfast by now." She carried a pile of fresh-laundered linen over her arm, than which there is no more fragrant article of domestic utility. She leaned over him as he sat on the bed and the smell of the fresh linen seemed a personal, clean and delightful scent, more enticing than any perfume worn in the boudoir; the smell of a newly made bed.

Steve had to exert all his will not to make a grab for her.

She fooled about with the sheets and the pillow-cases, bending close to him at every opportunity, and assuming the most vulnerable postures. He carried the memory of the girl's shape on the playing fields with him that day.

That evening he began to wonder for the first time whether, in certain circumstances, infidelity was justifiable.

It was no good discussing the question with that hedonist, Erskine, that pagan, Dick Sinclair, starchy Driffield, moralist Townsend or the conventionally minded Jeffers. Wilson was something of a liberal and they talked over the matter seriously, but of course both came to the same *impasse*: what would you say if the missus did it? Their reservation that infidelity was different for men was a half-hearted one. Both were too honest to believe that there were two codes of behaviour, one for men and another for women. "In any case," said Steve, "it's *women* you're being unfaithful with. She could be someone else's wife. There you are; you've gone round in a circle."

No possible conclusion.

Steve was sitting in his hotel suite, the curtains drawn against the light of evening so that he could rest his eyes after the exhausting concentration of the day in the glaring sunlight. The gramophone he always took with him on his trips abroad was playing record after record: Jack Teagarden, Bix Biedebecker, Jelly Roll Morton, Goodman, Ellington, the pick of the bunch, all his favourites. He had borrowed the drum from the hotel orchestra and was beating out the rhythm in quiet synchronisation; he kicked and heeled gently, his wrists throbbed staccato, mounting crescendo, accelerating tempo. At first he did not hear the ring at the door-bell.

When he opened the door, he stood rooted in astonishment. "Nesta!"

"Steve darling! Why are the curtains drawn? Have you got a woman in there? Am I intruding? What a lark. What about Lucienne? Does she know? Well, are you going to ask me in? For heaven's sake, don't just stand there."

Steve recovered himself slowly.

"Come in if you like. I was playing over some records."

She entered. He did not invite her to have a drink. He merely picked up the sticks and continued to tap out the rhythm.

She sat down, crossed her long legs and carried on as though she had only seen him yesterday. "I'm staying at the hotel. I'm on a tour with Gene's band. I'm singing for him regularly now."

"That's nice."

"Oh, Steve, don't be so stuffy. Why don't you take me in your arms and kiss me? Haven't we been divorced long enough?"

"Don't be silly."

She puckered her mouth humorously. "I've missed you. Thought about you a lot. Your name's in the papers all the time. Can't help thinking about you. When I heard you were staying at the same hotel . . . You don't mind me calling on you like this?"

"Does anybody know you're here?"

"A practical question. Of course not, silly. I'm not dumb about things like that."

"What do you want, Nesta?"

"Oh, come, darling. It's your fatal charm, of course. What else? Relax, I won't eat you."

"Are you broke? Is that it?"

"Oh, have a heart. As a matter of fact, I could do with fifty, but that's not why I'm here. Just thought I'd see how you were, have a chat."

"Well, you can see. And we've had one. Please go, Nesta."

"What's the rush? Why don't you ask me how I am? Silly boy, haven't you got over me yet? Why are you in such a hurry to push me out?"

"That's nonsense. I'm working."

"Working? Playing the drum?"

"It's work."

He increased the rolling rhythm, driving up to a frenzy of pyrotechnics, his face taut with concentration.

"My, you really mean it. Why do you do that, darling? Funny, you were playing the drums when we first met at the cabaret club. Remember?" She sighed. "Why do you do that? I always meant to ask you. A funny hobby."

"It's not a hobby, Nesta. It's part of my training and limbering up exercises. Everybody has his own method of training."

"I thought you'd be doing that on the field."

"No." Bix was going to town; the trumpet note quality was hard and crisp, like a shower of shining, freshly minted coins; he was supreme in that number, eclipsing the combination. Steve followed suit, his eyes closed, his muscles straining, the wrists and feet flickering. "It's in the wrists, the feet, the rhythm; everything is in the rhythm, really. Rhythm is co-ordination, a combination of muscular control, judgment, timing. That's cricket, football, any sport. You ought to know, you're an artist, a singer. It's timing and control there, isn't it? It's the same in sport; every movement must be part of a whole, fluent, rhythmic, perfect at any time, so that if you're frozen in mid-action it can be a subject for a sculptor like those figures by the Greeks throwing the discus. That's what I'm learning from this. My muscles are obeying a series of split-second instructions, instinctively, without being conscious of them really. And I can keep it up for hours because I enjoy it; it's not merely dull repetition."

"Well," she said quietly, "now I know. You never spoke to me like that before."

"Maybe you never listened."

"Steve, you are a great man. I've always known it. No wonder you're famous."

She dabbed a handkerchief to her eyes. He threw down the sticks and laughed. "What on earth are you crying for?"

"Oh, seeing you again. Hearing you talk. Nothing. It will pass in a minute." A little later she said, "I'm sorry, Steve. Truly, truly sorry. I was such a fool. There never was anyone else really. None of them meant anything. Before or since."

"Oh, shut up, Nesta."

"Steve, make love to me."

"Don't be an idiot."

"Did anyone else ever mean anything? Truly and honestly? Tell me that they did? Do you get anything out of that dull pudding of a wife of yours? Anything we had to give each other? You know I'm right. When you saw me in the doorway it hit you just as hard as ever, didn't it? Just the way it hit me." She put her hand at the pit of her stomach.

"You knew it would. That's why you didn't let yourself be announced. Sprung it on me cold. I could kill you, Nesta."

She got up. "If I go, you'll never see me again."

Steve groaned. Sexual attraction is almost entirely a matter of personality; whatever her other faults Nesta's personality was as perfect as one of those pieces of crystal, which, however you turned them, formed perfect patterns of brilliantly refracted light.

The love affair that commenced on that tour continued for several days until the never forgotten evening when Steve returned and found her in his suite. Unaccountably, he flew into a passion.

"Who let you in?"

"The night clerk had a pass key."

"Don't you realise what this might lead to?" He seized her arms. "Do you want to smash up my other marriage, too, Nesta?"

She disengaged herself. "It can't be Lucienne you're so het up about. . . . It's your son, isn't it, Steve?"

She sat in his lap as he sprawled into an armchair. She had drawn the curtains and they were in almost total darkness; he caressed her head, listening to the faint hiss of silk against nylon as she settled intimately, saw the blue spark flame from his hand as he went on stroking her hair.

"All over?" She murmured the words, her lips against his.

"You only want me for as long as some other woman has me."

"What other woman? I own you now, my pet. And you know it."

Steve wondered why, in spite of this addiction, this itch he had for this silken creature, he should continue to feel resentful, unhappy and frustrated.

He heard her chuckling hoarse laugh, her 'Tallulah' giggle that used to drive him to a frenzy, and the nostalgia invoked in him a conflict of love and rage. She flickered her eyelashes against his cheek. "Look! You're drawing sparks from me! What a man."

He said miserably, "Nesta, where is this getting us? Where are we going?"

"I don't know, darling. But it's fun getting there."

Steve liked to build his life as he planned a manœuvre on the field of play, with the opposition firmly established in his mind, the form of attack worked out with precision; he had to know where he was going.

But as Gene Carreras had said, with Nesta it was like trying to trap moonlight.

Twice he had decided to stop the new affair, it could only lead to trouble, but home was remote, the evenings were long,

93

empty and racked with memories and hunger. All around him his team-mates were living for the moment, enjoying their opportunities; he could not for ever sit in the empty suite with the curtains drawn, drowning the chemic rhythms of his longing with the drum-beat and the mental passion of Ellington. Then the thought of her shining mahogany-coloured hair, the wide gash of her mouth, began its spell and the sticks snapped in his pincer-like fingers.

What overcame his final resistance was the knowledge that at long last even the skipper had strayed, had succumbed to temptation. It was reliably reported that there was a female practically living in his suite; nobody had seen her with him because he smuggled her into the bedroom when there were visitors, but, heavily veiled, she had been observed hurrying late at night with him into the hotel and up to their rooms.

This was the final straw; the weight of responsibility of the team's reputation—even that was not enough to resist temptation.

It was a temptation that continually recurred, formed part of the perennial conflict in their professional lives. To be separated from your wife for months at a time, every other winter, when on tour was a systematic strain that proved too much for a number of the married men. They saw the playboys, senior and junior, Erskine and Dick Sinclair, walk off the cricket fields straight into the willing arms of eager girl friends or mistresses. After the tensions and drama of the big games emotions were drawn wire-tight; solace and comfort, encouragement and reassurance were even more important than the mere satisfaction of physical appetites, although the latter, in the case of these mettlesome athletes in their virile prime, was a major necessity.

It was an occupational problem that officialdom preferred to disregard, turned a blind eye to—and counted the pennies saved in the restriction of touring costs for the womenfolk left at home.

The men were extremely popular with the opposite sex; there were countless opportunities to meet sweet young things on their travels, provided by a large number of social occasions. Their colleagues on the opposing teams constantly invited them to their homes, to parties; some of them were besieged by fans lying in wait outside dressing-rooms; their eyes were caught by women in the hotels where they stayed, women who were dazzled by their notoriety as much as by their personalities.

At the beginning of every tour the married men started out with the strongest resolutions to resist temptations. Bets were made. The particular code used by the players for sexual congress, 'clearing your eye', became progressively in greater use as the weeks drifted by. "So-and-So couldn't care less; he was off like a shot as soon as the boat docked. ——er Number One." "As for X, he held out for six weeks, but after that he ran amok. There was no holding him. Had to call the fire brigade!"

"Did you clear your eye last night? I met a smasher at So-and-So's party. Got a pretty useful girl friend, too. Could fix it up for this evening if you like."

Conversations in the dressing-rooms.

Honest, conventionally-minded men like Jeffers or Wilson, deeply attached to their womenfolk, listened to the unconscious boasts of the younger men with vexation and resentment. The nerve strain of the big matches—and then the emptiness of the austere impersonal hotel rooms. Conflict and emotion, and then a monastic cubicle. Bed at ten o'clock on a soft summer night. The sound of chatter and music from the restaurant downstairs, whispering and feminine laughter in the corridors at midnight.

Indeed it was a long way from home.

Stavenden, who had little taste for casual adventure, had been an oddity almost, an ascetic figure. But the first abandonment to Nesta had touched off the deep longing, buried in the shaft of his mind. At home he would have resolved the problem after one hectic night. He would have guarded himself against a protracted affair by deliberately renewing his strong attachment to Lucienne. In the circumstances, this was impossible.

And now the skipper himself, the model of propriety, the proud and doting husband, genuinely in love with his wife —he, too, had succumbed.

When Steve heard about it he threw everything to the winds and that night Nesta and he had danced in the hotel supper-room to the early hours. He had held her tall, slender body in his arms, her hair against his cheek, till the tables were being cleared, till the band was almost deserted, till the lights were being dimmed, one by one, and till Philippe, the melancholy wine waiter, sat dozing and nodding at their table amidst the empty champagne buckets.

The murmuring in the hotel, the chatter that died down when he approached, the good-humoured jokes about carrying a torch for ex-flames, the surprised look on the skipper's face, and then the humorously apologetic one.

"Et tu, Brute?" said Driffield.

"Cæsar has already fallen," Steve said dryly, and the joke was repeated amongst the team.

"Steve gone the way of all flesh," murmured Sam Halliday, who was the only one to win money on the bet he had made this tour about Steve's powers of resistance.

The other married men shook their heads.

"He'll be unlucky. It's always the last one to hold the fort who gets slaughtered."

Their instincts were right. When Steve had finally seen Nesta back to her room in the early morning and, returning to his suite, switched the light on for the first time since he had returned to the hotel, he found a letter from a local solicitor. He had apparently received instructions by cable or phone from a London firm that their client, Lucienne Stavenden, had commenced proceedings for divorce against him.

Lucienne! A solicitor's letter from his wife! It was un-believable. Without a word from her, without a hint that he had been watched, that she suspected him in the slightest, without a murmur of suspicion, without any preliminary note, even of reproach, without giving the least chance to explain the situation, she had struck at him, as though she had been nursing the intention for all the years of their marriage. And she was claiming custody of his son! Could it be possible? Steve read and re-read the terrible, brief, formally worded communication; it was the second great shock of his life, the first being Nesta's infidelity . . . ironical: Nesta again. Always Nesta. Then he forgot his anger at the fear clutching at his belly. He would lose the boy. That he could not face. Unthinkable. The child worshipped him, they adored each other.

He had been a good and faithful husband to her all the years of their marriage till this lapse. He thought he understood her nature. She appeared to have been devoted to him. She was a rational, civilised person; he was not mistaken in that. Then, for God's sake, why? Why strike at him, literally, out of the night, as from under cover, as though he had been some enemy she had watched malevolently? *Why?*

And then he knew.

The sudden awareness was a flash of clarity, like a magnet drawn across the years. "So that's it. Yes."

Steve nodded curtly as though replying to a worded question.

"Can you spare a few minutes, skipper?"

"Surely. Come in and sit down. Have a drink?"

Steve regarded the captain of the team, the only man who could save the situation, whose authority and influence was considerable, whose word unchallengeable.

"Sydney, I'm having personal trouble."

"Lucienne?"

"Yes."

"Over that show-girl, what's her name. . . ? Nesta."

Steve nodded.

The skipper pushed a box of cigarettes over to him. "A pity, that. You weren't very discreet, though, Steve. Not like you at all. What on earth made you start all over again with that girl? She was poison to you in the old days."

"Don't lecture, Sydney. I've come for help, not advice."

"Of course. Sorry. Any way I can help you I'll be anxious to. Is it really serious?"

"Very."

He showed the letter. Driffield whistled; he sat up. "It *is* serious. But Lucienne . . . Why, she's absolutely charming. A most intelligent girl. . . . Why don't you get in touch with her personally? I'll write and speak with her, too, Steve, if you want me to. Surely, she'll understand. The temptation . . . the thousands of miles from home . . . men aren't made of cotton-wool, particularly chaps like you . . . some outlet necessary unfortunately . . . just a temporary lapse . . . doesn't mean anything at all, really. Of course, her pride must be hurt, but she's an understanding girl. No, I don't think it can be all that serious. Nothing we can't straighten out." He lit his pipe. "Hell, it's a damned nuisance, this wife problem. How on earth do they expect trained athletes at the peak of their form to go to bed with a good book each night? And those girls—they chuck themselves at us. Anyway, I know what to say."

Steve said, "I'm going to deny it."

The skipper was surprised. "Deny it? You won't get anywhere with that, Steve."

"Won't I?"

"You've been seen in that girl's company for days now, every free minute."

"Yes, in bars, restaurants, places like that. They don't know about the other thing. They can't prove anything."

"Are you sure? You might have been watched. She might have been seen with you in your suite. A waiter, a chamber-maid, perhaps."

"No. Nobody with us at any time."

"Well, she might have been seen going in with you late at night."

"I don't think so. Anyway, that's where you come in. You can say you were invited, too, that it was all innocent."

"How on earth can I do that?"

"Oh, I don't mean perjure yourself in a court of law. It will never come to that if you cover up for me. If you write and 'explain' they'll believe you; your word will be indisputable."

"I see."

"Sydney, you've got to do this for me. I'm desperate. It's Harry I'm thinking of."

"Your boy?"

Steve nodded miserably. "I can't lose my son. I just can't."

'Not Lucienne?' Driffield wondered.

"I know it's a lot to ask someone like you, but I would do it for anyone in the team, and I think any of them would do it for me."

"Must you ask me? Why not . . . well, one of the others?"

"You're the captain. Your word would be gospel."

"It might be. Might not. But don't you see that because it means so much I can't abuse it?"

"Of course I see it. But this is more important. This is real. This is happening to *me*."

"Steve, you're putting me in a terrible position. If I weren't skipper I'd do it like a shot. I'd alibi for my friends with their wives if I were at home and it was a private matter, but I'd be abusing a position of trust; they'd have to believe me *because* I'm the captain of the English team and what I say must be so. It doesn't matter if it's not in a court of law. I'd be writing to solicitors, and that would be evidence. If it goes further I can't back down. It's impossible, Steve."

"Impossible? When you know I'd do the same for you?"

Words of anger trembled on his tongue. He wondered; looked around the room, at the closed bedroom door, saw the tell-tale signs at last, a woman's gloves on an occasional table, a hand-mirror beside it.

Driffield looked uneasy.

"I know what you're thinking. You mustn't judge by appearances."

"I'm not making any judgment on you, skipper. But we're all in the same position."

Driffield shook his head. He said gently, "No, Steve."

"You and I are in the same boat, Mr. Driffield," said Steve, his anger finally crystallised to resentment.

"You're mistaken. It's different from what you imagine, Steve."

"She's your sister?"

"Oh, no, I'm not evading the issue, but believe me you've seen nothing. It's as I said, you can't possibly know what's involved here."

"Does anyone ever really know what's involved? Does anyone know the real story behind the way things look? I'm not even interested to know. I have no opinions, no comments; I'm not pronouncing judgment. I'd do what I had to to help, that's all. You are talking about being loyal to a trust. What about your loyalty to your friends?"

"You're asking me to do something that I simply cannot do. There's a principle involved here, bigger than any personality, bigger than you or I or any one member of the team."

Steve tried to control the rush of denunciation, suppress the anger. When he finally spoke, it was calm and reasoned.

"You don't have to give evidence if it ever goes to court."

"Then they'll know I lied and they'd subpœna me. What sort of reflection on English sport will it be to show up a national skipper as a liar? Think of the game."

"It probably would never come to that. They wouldn't have much case with evidence against them like that."

"I can't take the chance."

Steve's mouth was dry. "Is that final, Sydney?"

"I'm afraid so."

"You expect me to go out on that field tomorrow, with this on my mind, and play the game of my life?"

"I hope you will. I'm sure you will. You're a great player and you're a real pro. You'll do just that."

Steve got up; his face was pale under his tan. "You're asking too much, you know. Oh, I'll go out and play my best. And this won't hurt it. I'll see to that. But I'll never serve with you as skipper again, Sydney. Never. It's you or me. The selectors will have to decide. It's your word, but it's my son."

Driffield said, "You've just made an important decision."

The threat was not underestimated by Driffield. He was perfectly well aware that Steve, the number one attacking force in the English team, might do just what he threatened to do, kick the captaincy from right under him.

He re-lit his pipe. "As a matter of fact, Steve, I think you might be worrying unduly. I don't think this threat is so serious as it sounds. Lucienne must have got into a temper; this thing might be just the heat of the moment. It sounds that way to me. Else why should an intelligent girl do a thing like that? Why, she doesn't phone you or write or get in touch at all about a possible explanation. Obviously it's something done on the spur of the moment. She's probably regretting it right this minute."

"She means it," said Steve, shortly.

"But why? Surely the marriage means something to her? After all these years a woman doesn't just smash up her home over one lapse. I know you've been a model husband till now."

"She will," said Steve grimly. "If she can make it really hurt."

But he did not explain about the meeting on the wedding eve behind the summer-house.

"Steve's really working up a sweat tonight for tomorrow's game," the boys said, listening to the Drum Roll Blues that were shaking the suite. "Somebody ought to go and tell him to knock it off before the other guests start complaining."

They had never heard such an angry despairing commotion. "And all in swing time."

Nesta heard it when she pressed the bell of the suite. There was no reply. She rang again, but still no answer.

"Steve. . . ." she called. "I know you're there. Why don't you answer? I've phoned and rung all night. What have I done, darling? Why don't you answer the bell?"

After a while she realised that he really meant it. What had she done? She couldn't understand it.

Two or three doors were beginning to open along the corridor; most of the faces were sober and concerned, but one tall figure, in a resplendent red silk dressing-gown, looked cheerful enough.

He said, "Will I do?"

Then the smile was wiped off his face as he saw the expression on hers and the hot tears. It was not often that the four-star hotel corridor was haunted by a weeping woman in a sable cape. She passed him by in an aura of Chanel, the jewels glinting in her ears and flashing white flame on her wrists, her head held high, and her tears flowing unchecked.

The Skipper

"You close late," said Driffield to the girl in the florist shop which was a special feature of the resplendent hotel foyer.

"I was just putting them away in the cold room for the night, Mr. Driffield."

"How long do they keep in this weather? I should think it's a difficult line of business. They must perish in a matter of days, hours perhaps."

"Yes, we have to sell them quickly. But of course there is always a demand in a place like this. People are always buying flowers, the men before they go off on their dates. Usually at the last minute they remember they ought to."

"And who buys you flowers, mam'selle?"

"Well . . ."

"Or do you get bored with them? The young men bring you chocolates, is that it?"

"Oh, no. I adore flowers."

"Even though you deal in them all day long?"

"Even then. There's nothing like flowers for a girl. They're favourite, even with me."

"And which are your favourite?"

"The long-stemmed yellow roses, Mr. Driffield."

He nodded. "Take a dozen home with you, then."

"Why . . . *thank you.*"

Driffield went through the lounge into the coffee-room, sat down in a quiet corner, ordered brandy, and settled down to read Cynthia's last three letters for the fourth time. Well, natural that she should miss him as he missed her on these tours, but the tone of dejection was unusual for her. These trips were becoming progressively more difficult to announce to her. ('If you'll hate me being away, I'll turn it down. I can see you're bored with the idea.' 'But *why* can't I come with you? I know you love these tours. You seem to look forward to them so much; I don't want to spoil your amusement, darling, only share it. Can't I possibly go along? The boat trip would be fun. The long cruise, and I enjoy watching you play—in spells. It would be perfect.'

('I know, dearest. I would like nothing better. But you see . . . the others. The pros can't arrange it. . . . It's too expensive. I'd be the only one travelling with my wife.'

('Well, heavens, *I* don't mind. I'll find plenty of girl friends on the trip if I feel like a hen party.'

('That's not it, darling. Some of the pros who are married and can't afford to take their wives would resent the idea that we can be together.'

103

('Well, really, darling, that's just too bad, isn't it! Why don't you give away your money like Tolstoi? There are lots of people who resent us having things we can afford.'

('Please try and understand. This is different. It's a comradeship. It wouldn't be . . . friendly.'

('It wouldn't be *cricket*.'

(She added, a moment later, 'What have you done to Noel? When you went off on that West Indies trip that winter, he kept ringing me up to see if I was in. I thought he wanted to take me out, but all he wanted to know was whether I had any plans for the evening. When I said "No," he said, "Good. That's all right then," and rang off. He did that so often I was sick of it, so one evening when he rang I said I was going out. He began to ask me all sorts of things, particularly if I was going out with another chap. I told him I was. He said, "I'm coming over right away." He did, too; and we sat and listened to the records all the evening till about eleven. Then he got up and said, very formal, "Thank you for a splendid evening. I'll have to go now." Well, really! I couldn't care less, but after all—Noel! I ask you! That sort of behaviour from Noel is uncalled for.

('Well, I got to thinking, and it was a dreary long night without you, and then I began to think about Noel, too. You know how my mind wanders from one thing to another. I felt very depressed. "Heavens, I must be slipping," I thought. I didn't have it any more. So the *next evening* . . .'

('The next evening?'

('Yes, the next evening I rang him up and asked him if he had any plans. He said, "Why?" and I said, "If you're not free I'll make other arrangements." So he said, "No, that's not necessary." So I hung up quickly and put on my best taffeta—you know the off-the-shoulder one that sounds like a tree in a wind when I walk—then I tricked myself out with those long ear-rings that swing and jingle like sleigh bells, sprayed myself all over with the perfume you bought in Paris on our honeymoon, put on my tallest evening slippers, and I thought, "If that doesn't do it . . ." Well, when I arrived I stood in the doorway for a moment, one arm up, with my left profile slightly away, like in the photo Angus took, and I *knew* I must be getting across all right because Noel's left eyelid twitched a little as it always does when you're registering. *Well* . . . he was wearing a long black-and-gold dressing-gown, and a scarlet neckerchief with gold dragons on it, a black jade holder affair for his dreadful Russian cigarette, just like the other chap. *Well* . . . I floated in, brushing my hand under his chin, and looking up with my small girl look. I sank down into his longest chaise, put my feet up . . . and waited. *Well* . . . that's all!'

('That was all?'

('My *dear,* I might have had the plague! Oh, he was very sweet, and he gave me lots of his haggard hungry look, and a most scrumptious dinner. And then, when we reached the Chartreuse stage, he said the nicest things to me—things that were reassuring, anyway. But . . . *that's all!* When he saw me home he held my hand and murmured something about owing it to you or something, and I assured him that we weren't being watched, that you would never dream of such a thing, and he sort of sighed and said, "That's just it." *That's just it.* Who would have thought it? *Noel.* Darling, what *did* you do to him?'

('Nothing. I assure you.'

('Then it must be something you said. That it wouldn't be *cricket.* Something like that. Just like this business of not taking me with you because the pros can't afford it! That's it, isn't it?'

('Perhaps.'

('I knew it. Men! They're such children over that game. It's not a game, it's . . . it's a religion. Why on earth didn't you learn to play *football?*')

Driffield read the last letter intently, trying to see beyond the tender endearments, the gaiety, the devotion, to the heart of the conflict that she kept from him. It had been harder to tell her of his offer of captaincy for this last trip; she had got into a sort of panic about it, throwing up a smoke-screen of objections without ever coming out into the open about the real cause. His medical practice would be neglected, she insisted, although she well knew that, since the war, his work was merely administrative at the local hospital. "I have no patients to look after which my partners can't take care of. My job at the hospital is mainly organisational." Then she began to argue about his indifference to his father's business. "The firm bears your name, Sydney. Driffield and Son. Surely, Son ought to take some interest in it." Her reproachfulness surprised him; he did not realise that she felt so strongly about his complete lack of interest in the business. "Your father told me once," she went on, "that as a youngster, when he himself was seriously ill, you took charge at a moment's notice, and steered it through some big crisis or other. Darling, I wouldn't care a bit if you had no aptitude for these things, but when you set your mind to things you're a real force. You were a *bloody* fine doctor during the war when you were needed, you mastered the ins and outs of a big industrial concern when your father needed you. I want you to do something really big when you *don't* need to, because you *can,* for the sake of doing it, not because you have to." She was flushed; her mouth trembled as she said, "If all you could do was to play cricket, or even if you had to make a living by it, I wouldn't mind so much, but you've qualities in you that would make you a really big man, and you're not doing a thing about it. You play at your work and work at your silly game." She stopped suddenly and kissed him. "Don't look like that. All I want is your happiness really. It doesn't matter to me what you do, provided it's what you really want." He had said, "I want you to be happy about it, too."

'You play at your work and work at your silly game.' That he had carried in his mind all these weeks of travel; not a day passed that he did not think of it. The one reproach had almost made him decline the selectors' offer, the crowning achievement of his cricket career, captaincy of the English team against Australia. It was his last chance, too; at thirty-five he was still at his peak, but in a couple of years or so Stavenden would almost certainly be the choice of captain.

When he had told his father about Cynthia's reproach, and that he felt guilty about neglecting his duties as a director and partner of Driffield, the old man had unmistakably told him to accept the selectors' offer. "You've won your spurs, Sydney. What you did here when I was laid up is enough for me. And besides, the firm can't afford not to have you accept the offer to captain England. The publicity value to us is phenomenal. Ask me to dinner tonight and I'll slip it into the conversation for Cynthia's benefit."

And then there was the core of the problem: the continual separations during his tours abroad. The discussion about the lack of facilities for the professionals' wives was the key to her resentment. "I'm not asking you to decline the offer. That's what you want to do, it's important to you, and your father thinks it important to the firm. But why we should be separated because there are no travel allowances for the others? I don't understand. I think the management is damned mean. They must make tens of thousands of profits out of the tour; the least they can do is to pay out a bit of money for the comfort of the men and their wives."

"The money is devoted to helping the sport at home. These big tours make up some of the losses the smaller clubs suffer. Cricket is not a wealthy sport like soccer with millions of regular fans turning up at the grounds every week."

"If the smaller clubs can't even get the support of the public why should they be subsidised? They're not a national health scheme. It's not a basic necessity like agriculture or defence. And your sensitiveness about the way the other men feel—that's a bit much. How many of them really want their wives to come, as you do? How do you know they don't welcome these jaunts to get away from home? The way some of them behave when they're abroad—I *know* they do, so don't try to alibi. Noel told me all about it in the old days."

"That sort of thing is a gross exaggeration. And I'm sure he didn't tell you to repeat it."

"Well, I only told you. That doesn't count."

"And I bet you wormed it out of him, female like."

"Well, why not? I'm a female. Anyway, don't change the subject. When you went off for that first time I thought it was just the odd trip, but when it began to crop up almost every winter . . . I find it most unsettling. If it was *really* a job like exploring or archæology or building bridges and things, then I wouldn't mind, but to play games . . . well, something must be done about it. I can't see any good reason why I shouldn't join in the fun and hop on board the charabanc. I like games, too."

"You can't come, darling. I'd rather not go at all if you feel you're being denied something you're entitled to. I mean it. I'll tell the selectors I'm not available."

"No," she said, "you men find it so important. There is no doubt you must go."

During the next days she appeared to accept the situation philosophically; she insisted that he went on the trip; she pleaded that she would be far more miserable if he were to deny himself the honour of captaining the series. "I've thought it out finally," she said. "As it is your big triumph and you might not get another chance to be captain against the Aussies, I've decided that you really must accept."

"Do you really not mind me leaving you again?"

"No. I've decided, in the circs, that I don't. Truly."

"I wonder what has brought about this change of heart?"

Some weeks later, sitting in the coffee-room of the hotel, and with her last letters in front of him, he wondered again. Driffield had little understanding of the subtleties of the feminine heart, and there were times when he felt that his wife was a creature of Machiavellian inscrutability. In common with most men of a mainly extrovert character, he had been content to accept the mystique of female psychology as a standard fixture of the the universe, like the migration of the conger eel, the influence of the moon on the ocean currents, and other such immutable mysteries. But there were times when the shadow play and sleight of hand of his wife's attitude to him was uncomfortably near the bone. It became absolutely necessary to understand it for the sake of his peace of mind. The sudden lapse of resistance to his trip had left him with a vague sense of suspicion; and he was unhappy about that nagging thought that she believed he played at life and only took games seriously.

About this latter problem there was something that he could have told her, if he had believed it right for a man to protest his manhood, which of course one simply did not do.

He could have told her exactly why he had discontinued to give much more of his time and efforts to the firm. He could have answered her unspoken criticism that as he was a full partner and not a nominal shareholder, drawing very considerable remunerations, far greater than his earnings as a doctor, he was morally obliged to put himself at the disposal of Driffield and Son. He could have explained otherwise. He could also have explained that he had become a doctor on active service during the war for precisely the same reason that your genuine pacifist becomes a stretcher-bearer in the Commando or the Marines, giving courageous service but refusing to take life, so that when the war was over his medical work in peace time became a token service only. He could have explained but didn't. It was not in his nature to protest his integrity; his actions had to speak for themselves; that was the way he was made. His wife, his friends, knowing the man, would have to accept that. Usually, they did; but a woman, by her nature, could not see with his eyes, could not feel the way he felt; and there were times when she simply did not understand.

Misunderstandings.

When his friends or acquaintances had told him about the conflicts or incompatibilities in their marriages, he used to think it must reveal a weakness or fault in their natures. How could any outsider judge? This business of Cynthia and himself: each of them probably absolutely right according to their lights, and yet neither of them understood the other. If only she had faith in him, as he believed absolutely in her.

But did he? There was the suspicion and jealousy about Noel, which he had dealt with in a by no means forthright manner; there was his later suspicion after she capitulated about not going on tour with him. What was she up to? He hardly dared frame the thought in his mind. Was she planning to resume her association with anyone else in his absence? A dreadful, unworthy thought, yes, and probably a weakness of his own conventional upbringing. She had not come to him as a bride should; he had known—in fact, she had made no secret of her passionate affair with Noel. Was there no one else? Was she really incapable of breaking her vows of loyalty? Under normal circumstances, there was no doubt of her devotion, but when he repeatedly left her for what she felt was a frivolous reason, going away for months at a time to the ends of the earth to play a game with a bat and ball—let's face it, according to her own logic, it was no more than that—then, to her feminine way of thinking, was there not justification for her to take her consolation where she could find it?

There were her letters. There was the forced note of gaiety, ill concealing her depression about his absence. And there was something else, something even worse, something which he could not explain in any way, except one:

In the last five days, driven by his loneliness and longing for her, he had tried to telephone her from the hotel. "Mrs. Driffield is not at home. . . ." "But where is she? Is she in

London with friends? Perhaps she is with my parents? Or hers?" No one knew. He had phoned repeatedly, speaking with the butler, her personal maid, the housekeeper, all of whom must know where she was. He always got the same answer. They knew nothing. He dared not phone his parents or hers as that would put them in a panic. Besides, the domestic staff would most certainly know if she was with the family.

What possible explanation was there to this mystery? What explanation but one?

He recalled his own lonely evenings, the long almost intolerable nights. His body, accustomed to hers even in sleep, turned restlessly; the sheets were tangled in knots in the mornings; the ache in his bones, the sluggishness of his blood, the irritability during the day could only be tempered by hard physical exercise. Each evening he prayed for exhaustion.

Surely, surely, it must be the same with her. How well he knew the warmth of her physical nature; how often had he delighted in it. He cursed himself for a fool, a hundred times a fool for his failure to understand. Of course, she had got sick of it, gone off to find distraction, no doubt found it. There had been a swarm of suitors after the eclipse of her love affair with Noel. Any man worthy of the name could see the nature of such a creature almost at a glance; the languors of her walk, the indolence of her glance, the profound lines of her figure. He remembered a hundred things, his nerves, his blood, the roots of his hair remembered. Fool to think that because she was his wife, she was immune from temptation.

The brandy glass slipped from his moist grasp and clattered to the table. The wine waiter came over with a napkin to mop up the stain.

"Shall I fetch you another brandy, Mr. Driffield?"

"Storrington . . . England here. . . . Your personal call to Mrs. Driffield, sir. Sorry, Mrs. Driffield is still away. No news of her whereabouts yet. Is there any message? We shall call you the moment she arrives."

"Let me speak with Maynard, the housekeeper."

"Mr Driffield. . . . Can you hear me?"

"Speak up, please, Mrs. Maynard. I can hardly hear you. Still no news from Mrs. Driffield?"

"No, sir."

"But surely you must have some idea where she is?"

"I'm sorry. . . . Would you please repeat . . . ?"

"Some clue as to where she is? . . ."

". . . alarmed about it . . . sure she's with friends. . . ."

"Alarmed? Why are you alarmed? Is anything wrong? I said, is anything the matter?"

"No, I said there's no need to be alarmed, Mr. Driffield. I'm sure she's with friends."

"But what friends? Did she receive any invitation from anyone recently?"

". . . bags packed . . . nothing . . . hardly know what to say. . . ."

"I can't hear you. You're most indistinct. She couldn't have just gone off and told no one. She's not with anyone you know?"

". . . to say . . . but please don't worry."

"Worry? I'm worried like hell! What do you expect me to feel? You must find where she is. I've had no letter from her the last fortnight. Not a word! I'll call you again in a few hours! You *must* find out!"

The receiver fell from his hand. It was a conspiracy. The woman obviously knew something. Someone must know. The mistress did not just go off and leave a household without retaining communication with her staff. What if there was a telegram, something urgent that must be forwarded to her at once? It simply didn't make sense. Cynthia was a responsible person.

What a rotten trick to play on a man. Was she punishing

him? Didn't she realise the agony of mind he must be in? Who was she with at this moment whilst the cold sweat was on his back, making his shirt cling? Thank God, Noel was with them on this trip, otherwise he would be catching the next plane back to England with a loaded revolver. Did he really have an inferiority feeling about Noel, as she hinted? What the hell did it matter? What did anything matter? By God, what a way to behave when she knew he had the strain of the series on his mind, the whole responsibility . . . to hell with the series! This was something vital. God, how he loved that woman! Nothing else was really important compared with that.

He was in such a state of mind that he failed to hear the door-bell ring. It had been repeated whilst he was still on the phone; he had paid no attention. Now it was resumed, insistent, urgent.

He strode across to the door and threw it open.

He stared speechless at the woman standing before him.

"Hallo," she said. She lifted the little veil that covered her face. "Yes, it's me, all right. Stop standing with your mouth open and help the boy with those bags of mine."

It was Cynthia.

"Oh, no," she was saying some hours or so later, "I didn't exactly plan to come all the time. Nothing quite so definite. I simply thought, 'I'll see if I can last out this trip, and if I can't, I'll chuck a couple of nighties into a bag in case of fire and hop on a plane.' "

"I was thinking such dreadful things. Surely you could have told someone?"

"Well, seeing the way you felt about this thing I didn't want anyone to know. Not anyone who might talk. If the reporters found out it would have been in the papers and you would have been shot at. Dogs must be carried on the escalators, darling. No smoking. Please fasten your safety belts. Don't forget to adjust your dress before leaving. Wives simply not allowed. And all that."

"I'm glad you came."

"Just like that?"

"Just like that."

She said with a sigh of relief, "Thank goodness you put it so succinctly. If you'd have said, 'I'm glad you came, but——' I'd have walked out of your life. I mean it. That one word 'but' would have cost you a pretty good housewife and mother. So don't forget."

"No, my love."

"I'll stay under cover. I'll pretend to be your mistress. I'll go out with you wearing my veil. Oh, yes, please. Darling, this is simply splendid. I'll love it. We'll sneak out when no one is looking. Or if they do, they'll pretend not to. They're so discreet here! It's marvellous. We'll have champagne in buckets, and I'll slip into the bedroom when anyone calls. Darling, this is marvellous fun, much more interesting than being merely married. Do you think the veil's enough or can you get me a yashmak?"

Driffield had enough sense of humour to enjoy her preposterous suggestion. She had travelled in her maiden name and registered in the same way when she arrived at the hotel. She explained who she was to the hotel manager, whose discretion was boundless. She had told Samson, the butler, of her intentions, and swore him to secrecy (she did not trust the female domestic staff). Alone amongst her relatives, she informed her parents and his; she did not breathe a word to any of her friends.

She had thought his objections to her accompanying him on the trip quite unreal, but she respected his wishes in the matter absolutely. And then, after their reunion had been some hours old, and they were getting their breath back, he had wondered about how he would inform the other members of the team, and the team manager. He was planning to take the blame

114

himself and say that he had requested her to make the journey; she had suggested that she could spare everyone difficulties by the simple and charmingly fantastic expedient of pretending to be a casual girl friend he had picked up. "It's quite easy, really. It's a large hotel, this suite is quite self-supporting. I can go out when you chaps are playing cricket. No one else knows me. If we want to go out in the evening I could arrange to meet you at some out of the way place. We could easily get away with it. If we stay in we could have dinner sent up. I can make myself scarce in the bedroom if anyone calls. When you have to go off to the next playing date I'll travel alone and join you later. And think of the fun!" Her eyes sparkled. "It makes the whole thing twice as jolly, darling. Think of it! Dinner alone in a gentleman's hotel suite, Champagne, discreet knocks on the door. Tactful waiters, quietly smiling behind their hands. Secret rendezvous for the evening, dodging all our friends and acquaintances, false or practically false names in the hotel register. It's perfect. I've *always* wanted to know what it would be like. There is an Other Woman wearing a veil and black lace cami-knickers in the heart of every respectably married housewife. And don't pretend it wouldn't be fun for you. You'll be able to see me from quite a *different* angle, and after all, variety is the spice of life."

It was a French farce standing on its head.

Later that night he said to her, "I suppose I'm quite the happiest and luckiest man in the world. There's no one like you, my darling. If you hadn't walked in through that door when you did, I just don't know what I'd have done. You're wonderful."

"You just hang on to that and we'll be all right." She chuckled. "I admit it *was* good timing. But then I know enough about your personal thing to guess that two months away from me and you've just about had it."

"You, too?"

"Oh, yes. Me, too," she said.

The hours had slipped by in a stream of enchantment. Her hands and lips had never held such magic; fire fed fire; love was a rejuvenation.

"Well . . . and do you think you could manage a little strawberries and cream?"

"Strawberries and cream? I'm still on the smoked salmon. . . ."

Oasis.

The curtains moved in the night wind. She awoke with a start, searched frantically for him beside her, saw him standing in the starlight. The breeze was blowing the fragrant night air into the room, the curtains flapping on the balcony.

"Something interesting out there?" she said in a haughty tone.

"Hallo. I didn't know you were awake."

"I was asleep. I woke up as soon as I felt you gone." It was literally true; and the sweetness of the words caught at his heart.

"Why don't you say nice things to me?" she said after a while. Deep feeling had always made him speechless.

"You know how I feel about you. All right, I know. A woman wants to be told." He took one or two deep breaths. "This has been the most wonderful night of my life, and you have made it perfect."

"Mr. Driffield, *what would your wife say if she knew?*"

He tried to spank her and she threw a pillow at him; they scuffled on the bed like children. At length he trapped her. They stared into each other's eyes. She said, "All this . . . and you're still *not out!*"

"Darling! I didn't think you cared! You've been following the game!"

"Secretly. Don't think I'm not proud of you. John's doing well too. His report is better than last term. Seventh in class, and in the junior school second eleven for soccer.

There. And you, sixty-something *not out!*"

"Darling," she said, "will this be the last time?"

"The last tour. I think so. Yes, it will be the last. I'll chuck it in after this one."

"Not that I think you're getting old or anything. It's no reflection on your manly prowess." (He pretended to bow grave acknowledgment.) "But we can't obviously repeat this boudoir comedy . . . and I might run out of ideas." She stretched sleepily, patting the place beside her. "You're too far away. . . . . . . What was I saying? . . . . Oh, yes, I think you agree that after this tour. . . . . What was I saying? . . . . . . After this tour . . . Yes, I'm glad you agree. After all, you can't top this, can you? Finish on a high note. . . . . What was I . . . ? Oh, yes. Finish on a high note. . . . . Go on playing for the county in the summer . . . . in the summer. . . . . Where was I? Go on playing for the county and I'll be quite pleased to be a camp follower. We could stay at different county pubs . . . ."

(John was seventh in class, and he was sixty not out.)

"Darling," he said, "do you really think of me that way—the way you think of John?"

"Do you mind?"

"I don't know."

("You play at your work, and work at your games.")

The stars hung trembling in the deep pit of the night. When he was a child someone had told him that the stars were God's spy-holes to watch over him whilst he slept. Had anyone ever offered a better explanation? *(In the second eleven of the junior school. . . .)* He slept.

He dreamed that he was a boy once more, and the sun was hot in the sky, and he was partnering Noel in a great stand. Noel was five hundred not out, but Sydney was struggling for runs. He had only scored seven. The sun was so hot. Every time he tried to score, his father, who was the umpire, disallowed it. 'Leg bye!' he shouted after Sydney had played a perfectly sound shot, with the ball connecting squarely with the bat. Sometimes the bowler was his father, too, sending down unplayable googlies that hissed like snakes. And the sun was hot in the sky, so hot.

Suddenly, there was a downpour, a tremendous clap of thunder; the lightning flashed; the players ran for cover, even Noel, his bat under his arm, stalked off with that lean dignified stride of his. 'No more play!' his father shouted. And the cry was taken up all over the field. 'No more play!' He stood in the pelting rain, his head bowed, refusing to budge. 'Why doesn't that boy give up?' shouted a voice. The cry was echoed, 'Give up!' He wanted to give up; he refused to move. 'Why don't you give up? There will be no more play today. Why doesn't that boy move? Obstinate boy!' (Somewhere on a different level his mind was racing on, 'If only it will rain hard during the night and bind that turf. We could fight back. Fight back!') And the voices were calling in his dream that he could not fight back; he could not fight the storm. It was God's will, the storm and the lightning flash, and there was no fighting it.

He woke with a start, his heart racing. Yes, there was a sharp knock on the outer door of the suite. Who could it be at this time? Was it Noel? Noel in some sort of trouble? He jerked to full wakefulness. That it was trouble of some kind he was certain. Some member of his temperamental flock. Shepherding a band of athletes across the world was like transporting a string of mettlesome racehorses whose delicate ankles could be broken by one mis-step.

He threw on a dressing-gown, pacified Cynthia with a brief word, closed the bedroom door gently behind him, and opened the door of the suite. It was 'Steve' Stavenden, the star player and the apple of his eye.

"Sorry to bang like that. . . . Can I have a word with you, skipper?"

At a glance Driffield recognised a crisis.

"Can I have a few minutes with you?" repeated Stavenden.

When he had gone Driffield told the whole story to Cynthia, who listened with deep attention. He omitted nothing but the threat to his captaincy. That was an issue with which he did not wish to burden her.

"Poor Steve," she said. She had a soft spot for Steve. Everyone had; a charming fellow, and completely unspoiled.

"I think Lucienne must be mad," said Driffield, referring to the episode. "Now why should she want a divorce?"

"You never know with people," said Cynthia. "How well do you know her, darling? I only met her at the do's. She seemed a self-possessed piece. French, isn't she? A bit of a tight mouth. But I didn't pay a lot of attention." She sighed, "No, you never can tell."

"You don't know Nesta?"

"No, a bit before my time. I've seen her . . . perform. It was at the club we went to last New Year but one, I think. A high stepper. And Steve's a hot-blooded boy. Lucienne ought to understand." She suddenly laughed. "You know, I was thinking. . . . If Steve had wanted a good threat to make you play ball, he could have said he'd expose you to me with associating with an Unknown Woman!"

Driffield laughed. "Well, he didn't go as far as that."

"Then he *did* threaten you?"

Driffield was silent. She pressed him, and in the end he admitted the threat about the captaincy, almost apologetically. "I didn't take any notice of it. It's just the heat of battle. He was resentful at the thought that I was getting away with something he wasn't." He shrugged. "He'll calm down. He's a good chap."

She said slowly, "You know, I don't think my idea is such a good one. As long as he doesn't know it's me, he'll feel a real grudge. It will get worse later with the divorce, not better. You must tell him, darling."

He shook his head. "No."

"But why not? Don't be so obstinate. A simple explanation and he'll drop his threat."

Driffield said, shortly, "I'm not answerable to Stavenden for my actions."

"What an odd man you are. Proud, stiff-necked. Just like your father. Take it or leave it. And to hell with any explanation."

"I told him it wasn't what it seemed. That ought to be good enough for him."

"You're like a spoiled, stubborn child. You and your schoolboy code! For God's sake, grow up, Sydney. You're a grown man physically; it's terrifying to be so intolerant, so hide-bound. You are in a world of people with weaknesses, fears, vanities, jealousies; the world isn't just black and white. This man is suffering because he might lose his son. Don't you know what that means? How can you expect him to behave like a plaster saint and take your word? He'll fight you with all the weapons he has. He looked to you, his captain, to rally to his side, right or wrong, and you could only give him some public school slogan. He'll strike back at you. You've got to be supple, darling. Bend with the wind or you'll break. Don't be such a monument!"

Driffield stared at his wife; it was as though he was seeing her for the first time.

PART TWO

Batting Honours

"Very chancy, skipper. Very. With the pitch like concrete . . .
it will be churned up later in the day. . . . You don't know
what you'll be in for. Anything goes. It will play tricks with
fast bowling or spin."

They were coming in from the field, Driffield and Wilson,
and discussing the plan of campaign.

Driffield said, "I hate to miss a chance like this, and we still
have a good one. If we can keep it up until the bowling is
worn down a bit Steve and the others may break through."

"I'll attack, but I'm warning you, I haven't got my eye in as
I had yesterday. Anything might happen."

"All right, Ben. You've made your point. You've covered
yourself every way. If you flop, I'll know why. There's no need
to go all out to start with. Wait till you're fairly comfortable."

No rain in the night; the pitch dry as a bone. No dew, no
moisture to bind the turf. By mid-morning at the resumption
of play it would be a battlefield. Ryder could make his bumpers
fly; the spin bowlers could get real bite into the turn of the
ball.

Driffield said, "If it had rained a bit it might be still worse.
A little shine and that ball would be shooting like a rocket."

It was not real consolation and the others knew it.

"Steve . . . Dick . . . Noel . . . this is just the sort of game
to suit your style. . . . I know you chaps aren't worrying about
your averages."

"Had your coffee this morning?" Jeffers was saying as Sam Halliday joined him. "Had a look at the pitch?"

"Bumps-a-daisy."

Jeffers nodded. "I reckon that's the main danger. The spin will take all right, but it's manageable. It's the flyers I'm worried about."

Jeffers was a master of defence against spin bowling; his tremendous experience stood him so well that he could anticipate the movement of the ball at the moment it left the bowler's hand; no googly had fooled him in years. But the 'bumpers' were different; no one could predict the outcome of a ball gone berserk; it made nonsense of all calculation, negated experience. Only the supremely swift, the very young with superhuman skill, could cope with that sort of stuff. Dick Sinclair, with the youngest, keenest eye in the game, hit a tremendous century in such circumstances during the second Test whilst players like Jeffers were groping and flinching.

Sam Halliday read Jeffers's expression and pushed a cup of coffee in front of him. "Don't brood about it, Bob. What will happen, will happen."

"A beautiful thought."

". . . Not that it will worry a bright boy like you," Noel was saying to Dick Sinclair. "The faster they come off the pitch the quicker you can send them to the boundary.—How are the ladies?"

"How are the horses?"

"Ah . . . *touché*. That means you've scored a point."

"Oh, hell, everyone knows what *touché* means."

". . . . And try and remember not to jump out to Carmichael. He works closely with Fallon behind the stumps. . . ."

". . . My favourite hook shot. I swore on a stack of Bibles I wouldn't do it in the second innings. And what happened? I was like a mesmerised rabbit. Same thing happened, same sort of ball, hanging up there like an apple in the Garden of Eden. . . ."

Driffield and Wilson walking out together; applause; the same faces all around them; in a few minutes the interruption of last night, the interrupted enchantment with Cynthia, the drama of Stavenden, would be wiped from his mind. By lunchtime, if he survived the ordeal, he would know no other reality; there would be no time, no other way of life; the universe would be this green bowl beneath the dome of the sky, the changing patterns of the white figures, the red sphere, all the drama and action and conflict, the whole of the law, that guided him.

"Fifty to one against us winning last night. I put two quid down. . . ."

"Plunger!"

". . . and if I win, there'll be Champagne all round tonight."

Wilson was struggling. The confidence of the previous day was lost in the first onslaught of Ryder's and Sterndale's fury, the ball lifting waist-high, and swinging. Wilson whistled with relief at the end of the second over, knowing he had had two narrow escapes, the first time from one that was a few inches above his wicket, the second when he got the thick end of the bat to an outswinger, and Reynolds, at fine leg could only get the tips of his fingers to it. It was almost the same with Driffield, who, getting off the mark with a quick single and a boundary later in the over, was forced to defensive back play, granting Sterndale his second maiden of the morning.

About ten minutes later the inevitable happened. Wilson pushed forward to a yorker; the ball beat him, and his leg stump was knocked clean out of the ground.

The applause for the bowler merged into an even louder roar for the retiring batsman, who had made his best score for the

123

series. A hundred and thirty-eight for one, Wilson fifty-nine; the shift of fortune favouring the Australians once again.

Stavenden, padded and gloved, held the receiver to his ear; Cynthia's voice was drowned in the roar of applause as Wilson was bowled. "Just a minute . . . there's a lot of noise outside. . . ."

"So you see, Steve, that pig-headed husband of mine was in a sense covering up for me. You do understand, don't you?"

She went on, "If I can be of any help to you . . . see Lucienne when we get back?"

"It's very kind of you, Mrs. Driffield, but I'd rather not talk about it."

"You do understand about the other thing, don't you?"

"Yes, of course."

"Steve . . . no hard feelings?"

"No, Mrs. Driffield. Of course not. Forgive me, I have to go now."

Steve picked up his bat.

The skipper covering up for his wife, his wife covering for him, nobody covering for Steve; but no, no hard feelings. Not that he would have implemented his threat about the captaincy. He'd had second thoughts about it. Well, the skipper had been clever enough to solve his problems; clever enough to marry the right woman; more than he deserved. Still, there was no point in envying the man his luck. Stavenden balanced the bat in his hand. Luck.

The skipper was lucky: wife and home, fame and fortune. Steve wasn't so lucky. Nesta, Lucienne . . . even Harry, perhaps, his only child. No, he hadn't had much luck. There was only the piece of shining willow in his hand. That was his luck, that and nothing else. Not much for a man, perhaps, but all his. The flexible muscles of his wrists tightened as he gripped the handle; he swung it in his grasp. In the old days a two-handed sword would have been right, it would have been better, far better; they only handed out wooden swords these days. Not much; better than nothing. A man was never quite alone.

He tucked it under his arm and stepped out of the pavilion. The heat, the glare of the sun, hit him; that, and the roar, the shout from the crowd, with something about it that was different from the sound it made when it greeted the other players. Special for Steve. It had edge to it. It told him something that no man could ever forget; in years to come he would still hear it; even when he was finished, retired, out of the game, too old for the struggle, too tired, it would be there with him, till the end of his days. Special for Steve. (*How does it feel to be just a bit better at something than any man in the world?*' That's how Bob Jeffers once put it to him. Bob knew; there was little he didn't understand about it.)

Well, he would show them all today. Lucienne would hear about it and understand; it would make no difference to her, it wouldn't shake her passion to hurt him, but it would taint her triumph. And Harry. He was too young now, but in the years to come he would hear it all over again, and understand. Harry would never really be lost to him. Whatever poison she would drop into her son's soul, *his* son would not be lost to him; never.

"He's got a bit of greatness today, have you noticed?" Bill Townsend was saying to Jeffers. "Even the way he walked to the crease, the way he holds himself. A touch of majesty."

"Just about the best in the world . . . only about once in a decade." ('*How does it feel to be the best there is, Steve?*')

"I guess," said young Gogarty, "he must feel the happiest man in the world on a day like this."

Stavenden approached the crease, and with every step he felt lighter, calmer, more rested. There would be nothing in his mind but the game from now on until the end of his innings; he would know nothing but the friendly rivalry of a great contest of skill, feel nothing but the deep respect and comradeship of the players—yes, even his antagonists were comrades, for it was a battle without a moment's real bitterness. Even in the heat of the most ferocious tussle for mastery there would not be a shred of ill will, not a particle of bad faith, not a blow struck in anger, not an effort but to establish supremacy of skill, and defeat carried no humiliation with it, no indignity.

The Australians grinned and nodded their welcomes to the approaching giant; Raeburn greeted him, Fallon muttered a friendly threat behind the stumps, 'Scissors' Sterndale gave the ball an extra rub on his rump and moistened the index and middle fingers that gripped the seam. They watched him, easy, confident, without a trace of conceit in his bearing, broadshouldered as a barn door, long in the back, deep in the forearm, the strongest, most majestically competent English batsman since Hammond. He looked a trifle older than his twenty-eight years; he had matured under fire.

And then they looked instinctively towards Ken Travers, the tall, lithe youngster, whose first Test this was. Travers was their Joker, their Dark Horse, the ace in the hole, the one they had been saving up for Stavenden, the bowler with the double-jointed wrists. He had been held back in the first innings till the wicket had begun to show some wear, and then had taken four batsmen's lives for eighteen runs. Both Hallidays, Townsend and Wilson had fallen to him in less than six overs, a complete collapse of the middle batting. His first Test—at nineteen he was the youngest player on the field, younger than Sinclair, younger than Gogarty—only his second year in big League cricket, and already an international player. He had performed wonders in the inter-State games, and was hurriedly thrown into the conflict of the Tests after the failure of an experienced bowler who had been an automatic selection for ten years past. His first spell had shattered the English hopes of a respectable score, was a triumph for a novice. At nineteen he had a whole lifetime in which to harry future English teams.

All the English batsmen had felt the shadow of his presence after that incredible break-through. ("That young chap . . . what's his name? . . . he's good. He'll prove a menace to us if he's not nipped in the bud," Driffield had said to Stavenden. "Make him your special target, Steve. Hammer him. Knock him off his length. *Knock him out of Test cricket.*") Thus within the compass of a single Test a whole long-term policy was envisaged. What Jardine and Hammond plotted and succeeded in the eclipse of Fleetwood-Smith, Driffield and Stavenden conspired to do with this dangerous youngster for the benefit of England teams of the future. The short-term policy and the long-term plan; the strategy within a strategy; the echo of Stavenden's bat would be heard in English and Australian cricket fields in years to come.

This was Stavenden's task, his double burden. The broadest batting shoulders in the England team would carry this load gladly: to beat the clock and break through the Australian attack, to shatter the morale of the newcomer before he had a chance to establish real confidence in international cricket. Not Erskine with his temperamental genius—he hadn't the concentration for such a task; not young Sinclair with his uncanny eye and superlative speed—he had neither the experience nor the resource. The skipper's choice had been Stavenden. Only Stavenden. The honour was to be his. It was a responsibility he welcomed gladly.

None of that vast audience, not one of the sports critics, broadcasters or experts would appreciate the extent of the responsibility he was carrying that day; it was a secret between the initiated, between the privileged few, and that they should know in years to come what he would achieve was worth more to Stavenden than all the plaudits from the thousands and the praise of the publicists.

Perhaps one day, too, Harry would know.

Stavenden, locked within his moment of realisation, faced the bowler.

He gave his monosyllabic instruction to the umpire and took guard. There was one ball only left of that over, Sterndale bowling, who had made Wilson peck like a chicken picking corn that morning, Sterndale making a big effort with the last ball. What a moment of triumph if he could. . . . No, it was too much to hope for. Still, with Wilson floundering, the pitch baked dry and beginning to flake, the old leg-trap experts hungry as wolves for the kill. . . . Sterndale sent down his best one of the morning, a very fast one, and flying out like a racing car skidding at the turn, shooting away, the sort of ball that Wilson was mistiming, fumbling with or leaving alone; and Stavenden, his bat shoulder-high, his body shifting into position easily, naturally, poised almost negligently, all-the-time-in-the-world ease, and the bat dropping down like the swoop of a hawk, and the sound of willow meeting leather clean and crisp on the morning air, and the ball flashing past square leg to the boundary at its nearest point, and the shout of sheer admiration, and the sheer frustration of the bowler at this demonstration of instant mastery, and the knowledge that this was no longer Wilson, no longer a struggling victim but a smoothly accomplished veteran.

And the unpalatable certainty that he would survive any ball like that from here to the end of the long day.

Sterndale swallowed the pill; Raeburn, shaking his head, swallowed it also; the boys in the leg trap relaxed and shuffled off to their new positions in the field, their backs a little bent.

It would be a long day.

Driffield played Ryder with respect for a couple of balls, then slipped one through the leg field for a single. He relaxed mentally and physically with the arrival of his new partner. The main task of the batting would be transferred to the younger man from now on. He watched Ryder treated in the same way as Sterndale, with flawless clarity of style. He leaned back on his bat, gave himself up to the pleasure of a privileged spectator at close quarters; Ryder driving himself with increasing determination, bordering on the desperate, Stavenden waiting for the one that could be driven away comfortably, getting on top of the rising ones with a favourite chop stroke that dropped them with the precision of a pellet from a gun. Driffield, who had been a tennis player before he had mastered cricket, knew how much of this was in the wrists; it was not merely a question of strength, although strength played its great part, but in such sensitive control as would have done credit to a violinist. He had seen Stavenden juggle with a bat, the handle propelled by three fingers, spinning it with the ease of an Astaire twirling a cane; he had seen him flip a set of playing cards from twelve paces into a hat, and collect two pounds twelve shillings from Noel; he had watched him drive a chalked ball against a concrete wall and mark a target the size of a cabin port-hole with six consecutive strokes; he had seen all that, and he still marvelled at the movement of the bat in those hands, the curious magnetic law that made the ball meet it soundly at the punishing centre whose fruity impact was like no other music in sport.

To see a batsman playing with perfect confidence a really fast bowler who can make the ball swing is the acme of pleasure to a cricket spectator, and the strokes Stavenden was producing with such economy of movement—a mere deflection of the angle of the bat to glance the ball at flashing speed to leg, a last-moment flick to send it swinging through the covers, a powerful stabbing move downwards to drive it away off the toes, inch-high above the ground—were not mere counter-attacks, but forcing shots increasing the pressure against the bowler, taking toll of him, using *his* speed against him, turning his spearhead against himself. Nine runs against Ryder in the first over, including a boundary.

And now the moment of testing was about to begin. Young Ken Travers was thrown the ball; the Australians were playing their trump card. Travers caught the ball; waiting for the field to change he tossed it above his head and, to the delight of the crowd, let it roll down his back to be caught off the thigh. He danced a little jig, flopped down at his bowling mark, completely relaxed; double-jointed in both arms, he joined his hands in an 'impossible' position behind him, smiling at the crowd's banter. The field had taken positions according to some pre-arranged formula; he issued no instructions. A first slip fielding eight feet from the bat, a second slip, gully, silly mid-off, deep fine leg and short square leg. A run up of only three or four strides and a hop, and the ball came off the back of his hand very late, round the wicket, short-pitched, whipping away all of three feet from the original direction of flight; a terrific off-spin and rising sharply.

(When Sam Halliday, the first of this youngster's victims, returned to the pavilion in the first innings, Sinclair had said, 'Hard luck.'

('Hard luck nothing. It was a beautiful ball. He worked up to it like an old pro. Flight, length, turn like clockwork for about three balls, and just as I thought I got the hang of it the next one waggled its rump and hopped up like a sparrow.'

(Driffield said, 'Well, let's put salt on its tail. You heard that, Steve?'

('I heard.')

But the spin wasn't the thing. With a first-class batsman no spin, however vicious, is unplayable if the pace isn't there with it; if a ball can be seen all the way it can be mastered and attacked whatever it does. But young Travers (who had been described as a slow bowler to confuse the opposition) bowled anything, free style; the pace was there, all right, and for his short run it was quite startling. For the first time Stavenden had to change his intended stroke at the last split second. He got the turn well in sight, but that sudden rise was something else. He had intended a late cut; he whipped his bat away p.d.q.; real danger there. He heard young Travers laugh happily like a schoolboy who had got away with an apple from a fruit stall. Cricket was such fun.

The next one was different, too. It seemed to float as though airborne, hissing faintly, the movement of the fingers deceptive. When it touched the turf it snaked *inwards*; sudden death. But Stavenden had seen short square leg on the move out of the corner of his eye, suspected something. Fallon, behind him on the move, too. But the bat struck curtly, precisely, freezing it. The vast crowd was still and silent. You could hear a programme card drop.

The run again, a long loose swing this time and it whistled down. This was the joker. It was as fast as Sterndale, with all his twenty-yard run, and deadly in its accuracy, pitched on the leg stump and breaking away to the off stump. But Stavenden suddenly became galvanised. The bat met the ball on the hop, clean and hard, killing the vicious turn, driving it ankle-high past mid-on, inexorably to the boundary. A roar of appreciation, whilst the boys in the pavilion were going wild.

The youngster smiled, friendly. A nice plucky stroke. Would you like to try it again, perhaps? How good are your nerves? The same ball. Not quite the same, of course. This was pitched just a little longer. See if you can step out to this one. . . . The batsman stepped *back* . . . and it was a long hop that he was going to hook yards off fine leg. Reynolds chased it, stepped on it inches from the boundary and they only took two.

The youngster moved a slip fielder a little farther from the wicket. He was not quite satisfied. He wanted him there—no, there, not so near, a couple of feet only. . . . Stavenden ignored the abracadabra with an Olympian frozen stare ahead. The youngster was running up to the wicket confidently. The response was so unexpected that the crowd half rose to its feet. Stavenden was a third way down the pitch to meet the ball, moving at the moment it left the bowler's hand. He caught it full toss, the bat a golden scythe, a powerful unorthodox slash. The ball was skied over the boundary. Stavenden calmly dropped his bat between wickets, adjusted his pads, and in mid-field, in the most ostentatious manner in the world, began to peel off his sweater.

The umpire ran forward to collect it from him.

The youngster stared earnestly at Stavenden, a long look. He didn't believe a word of it. Nobody knew what he thought. He was not as green as that grass, anyway. Courage he admired, but plain impudence—no. That would not be tolerated.

He caught the ball with a quick impatient movement. Running up again now, unperturbed by the fireworks, the poker face, the strip-tease. He ran and suddenly stumbled. No . . . impossible. Yes! He had misjudged his run. He must start again. No, he was carrying on. Oh, silly youth! He should have taken his time, not worried. How Stavenden would cane him for that schoolboy slip. Yes, the bat swung in a characteristic manner. . . .

The crowd was on its feet, yelling. The ball was curving up into the blue, high, higher. Grant was running, Sebastien was running, Foreman was running, the batsmen were running once, they might cross before it dropped. Two of the fielders collided, but Sebastien had the ball, he had the ball, he could make it, he was there, almost . . . yes. . . . Oh, the blithering idiot had crossed the boundary. He had outrun himself. The oaf couldn't control his own strength. The ball had dropped four feet within the boundary and Stavenden had crossed three times with Driffield, who was grinning. Raeburn looked grim and unhappy, the fielders dejected, the youngster looked at that moment as though he could cry.

This had been his trump card. Not the 'joker', not the 'ace', *this* was the special one that he wanted to keep hidden up his sleeve till some such time as there was a challenge that was proving really dangerous. A challenge like Stavenden. A real, dangerous man after blood. And they had muffed it! The greatest fielders in the world! Three of them! And they had let it slip through their blundering stupid hands!

132

It would have been perfect, magnificent. Everything had been planned; the whole of that wonderful secret move had been planned beautifully: the pretended mis-step, the hesitation, the lost-boy look, and then the lovely, lovely googly, dead on wicket, beautifully pitched and humming like a wasp. He had fooled them all, even Stavenden.

And he couldn't repeat it. He couldn't fool Stavenden again with it. At that moment he looked not a day older than his nineteen years.

Of course, the duel was not over yet. By no means. Except that a man like Stavenden doesn't make a mistake like that more than once in any innings. The odds were with him now. It had shaken Travers, but it had strengthened Stavenden, made him more formidable, more like some impregnable bastion bristling with ten-pounders. (Travers was beginning to hope they might take him off for a spell. It might be best. Give him a chance to regain his nerve a bit. . . . No, they mustn't do that. It was like after a motor accident in which you were driving. The best thing would be to go back behind that wheel right away.)

None of what he was thinking was possible to tell from Travers's expression. Unconsciously he was modelling himself on Stavenden, learning something from him, too. That hard withdrawn look emphasised by the severe angle of the low-pulled peaked cap that hooded the eyes. The hooded eyes of a falcon, intent, moveless, unwinking, seeing every detail and sub-detail of movement. Without looking round feeling the presence of any close moving fielder, registering and pinpointing him in the map within the mind's eye.

Now the over was finished and Goodger was bowling to Driffield. It looked like a maiden—only two runs—compared with Stavenden's stuff. Another single.

How quickly that over had sped by, and he had to have the ball again. Bowling to Driffield . . . he, at any rate, respected him. Driffield pushed his third ball through slips for an easy couple, but Stavenden froze, checked the second run. He lazily signalled Driffield to remain were he was. Driffield grinned and perched astride his bat. Why was the ape grinning like that? What did he expect to see, squatting there?

Running up to bowl to Stavenden. An easy action, a well pitched leg-break with an off-spin movement. He could see Stavenden shaping for it, the bat shoulder-high, left shoulder forward, both hands equally dividing the guidance of the stroke. No, Stavenden didn't want that one. He let the ball move away harmlessly. He could have guided it, cut it or simply let it drop from his bat with that abrupt curt stroke that was like the fall of a judge's gavel, pronouncing it judged and sentenced, all in one movement; he preferred to deal with one he could send away like a bullet, cracking through the out-field or the gully. Stavenden, the Iron Man, the Adding Machine. What were the fancy names the press boys called him? Well, he had to admit it. They suited him.

Another ball—and this was it. This was what he feared. That damned man had seen it all the way, watched it turn from leg exactly as before, and he did not need a second lesson. He flicked it with a wristy beautiful movement to the boundary. so damned easy, so insolent! The crowd was in ecstasy. Yes, his own people! The crowd who had come to see him bowl the Englishmen into the ground. Wasn't *he* their hero? How fickle they were. That damned score-board rattling like a loose shutter in the wind, the clock standing still, Raeburn moving restively.

Why did they force him to go on? He was too young, after all. They should have blooded him before making him face a man like that.

What now? The ball was heavy in his hand. Fast off-break? He had tried those. A hanger? No, that was the one he stepped out to. Quickly now. He was beginning his run, he must make up his mind. The important thing was to keep the runs down now. But he had never bowled to such a policy before. That was Goodger's job. Why did they make him. . . ?

134

In the pavilion the watchers sat in complete silence. The end of the over was greeted with stormy applause. Travers, the dark horse, was being systematically slaughtered. Steve had got the hang of him and was mercilessly knocking him off his length. When the ball was short-pitched he jumped out to it; when it was long-pitched he stepped back and the long handle of the bat slipped into his grip for a tremendous drive. The boy bowled and bowled without a glimmer of hope, transfixed by the hypnotic supremacy of his opponent.

The break-through had begun.

The clock stood still, and the score board raced forward pronouncing inexorable judgment, testimony to the peak greatness of a supreme batsman.

Driffield, watching this *tour de force,* joining in some of the enthusiastic applause from the pavilion, had a sense of reassurance about Stavenden, although last night's episode still haunted him. He had exchanged greetings with him that morning before he had gone in to bat and it seemed to him that Steve was beginning to accept his domestic problem philosophically; but Cynthia's observation that he had let down his team-mate in his need persisted in his memory. Was she right? Had he failed Steve, or was the situation irresolvable? To provide an alibi for his friend according to his request of last night still seemed to him unthinkable. He went over the arguments once again in his mind, that the England captain had a special burden of responsibility and so on, and it still seemed to him that there was nothing else to be said at the time. Surely, to use his position in the way Steve had urged him was a clear breach of trust vested in him—well, by millions of his countrymen. The very phrasing of the words immediately made him think of Cynthia's—and Noel's—reaction to them. He had a sense of discomfort, of embarrassment. Trust vested in him by millions of his countrymen! Cynthia's indulgent smile, Noel's quick ironic grin. . . . It was, veritably, a ministerial phrase. Sydney and the Right Hon. Sir Anthony Eden!

Driffield grimaced thoughtfully. Was he making a bit of an ass of himself? Was this position of trust such a momentous burden? Or was Steve's domestic happiness, the real problem of any individual, of far greater importance than the observance of the rules of these schoolboy contests? Was he the overgrown schoolboy she had so contemptuously dubbed him? He had a sense of weariness, of frustration. Here was another test; a test within a test. His maturity.

There are times in every man's life when he takes stock of himself, when circumstances forces him to draw up a balance sheet. Driffield, confronted by Cynthia's accusation, was compelled to examine himself, his values, the profit and loss of his achievements, the very core of his nature.

There had been an earlier episode with Dick Sinclair when he felt he had failed, as Cynthia had pronounced his failure over Stavenden. Then the issue had been even more clearly defined. Once again it had been a question of values, of understanding of adult problems, and he had been proved deficient and inadequate. Then, it had been a simple lack of worldly understanding. Driffield had blamed himself.

During an earlier Test Dick Sinclair had arrived at the ground wearing an unusual expression of perplexity. Driffield and the others did not remark it, but Harry Halliday, alone in the pavilion, was sought by Dick, who wanted to have advice in a personal matter.

Dick showed a crumpled piece of paper to Harry, who read it fascinated. It was from a lady friend of Dick's and full of reproach.

Harry said, at length: "Do you know this girl well?"

"I swear I didn't do it," said Dick earnestly.

"Would she threaten you with a lawsuit?"

"That's the part I don't understand. I met her at some dance. You know how these girls buzz round you, Harry. I think we went on to some club later. The usual sort of thing."

Sinclair added, "She's not suggesting I did anything really

wrong. I mean, I know she was of age. I've always been careful."

"It's only a paternity claim. They can't do anything about that, apart from compensation, that is."

"Well, what? Even if I am—which I'm not—I can't be— what can they do?"

"So much a week for the kid when it comes."

"For how long?"

"Till it's grown up."

"What! For twenty years? Good Lord, no!"

"Well, what do you think? It's only fair, isn't it?"

"No, never. I'm not the father, and that's that! I won't give a penny."

Harry shook his head solemnly. "You might have to. But never mind. It's not the end of the world. Probably no more than a couple of quid a week."

"Yes, but for all those years. Why . . . that'll be . . ."

"About two thousand pounds in all," said Harry, with a glimmer in his eye.

"Well . . . you worked that out quick!"

The young man considered the awful prospect. He glowered. "Two thousand smackers . . . just for the privilege of dancing with some dame. I'll see her in hell."

"And if she takes you to court? That wouldn't be nice."

"The newspaper boys will get hold of it. Will it be a scandal, do you think?"

"Well, it won't look good."

"The disgrace . . . my folks. . . . No, it mustn't go to court. Gosh, I can just see the headlines. 'Test Player: Paternity Claim!'"

"'Sinclair in the Box,'" embellished Harry.

"What will my fans think!"

"Well, if that's the way you feel about it, don't let it go to court. After all, did you think of the girl?"

"You believe I did it, Harry!" Sinclair's accusing look made Harry a little uncomfortable.

"Listen, my boy, you have a reputation for running about with girls. What do you think I'd think?"

"Damn you, I'd have thought you knew me better than that."

"All right, I believe you. Millions wouldn't."

Harry went on with his letter.

Sinclair said: "Harry . . ."

"Well?"

"What can I do about it?"

Harry put down his pen again and said seriously, "You know what I'd do? Speak to the skipper."

A little later that day Driffield sought out the youngster.

"What's the matter, Dick? Harry tells me you're worried about something."

The skipper, his arm on his, steered Dick Sinclair remorselessly out of the lunch room. "Out with it. You don't have to worry about it going any further."

Sinclair explained in halting words, not meeting the captain's eye. ('Why does everyone make me *feel* so damned guilty?' Even his choice of words . . . 'bit of fun' . . . 'you know how it is, skip,' and the slightly foolish smile that was almost a smirk on his face. The captain did not respond to this like Harry; he was taking it absolutely straight. He hadn't seen him look so grave and long-faced before; usually the skipper was almost cordial to him. He never till this moment had understood why some of his team-mates looked upon him as a bit of a tartar; but now . . .)

"May I see the letter?"

Sinclair handed it to him; he could not understand the look the captain gave him. He had dropped his arm and looked sideways, oddly, at him.

"You say you did not have intimate relations with this girl?"

('Intimate relations!' The skipper must really be angry with him, talking like a blank text-book.)

"No, sir."

"Did you ever spend any time with her alone?"

He hesitated.

"You don't mind answering my questions, do you? I can't be of any help unless you do."

"Yes . . . I spent some time with her."

"Where?"

"At her flat."

"How long did you stay with her?"

"Half an hour . . . an hour, maybe."

"Not all night?"

"No. Oh, no."

"Anyone ever see you there with her?"

"I don't remember that. In fact, I hardly remember the girl. Do you think she can do anything, skipper?"

"The trouble is that anyone can start a legal action, with or without justification. Is this the only letter you've had from her?"

"No . . . it's the first one she's threatened anything."

"Have you got the others she wrote to you?"

"I . . . got rid of them."

The captain looked hard at him. "What," he said, testily, "if anything, did you write to her, in answer?"

"I . . . didn't reply."

"Nothing at all?"

"No. Should I have done?"

"If you were certain you're not the father of the child, why didn't you write at once and tell her that?"

"I meant to, skipper . . . at the time I got them . . . there were only two others. . . . I felt at the time I should have done. . . ."

"Why on earth didn't you?"

Sinclair was silent, tongue-tied. Had he been slightly sorry for her? Had he felt a little sentimental about her? Or was it, as the captain hinted, that he was not really certain?

"You're not very sure whether you're the father of this child or not, are you? Would you swear to it in court?"

"Yes . . . I think so."

The captain shook his head. "You *think* you're sure?"

"I'm *almost* sure."

"Dick, this didn't happen so long ago that you can't remember. You either did or you didn't."

"I certainly don't remember that I did."

The captain shrugged. "I suppose that's good enough. Still, all the evenings with her, in her flat, in restaurants, have to be accounted for, you know."

"But surely you don't suppose . . . "

"You're in the public eye, Dick. It's not my business to read you a lecture on morals, but you should have enough sense to know that anyone in our position is highly vulnerable to criticism. You have never been discreet, have you? I know all this . . . is a great temptation to a young man, but that should have made you doubly careful not to give anyone a chance to gossip.

"I see. May I ask you something, skipper?"

"Well?"

"Do you believe I did it?"

"Did you?"

"I give you my word. I'd *know*."

"Very well."

"Then what shall I do, sir?"

"I'll get you a solicitor to write to this girl. On no account answer her yourself."

"Do you think it will go to court? I hate starting with solicitors; it might force her hand, you know. What if she goes ahead?"

"Let the solicitors deal with it."

"Do you think it'll go to court?"

"It may."

"But don't you see? That will mean publicity, a scandal, even if I'm acquitted."

"That's possible. I shall do my best to keep it quiet. I have friends in the press. We all have."

"It would be impossible to guarantee that."

"We can guarantee nothing."

Dick was not too insensitive to see that the whole subject was extremely distasteful to the skipper. He flushed. "I'm sorry to burden you with my difficulties," he said stiffly. The captain made a gesture.

"I'll phone a solicitor right away for you, Dick. Let me keep this letter."

"Wouldn't it be better if . . . I made a deal with her?"

"What are you trying to say?"

"Why must she hurt my career . . . dragging me into the limelight with this thing? What if I settled some cash on her?"

"Are you telling me that you may have done it?"

"No, I'm certainly not admitting that. But if it goes to law it will affect my future."

"Your cricket? It can't affect that."

"No, sir, but other things. . . . I mean, exploitation. Sponsoring ads., writing for the press, things like that. I have a reputation to uphold . . . English sportsman, and all that."

"I see," said the captain. "I'm afraid I can't advise you about the by-products of your cricket success. To most of us, the game is enough."

"Yes, sir," said the young man hotly, "it's a game to you. It's my living."

Driffield said coldly, "I'm afraid I can't give you any other advice. Whether you did this or not is between you and your conscience. If you didn't, then you should not hesitate to deny it, even in a public courtroom, if necessary. What effect this may have on your exploitable value as a sponsor of cigarettes you don't smoke, shirts you don't wear, or as an author of articles you don't write, should not influence you."

"That's very nice for you, Mr. Driffield." ('I didn't have a rich father to make me so independent.') "I've got a few short years in front of me, and then what? I don't want to end up like Bob Jeffers, finished at forty."

Driffield made a gesture of revulsion. "Professionalism! My God, man, isn't playing for England enough? That you can say, 'I have done my best for England.' With the eyes of your countrymen on you, isn't it enough?"

Dick turned away. "The eyes of my countrymen are on me just as long as I can make runs. You'll be a better doctor at fifty than at thirty-five. I've got to make the best of the few years ahead. If they want me to sign testimonials for cigarettes or chewing-gum or hair-oil I can't argue."

Driffield nodded coldly. "Then make your deal, arrange your settlement." He added, sorry for the young man in his distress, "Maybe it won't cost you so much, you know."

"Any ideas what I should offer?"

"I've had no experience of this sort of thing."

"You're a man of business, Mr. Driffield. What do you think I ought to offer?"

"Well, a paternity claim, if established, wouldn't amount to more than a couple of pounds a week. She would probably be willing to take a cash settlement of three or four hundred pounds. Five, at the most."

Sinclair was shocked. "They've got me over a barrel. How on earth can I raise five hundred?"

"You haven't got it?"

"I've just started my career. I've not much money put away."

Driffield hesitated. "Dick, try not to be bitter about this. We all do silly things we're sorry for. That's growing up."

"I'll try not to be," said the young man dryly. "Is that all?"

"Well . . . if you're in difficulty about the money, let me know."

"You mean you'd help me? With the eyes of my country-men on me? Maybe I am a professional, but I don't accept handouts. No, thank you. I'd rather sign soft drink ads."

Driffield stared at the proud young back of the man walking

142

away from him; he thought he had a remarkably straight figure.

Later in the day there was tension on the veranda. Dick Sinclair was batting without confidence or concentration.

Noel put his binoculars to his eyes. "Kid Twinkletoes is off form. Anything wrong?"

Driffield hesitated, then took the letter. He passed it to Noel without comment. Noel read it, expressionless, folded it up and began to make a daisy chain.

"Look," said Noel. He pulled out the chain. "Teeny, tiny popsies."

"That might be an important document," remonstrated Driffield.

"You're joking."

Driffield exchanged glances with Sam and Harry Halliday. Noel caught their look.

"Hey, what's the matter with you lot? You're not worried over this piece of nonsense, are you?"

"The kid's worried."

Noel laughed. "No! That old paternity fraud? It's one of the oldest try-outs in the business. He didn't fall for this one, did he?"

"Fall for it?" said Driffield, genuinely startled. "Isn't it genuine?"

"Of course not. Everybody gets them. I mean, all the *personalities*. At least once a year. It's the same with chaps on the stage or films. Some fan who waited at the stage door or the foyer of some hotel, got an autograph, claims to have known the chap, then tries it on through a shyster lawyer. Surely, you chaps know all about it?"

Harry Halliday said, "It never happened to me."

"Forgive me, Harry, but you're not the type. You have to have the playboy personality. A kid like Dick is wide open. I've had at least six in my time; Steve's had a couple: we compared notes the other day. There's only one thing to do. Phone the Yard. It's nothing but petty blackmail. A C.I.D. makes one call on the girl—she often tried it before—and you never hear about it again."

Harry said, "I didn't know."

"Mind you," said Noel, warming up to his lecture, "the interesting thing about some of these girls is that they sometimes think it's true. Some of them actually believe it happened. Then it's a case for a psychiatrist. Wishful fantasy stuff. Do you know how many women every year think they've been followed in the street by Gregory Peck?"

In the strained silence that greeted this, Noel looked at the others in bewilderment, then at Driffield with dawning realisation.

"Sydney, you didn't take the kid to task over this thing?" At Driffield's embarrassed look Noel said, "Really, this is a bit much. After all, you're a *doctor*."

As it was determined later, Noel was absolutely correct in his view of the matter. Not only was Sinclair quite blameless in his relations with the girl, but it was established that she was not even expecting a child.

At the recollection of his rôle in the matter Driffield flushed with embarrassment. He had not told Cynthia about the episode; he could too clearly visualise her response.

Sinclair . . . and now Stavenden. Failure in the case of one, perhaps in the other. Unforgivable failure. Driffield was a man of affairs, a business man, a medical man, and yet in spite of his knowledge of the world there was something curiously naïve, almost childlike about him. Yes, perhaps she was right. . . .

After lunch Goodger found the worn pitch gripping, and his spin was raising little spurts of dust. He tossed the ball off the back of his hand, giving it a lot of air. Sometimes it shot; then it hung. Driffield, instinctively playing forward, caught one rising up suddenly; he saw Goodger darting forward, anticipat-

ing the stroke, but he saw it too late. It kicked off the shoulder
of his bat. Goodger dived. The ball hit his wrist, bounced up;
Goodger took it left-handed.

Caught and bowled.

A beautiful classical piece of strategy, skill, craft, deception:
Driffield had fallen at last. He could not have wished for a
finer curtain to his innings.

He made his way back to the pavilion, smiling. The applause
rose and rose as he approached his team-mates sitting on the
veranda. The score board showed two hundred and seventy-
eight for two, the last man eighty-five. He had batted nearly
four and a half hours.

Sinclair walked down the steps, swinging his bat, his cap
pulled down. The crowd greeted him happily, and there was
a curious high-pitched sound in it.

"Listen to those bobby soxers. *'Dickie!'* "

". . . So I told Steve everything. He's the only one who
knows I'm here. Don't be cross, darling. I'll meet you for a
drink after the match. Say seven-thirty. If you've got anything
to celebrate, celebrate with me."

Her voice in miniature always made him think she was
about six inches high.

He arranged the meeting with her. There was not a suggestion of any criticism in her voice after last night's outburst.
Surely, she hadn't forgotten?

"Tell me this. . . . As you don't want me to have the
captaincy after this tour why square me with Steve? I was
playing right into your hands."

"That's different."

"Well, I don't see it."

"Don't you?"

"I suppose I do. You want me to be offered the captaincy
again so that I could turn it down for your sake."

"A brilliant piece of perception."

145

"I'd rather cope with Goodger's backhanded spinners any day."

"I'm glad you're deriving some intellectual benefit from playing cricket."

He replaced the receiver, smiling; then he ceased to smile. She had forgotten to ask him how much he had scored.

A few minutes later, whilst he was standing under the shower, Noel came into the wash-room.

"Get out from under there, Sydney. I want you to hear what I'm going to say to you."

Driffield began to rub himself down with a rough towel.

"It's about Bob Jeffers," said Noel.

"I see."

"Sydney: a straight question."

"Well?"

"If the captaincy of the team was up to the players, who do you think would be elected?"

"Go on."

"Does it hurt?"

"Not particularly."

"Jeffers would have their vote. You know his knowledge of the game is streets ahead of anyone else's. He's obsessed by it. You're a first-class amateur, but between the gifted amateur and the thorough-going professional there is a space as broad as the Pacific."

"All this amateur-professional prejudice was exploded when Hutton led England."

"The selectors will always choose an amateur if there is the least justification. Prejudices like that die hard and you know it. That's why you'd get my vote. But believe me, Sydney, mine would be the only one."

"I'm sorry you think that."

"Not that the others would murmur. There isn't a word from any of them."

"Not Jeffers?"

"*Particularly* not Jeffers."

146

"Well, my instincts tell me he is resentful."

"He can't choose the way he feels about it, but he can control it."

"What do you want to say to me, Noel?"

"Jeffers is going to retire from cricket soon. This will without doubt be his last series as a Test player. He's a frightened man since you demoted him to number eight."

"My policy was correct. Wilson made the highest score of his career in a Test."

"Of course your policy was correct, Sydney. But there's something even more important than cricket. He's given his life to the game. Twenty-five years' service. It means everything to him to see the series through."

"Yes, I can see that."

"I want you to promise him your support at the selection of the team for the final Test."

"You should know I can't let sentiment interfere with the choice of the team."

"For God's sake, Sydney, it's only a game!"

Shades of Cynthia!

Driffield was silent; the painfulness of the memory took his breath away.

"Noel . . ." he began. His friend suddenly touched his arm. Neither of them spoke for a while. Driffield recovered himself with difficulty.

"How are the horses?" he said at last.

The tension was broken.

They had taken young Travers off. He was finished for the day. Finished for the series. The young man would have a long road to travel before his nerve and confidence were sufficiently restored to be given another chance in big cricket. Stavenden surveyed the field like a conqueror, plotting new destruction. The break-through he had initiated had been in full swing for nearly two hours now, the clock was well and truly beaten, the England team's hopes high. After the fast bowlers, the spin bowlers, after the spin bowlers, the change bowlers. None of them could make an impression on the Scoring Machine, cruising at high speed.

Foreman, Carmichael, and finally back to Goodger, the only one who could keep the runs down. For some reason Stavenden found Goodger awkward to get away. There was an imperturbable quality about his style that wore on the nerves. Goodger was a highly intelligent player with a good deal of subtlety in the variation of his deliveries; he was acutely sensitive to a batsman's weaknesses. Every batsman, even the best, had certain chinks in his armour, and Goodger's technique was to probe and feel his way until they were brought to light. He had studied Stavenden's technique since the commencement of the Tests; it had taken him three innings to get to know his style of play, his mannerisms, his eccentricities, his likes and dislikes. Although he had not taken his wicket, he had learned to read his handwriting until he could almost anticipate his stroke for any ball. Stavenden was quite a rare specimen, strong all round the wicket, superb as a hooker, and his cutting perfectly timed; on- and off-driving excellent. There appeared no weakness, no positive preference of stroke play, but Goodger was aware of a propensity of the great man's to play forward when he was fresh, and back when he was tired. To catch him on the borderline of fatigue, in a moment of indecision . . . forward or back . . . forward or back . . . that would be the trick.

Goodger's plans were deep-seated, long-term; he was as patient as a spider spinning his web. Every batsman must fall in the end to a bowler. The fly would find its way towards the tempting morsel and catch its wings in the invisible threads . . . forward or back. . . .

Goodger waited and spun; he was content to be patient; meanwhile, to keep the runs down.

"Well, it looks more than promising now," said Driffield.

Noel Erskine nodded contentedly, sprawling his long legs in front of him, padded and relaxed.

"What time did you get in . . . this morning?"

"Come now, Sydney. You know it takes more than a night out to put me off my game."

"You were snoring happily a few moments ago."

"It's the heat."

Driffield said, "How much did you lose?"

"A little."

"How little?"

"Oh, not that old thing, Sydney."

Driffield said, "As a matter of interest, how much do you reckon to spend in a year?"

"You know, I never dared to think."

Although Driffield's manner was light enough he was genuinely oncerned by certain rumours he had been hearing about his friend's gambling losses and some Stock Exchange investments that had suffered heavily in recent months. But usually Noel's financial fortunes suffered dramatic changes and he could repair them practically overnight.

"You must have some idea how much you spend a year. What is it? Five thousand? Ten?"

"Well, maybe a little more than that."

"More than what? Five or ten?"

"Both."

Erskine grinned at his friend happily; it amused him to shock him in the way that rich men were always shocked by losses of money.

"Prodigal!" Driffield shook his head. "What on earth can you spend it on?"

"I like to live like a gentleman." He added, "You know what's been my ruin?"

Driffield contemplated him with mild wonder. "Well?"

"Cricket," said Noel.

"The one steadying influence in your life."

"This will be a shock to you, Sydney, but if I had a son I'd teach him to play chess."

Driffield blew out a cloud of smoke; this was Noel being humorously outrageous and Driffield was quietly enjoying it.

"You should stop chasing about on the continent," he admonished.

"Oh, England's all right. The only thing I've got against it is it's an impossible country to live in."

Driffield said, smiling, "I suppose affectation is part of that charm of yours."

"The fatal Erskine charm. That is, fatal to Erskine. I didn't know it had any effect on a strong man like you."

"You ought to settle down with some decent girl, good County type. Country life, regular habits. It's long overdue, Noel. All this gallivanting will lead to trouble. Don't want to sound stuffy, personally I think you'll grow to like the life. I'm not misled by all those rumours about your continental escapades, that ballet dancer, what's her name, you were mixed up with. Is that finished, by the way?"

"Is anything ever finished?"

"I'm not misled by your manner. I know that basically you're an Englishman."

"What is an Englishman, Sydney? Drake was an Englishman, but then so was Crippen. So was Guy Fawkes. How about Lord Haw Haw? They convicted him because he turned out to be English."

Driffield grinned. "Well, let's say none of them played cricket for England."

"You've got me there."

Driffield said, "Come and stay with us at Storrington when we get back. A month in the country would do you a world of good. Riding, fishing; there's the hunt. We're not backwoodsmen, you know. There's quite a decent social life. The annual ball."

"Yes, and we mustn't forget the Ladies' Garden Party for the church bazaar. Sydney, I'll make you a counter-offer. Come to Paris with me in September. We'll spend a week-end there and then hi-tail it to the Côte d'Azur. A flutter at the tables, and then south once more to San Sebastian, where I will introduce you to the most spectacular torch singer in Europe. Then to a little village off the coast where the local sultan still exercises *les droits de seigneur*. On to Seville for the bullfights, and finally to Morocco just for the devil of it. What do you say?"

"You're incorrigible."

"But, Sydney, think of it. In not one of those places have they even heard of Bradman."

Driffield strapped on his watch; he was ready.

"I'll be in the pavilion, Noel. Ask Bob to come and have a word with me."

Foreman was bowling to Dick Sinclair, who was playing him easily enough, but without the thrust of his usual game. Stavenden, relaxing a little at his end, wondered at the lack of spirit in Sinclair's attack. Goodger had him in a bit of trouble the last over; the boy was not his usual sparkling self.

Stavenden's partnerships with Sinclair had proved exciting. Often it had been almost a tug-of-war, a race for runs between them; an implicit challenge, an unconscious rivalry. One of these days it would be a real struggle for supremacy. There would inevitably follow a slight adjustment in the batting order. Sinclair would hit peak form for a series of games, Stavenden fall off a little; and the batting order would read, Sinclair, Stavenden—Sinclair at number three, Stavenden at the more comfortable position of four. . . .

Such an adjustment had taken place that day with Erskine down one place. The original order had read: Stavenden, Erskine, Sinclair. . . . Driffield had considered policy carefully. Erskine's number four position had seemed a fixture for the series, but Sinclair had been consistently, startlingly brilliant, beyond everybody's highest hopes, and Driffield had said to Noel, "I'd like to try Dick at number four this time; I think he's really got his eye in this season. How do you feel about it?" And Erskine had graciously accepted the minor demotion, the subtlest suggestion of criticism of the erratic nature of his genius.

But this didn't look like Sinclair's game. A pity. This was one where he was specially needed; they all had to come off. Driffield had set a standard by playing his finest innings of the tour; Wilson had played his best game, too. The skipper's policy of playing to win was a real test to them all; it would be a great pity if Dick failed. And Foreman wasn't much. Stavenden had even eased up a little in his attack of Foreman's bowling to encourage the Aussie skipper to think there was something to him, to give Dick a chance to settle down in easy conditions. A routine off-spinner, Foreman had only been successful in tying down the opposition by the accuracy of his length; he had never seriously worried the top-flight batsmen.

Foreman dropped one a little short, on the leg stump, turning to the off as usual. Stavenden would have late-cut it automatically. Dick hesitated, let the ball go away without playing a stroke. It had been like that from the beginning, a lack of spirit that was unusual for the young batsman. Noel had brought out a fresh bat between the overs and whispered something to him. Stavenden thought it had been an excuse to pass on some message. It could not have meant that the skipper was asking him to go after the runs; they all knew the score. Still, a new bat was a hint.

But Dick was not taking it; his total remained at three, and he had been in for nearly fifteen minutes now. Stavenden did not have to refer to the clock to realise that they would soon be falling behind schedule.

Stavenden watched the next ball, a trifle better length, but by no means as accurate as Foreman's usual ball. Dick flicked it through the covers, an easy two runs. Stavenden crossed once, then signalled Dick to remain where he was. It was necessary to set an example. Foreman bowled an accurate length, but Stavenden could see it clearly. He judged flight and spin to a millimetre; he stepped across it, his bat flashed, powered high from a shoulder stroke, driving down on the ball. It whistled past first slip so fast that it crossed the boundary before a single fieldsman had time to turn his head.

Stavenden looked innocently at Dick, who nodded.

"Still going strong out there, I see," said Driffield to Jeffers, who had sat down beside him in the pavilion.

Jeffers tapped wood. "Don't say it, skipper."

Driffield said, "I was holding my pipe," and both men grinned.

Driffield pushed across a box of cigarettes and Jeffers lit up.

"You know," said the skipper, "I seem to have been so busy lately I haven't had a proper talk with you."

"Well, I think I understand."

"You do? Good. As a matter of fact, I had one or two problems I thought we might discuss."

"Yes, of course."

"Wilson seems to have shaped nicely. . . . I don't want you to think that I'm considering him as a permanent opener. As you know, it was just in those particular—circumstances."

"Quite."

"And it seemed to have worked out."

"By temperament Wilson is a hitter. He usually makes his runs in about half an hour. A concentrated effort doesn't suit him. An opener's chief strength must be stamina."

"You really think that?"

"I do, most sincerely."

"Well, he was in there for about three hours this time."

"In two sessions, skipper. Don't forget that."

"Mm. That's a point, of course. About young Gogarty. What did you think of his bowling yesterday?"

"Hard to tell. He's all right with the shine on the ball, but I think we need to use him in short spells."

"He kept a length all the afternoon."

"There wasn't much edge after the first eight or nine overs. I suggest we use Mac to tie them down one end and Bill Townsend and Gogarty to keep up a permanent attack of fast stuff in brief spells; then alternate with Sam Halliday and Harry when the shine's off the ball."

"It all depends on the circumstances."

"Of course. I was talking generally."

"You think he was kept on too long yesterday?"

"Yes, I do. You didn't see the state he was in later. He was right out."

"Why on earth didn't he speak up?"

"Well, Mr. Driffield," said Jeffers, "if you feel he ought to keep going it's not up to him to confess he's tiring."

"Why not?"

"Because," said Jeffers, coldly, "he's got to think of his place in the team."

Driffield said, "I think he kept going because he felt he was needed."

"He was worried you might think he lacked stamina."

"I'm sure young Gogarty puts his interests after the good of the team."

"Why don't you ask him?" snapped Jeffers.

There was a pause.

Jeffers said, with difficulty, "If you want my professional opinion, he's scared to talk to you."

Driffield said, "There isn't much point in this, Bob."

"No," said Jeffers. "You ask me about Wilson as opener. You think it's a bright idea to put in as opener a man who's played number eight all his life, and because he makes fifty-odd runs, he's a success. I've made nearly three thousand runs opening for England, but that means nothing. As for Gogarty, he's worried about his place in the team, Mr. Driffield, and that's the only reason he won't admit he can't bowl two hours flat in a temperature of ninety-eight fahrenheit."

"You refuse to think that there are some players who only think of the team?"

"Yes, Mr. Driffield, amateurs."

"All right, Bob," said Driffield, "I tried."

Jeffers said in a more reasonable tone, "Yes, you did. I'm sorry we don't see eye to eye."

"Tell me this," he said, rising, "am I opening for England in the last Test of my career?"

"I don't know yet."

"Or will you hold this against me?"

"Certainly not," said Driffield shortly. "I can only consider what's best for the team."

A little before three, the sun like brass in the sky, the concentrated attention on the patch of pale green in the centre of the field, the magnetised impulse of tens of thousands of white-shirted spectators, Stavenden reached his ninety-eighth run with a leg glance to the boundary so smooth, so immaculate, that it had an almost mechanical precision. Then, with the last ball of the over, with the field on tenterhooks, closing in on a packed slip field, he pushed to square leg, and took another single.

This was the moment the Aussie skipper decided to call for the new ball; and Ryder, a refreshed giant, who had not bowled a ball since the morning, marked out his thirty-yard run to five men in the leg trap.

There was perfect silence over the whole of the vast stadium, silence in the changing-rooms, silence in the press box, in the pavilion, at the millions of receiving sets.

Ryder's leaping stride lengthened panther-like. He hurled himself at the crease, his arm like the lash of a whip in the hand of a circus master. The ball he sent down was the fastest he had bowled in his career, and it shot off the pitch as lethal as a bullet, chest-high. Stavenden stood like a rock; his bat

155

was raised like a shield to the flying javelin, and in the briefest fragment of time that the ball met willow he deflected the blade with the most exquisitely sensitised movement of the wrists, and the ball flashed past the five men so fast that it was seconds after it had been recovered by a spectator that the crowd realised what had happened.

Erskine put down his binoculars.

"I'm glad," he said, when he could hear himself speak the words, "I'm glad it was Steve out there. No one else in the world could have faced that ball . . . and survived."

The pitch was becoming a battleground; the ball was popping, shooting and bumping like a demented thing. Sinclair was still groping and stumbling, and Stavenden, his mouth dry as leather with the heat and tension, stood red-eyed, parched, his head aching as though it would split, playing an immortal innings under fantastic conditions. With Ryder, with the medium spin bowlers, there was never time to shape for a stroke; the ball came off without rhyme or reason, turning and hanging, swinging out or in, according to no natural law of bowling, off a pitch so worn that it was almost unplayable. The ball had to be seen all the way to the bat; defensive play, with the field risking life and limb to harry the batsmen at close quarters, was out of the question. Survival was only possible by forcing the ball away, time and again.

Sinclair was only able to survive through sheer agility and keenness of eye. He stabbed the ball to the ground at the last moment, a few feet beyond the reach of the fieldsmen, but he could not get it away. That was beyond his powers. Stavenden's supreme skill and experience, his inflexible concentration, made it possible for him to beat the field. He was scoring for both of them, six runs to Sinclair's one. Every half-hour a tray of drinks was rushed out on to the field.

By half-past three, when the tray was brought out afresh, Stavenden spoke to the Australian captain. He wanted nothing more for the rest of his innings. The clock was against them.

156

"If I can do without it, so can you lot."

"Very well."

The struggle proceeded with unremitting tension.

Noel said to Driffield:

"What do you really feel about all this, Sydney? The comradeship? The applause? It's the English summer, the green fields, the hush when the game's in the balance. We are reliving our childhood days, Sydney. Running away from reality, you from your patients, I from myself, from life itself, into the boyhood world of make-believe, where the problems are not real problems, defeats are not real defeats, and behind it all is the sound of perpetual applause. It's a sky-blue life, isn't it, Sydney?"

Driffield looked at him closely. "Is there anything wrong, Noel?"

"I'm going to cry off when this series is over."

"You mean . . . the tours?"

"No, I mean cricket. I've had it."

"Noel, surely I can rely on you for the County?"

Noel shook his head. "No."

"But why?"

"Sydney, stop pretending you don't know about me. I've never done a day's work in my life. But I've lived at a higher rate that the Archbishop of York, bless his heart. And you know how I did it? Half a dozen guinea-pig directorships, Stock Exchange tips for the honour of accepting invitations to dinner, a free winter cruise when I'm on tour, standing invitations from a dozen hostesses from Bucks to anywhere in the South of France. It's been too easy. It's always been too easy. Since school. . . . Do you remember a chap called Pattison?"

Driffield remembered. "He was sacked."

"Remember why?"

"Yes."

"Well, there was another chap mixed up in it. Yes, Sydney,

it was me. Pattison got expelled. I'd made eighty not out against Harrow the day before the thing happened and the Head let me off with a wigging. It was the same at the 'Varsity. In my four years I doubt whether I attended a couple of dozen lectures, but I passed my exams all right. They daren't fail me. The match against Cambridge was far too important for me to waste time on books.

"I got into some bother afterwards, you remember. So I made a hundred and thirty runs in eighty-seven minutes playing against the clock, in that Surrey match: my father paid all my gambling debts.

"Next summer I'll be thirty-seven. I'll have lived half my life, and what have I achieved? What have I done with it? Well, it's caught up with me now."

"You mean . . . ?"

"Yes, I'm bust."

"I'm sorry. If it's only a question of money . . ."

"No, I value our friendship too much for that."

"But the scandal?"

"Don't worry. There won't be any. It will be kept quiet. There is an uncle who has a soft spot for me; he's a banker. He will arrange something . . . so much in the pound, I think. All my creditors have a lively respect for the fair name of English cricket; they will accept what they're offered. But no more invitations to the South of France, no more cruises on other people's yachts, no more guinea-pig directorships. I've gone too far this time."

"My dear man," said Driffield in alarm, "how are you going to manage?"

"You know, Sydney, this will kill you. If I said I'd do the honest thing and turn pro, you'd throw a fit, wouldn't you?"

Driffield said in alarm, "Turn professional? Good God, you can't mean it!"

"But that's all I know, Sydney. What else is there?"

Dick Sinclair touched one to first slip, who held it effortlessly. He had never got going that day. He had not been able to recover from a false start. There had been too much wear on the pitch, too much venom in the desperate attack; whatever the explanation, he had lost that fine edge necessary for trigger-tension alertness. So brilliant in the first innings, so uninspired now. Quite inexplicable. A change of temperature of the spirit, something missing from the tempo of reaction. Every athlete, virtuoso on the platform, orator in parliament or the court-room knows this occasional chemic change that lowers the blood heat and transforms passion to dullness. It had not been his day. Perhaps he had been standing in Stavenden's shadow that morning, dominated by a superlative model of skill. . . .

He trailed his bat. Last man eleven.

"Good luck, Noel," said Driffield in the pavilion. "Don't let that thing worry you. But don't take any unnecessary chances."

"Hang on to your hat."

"Noel . . . this is important."

"It's important to Mr. Stavenden with his sports shirt advertisement and to Mr. Jeffers with his pension, but I am an amateur and a gentleman. I dazzle them."

Driffield watched the tall, lean figure saunter out into the sun, six feet three inches of matador-like elegance.

Sterndale was bowling; Noel liked Sterndale's steely control of the ball. He was tall enough to get on top of the fluent, high-flying, long-lengthed deliveries. Sterndale didn't pack his leg field as closely as Ryder; he didn't have Ryder's powers of intimidation.

He bowled his true, fine-paced leg ball, and it whipped up knee-high, kicking up a little puff of dust like gunsmoke. Noel leaned towards it, his long wrists, all sinew and suppleness, tensing; the ball connected squarely, deflected towards long leg. Two runs; two runs and first blood. A couple of balls later he late-cut a loose one for another couple. The last ball of the over, he met a long-hop with a superb sweeping stroke for three runs.

He faced Foreman.

It took him less than half an over to master the off-spinner's turn of the ball. He straight-drove him for two, a boundary, and then came down the pitch to meet the ball on the hop. He lifted it clean into the stands. Foreman's chagrin was complete.

He faced Sterndale. The second ball, a little over-pitched, was driven inches off the ground, the grass nodding in its path. Then, a little later, another raking shot through the covers, the bat describing a perfect arc in the noble follow-through. Stavenden trained with the baton, Noel with the rapier. Shades of Ranjitsinhji! He transformed cricket into choreography; strength, timing, judgment. "The D'Artagnan of the willow," as Moncrieff of the *Gazette* had called him in a lyrical moment, was meeting the challenge of the clock as even Stavenden had met it in the first tremendous breakthrough; and even Stavenden's efficiency seemed dull by comparison. The stylist, the sportsman *par excellence,* was eclipsing the machine-like professional.

The crowd were in ecstasy; the grimness of the tight-lipped contest yielded before the charm of the elegant fireworks.

There was a haze in the sky, a sort of milky haze that hurt the eyes, like steam seen through sunlight. The humidity was so great that the players sweated as though in a Turkish bath. The bowlers appeared to flight the ball oddly. Not for long; breaking point was inevitable. Lightning quivered in the sky; on and on. Would it never break through that bath-tub saturating heat? Stavenden's head was a crucible of pain. The rim of Noel's cap pressed down like an iron band on his brow.

When the storm broke it was like an eruption; the thunder was massed artillery, the rain pelted down in a stream, the players ran for cover, the stands were in a turmoil. Only the fanatics stood in their silent ranks like sentinels. Noel was the last to leave the field; he stood a solitary figure for a moment, then he walked slowly back to the pavilion.

Although Driffield had forgotten his dream of last night, somewhere in the subterranean reaches of his mind there was a faint stirring, an evocation, a psychical discomfort. An unaccountable melancholy came over him. When he saw Noel standing on the field alone, he felt a sudden desire to run out to him, to reassure him of his friendship and goodwill. He shook off the strange mood with difficulty. And then as Noel left the field a poignant moment of panic, fear, hatred, came over him, clutched at his entrails, and was gone; baffling; incomprehensible.

He raised a hand to a moist brow.

"You all right, skipper?"

He turned to the concerned face of Bill Townsend, had a momentary blankness of recognition.

"Yes, of course."

"I know one sometimes has that feeling," said Townsend.

"What feeling?"

Driffield was 'himself' again.

"A shadow. A sense of end-of-the-worldness," said Townsend.

Stavenden interrupted the conversation with a hurried word to Townsend about Ryder's technique on a wet wicket.

"Now we're in for it," said Bob Jeffers.

"You never know. It might be a wash-out."

"It will be over in ten minutes. An Aussie speciality, this downpour. Specially designed to help the bowlers when they're in difficulty."

"Anyway, it will clear the air," said Stavenden. "Anything's better than that humidity."

"Sure, Steve," said Jeffers, soothing.

Driffield, his head throbbing, went into the lounge of the pavilion to relax. He sank into an armchair, closing his eyes. His disturbed night, the reunion with Cynthia, the exertions of the day, were beginning to have their effect on him. He was not aware how tired he was till his head fell forward, and he sat up with a start.

The other players, on the veranda, were deep in discussion of the game. He let his mind wander to his meeting with Cynthia this evening.

('An overgrown schoolboy. . . .' she had called him. And Noel: 'We are re-living our boyhood days. . . . It's a sky-blue life, Sydney.')

Driffield thought about his childhood. His boyhood days were gloomy ones, on the whole, with his Methodist father, of whom the whole family were very much in awe. His mother, a pallid creature, his younger sisters, both rather quiet, serious girls, dropped their voices a little when speaking of Father. Not that Father was a tyrant or disciplinarian. Father was a just figure; a figure respected in the community. There was a sense of this fearsome respect always about him like an aura, in the town when he went visiting with the family, in church, in the factory, which employed many hundreds of respectful employees. Sydney was always conscious of it.

Outside the factory, on the main gate was the wording wrought in letters of iron DRIFFIELD & SON . . . and son. But who was the Son? Surely, not he? So quiet, serious, just like his mother's side of the family, like his sisters—which of them was the more *pallid?*—who vied with one another for obscurity when Father conducted family prayers, an awesome ritual with all the domestic staff present. On one occasion there had been a weeping maid. She had begun to cry into her hymn-book in the middle of the ceremony; but Father would not stop. Sydney would have wanted to stop. Had someone been unkind to her? Although he knew Father was Right, that the Word must not be interrupted, he would have liked to stop and comfort the hysterical silly unhappy girl. But Father did not stop; he carried on, raising his voice in the brief sermon a little, drowning the foolish noises of the girl. *'Stop, Father, please, Father, stop . . . I can't bear it. . . .'* he had wanted to cry out, but he kept the words to himself. Afterwards he had tried to find out why she had been crying, but his sisters, who knew, were very secretive about it. But it must have had something to do with the sermon, because the next time they foregathered there was a prayer said for the girl, who was no longer with them; and still no one would explain why she had wept, or what had happened to her. She had been the gayest one in the household, had met him in the garden, after midday dinner one morning, and pressed a bunch of sweet black grapes into his hand, which had been his favourite fruit. "Take them. Don't be silly, Master Sydney. No one can see." She said this because she knew he was only allowed to have them on special occasions, and then he never had enough of them. What was her name now? Sally . . . Doris . . . Gladys . . . a name like that, he couldn't for the life of him remember what it was. But he remembered there was a vitality about her, that her cheeks were rosy, her eyes full of sparkling good humour; she had been very pretty, even as a boy he could see that. Once, too, when his parents were away for the day, and he had friends to tea from the prep school, she had produced a meal that had taken his breath away, candies and chocolate cake, strawberries and cream, coloured jellies, and when the chaps horsed around and shouted and spoiled things, she had only laughed. She had pressed him to eat everything he could cram inside him. "Doesn't matter if you are sick. It's worth it."

Father had sent her away. The realisation came to him gradually. Father, in his black frock-coat, the ebony and silver cane, the wing collar, the stiff straight back, just like the life-size portrait of him that hung in the drawing-room, and the duplicate one in the board room of DRIFFIELD & SON, beneath which it said 'Founder'. Father had dismissed the silly creature, banished her from Sydney's life. When he first knew that, he had felt a deep bitterness and anger, had wept into his pillow at night, but of course he said nothing about the way he felt to Father, or anyone. Father no doubt had been Right, had had good Reasons for sending her away. Sydney realised that.

DRIFFIELD & SON. He had sat on his father's right hand at the family table, his mother sat opposite. When they drove, he had sat beside Father, the women in the back of the car. He stood beside Father in the family pew; when they sent the collection plate round, the girls put silver, but Father had given him a golden sovereign each Sunday to put on the plate.

DRIFFIELD & SON. Surely, it could not be he who was the Son? The boys had ragged him about it in the prep school, and the teachers had hinted at it, but he was certain it could not mean him. He thought that all firms and businesses put & Son or & Company, as a standard description, like Mr. in front of a grown-up chap's name, something ordinary and meaningless like that. But one day, when they were driving through the town, and they passed the main gate, he turned to his father and said—he was nine at the time—"Father, who is Son?" and his father had patted his knee and said, "I put that sign up on the day you were born, Sydney. One of these days, when you are older, you will step into my shoes." And he was terrified by the thought. For nights afterwards he had dreamed of the horrible black factory with its great screaming plant, like an express train bearing down in the night, and the furnaces roaring like hell fire. He didn't want to be Son, to step into Father's black glittering shoes, to control this monster. And his mother had visited him in her nightgown, like a ghost, and pressed his wet face to her breast, and spoken to him gentle, meaningless words.

He had looked forward like anything to going to public school, but when he got there he found it dull and horrid, and the early terms were dreadful with the bullying, the ragging and the fagging. But then in the second year he had been befriended by an older boy, a brilliant boy who could do anything, and whom the other boys respected and even feared a little. They had been making up a game of tennis; Sydney wasn't much good, and this boy had chosen him as his partner when he could have chosen any of the others. "I'll have young Driffield," he said, and dropped his hand on Sydney's shoulder, and all the others had looked surprised, and Sydney's heart beat like anything. It was a terrifying but wonderful game; and Sydney had never played better in all his life. The boy who was his partner didn't rag him when he double-faulted or missed a sitter, but laughed and said something to encourage him. For weeks afterwards Sydney was up at half-past five in the morning in that summer term, practising with a squash racket, alone in that huge gymnasium, and later in the term he had the thrill of that boy saying to him casually that he was "pretty good".

During the holidays the boy had invited him to stay with his people. They were rather a grand family, with an old country mansion; his father was Sir Lionel Erskine, the barrister, a wonderful figure of a man, and they had lots of servants in uniform, and horses, and his sisters were jolly girls, full of fun and very pretty. Altogether it was a wonderful holiday for him, although he dreaded what his friend would think of his home, with the dark cold rooms, the morning prayers for the whole household, the way everything was done to time (his father taking out the massive gold watch every now and then which chimed when it was opened and clicked like a heavy lock turning when snapped shut).

Of course he did invite him—he had to repay the former invite—and it turned out all right because his friend had an easy natural manner, and seemed never at a loss in any situation. Until some years later when he visited him in the Christmas holiday and one evening, when Father was giving Advice to the youngsters, his friend Noel had suddenly interrupted and said, "My pater gave me some advice, Mr. Driffield." "And what is that?" "Three things I must remember: never drink red wine with fish, always remove the band of your cigar when you smoke, and refrain from exercising marital rights in the morning because you never know what will turn up during the day."

Sydney had never forgotten the dreadful silence that greeted this remark.

Fortunately there were no womenfolk present at the time, and although Noel had apologised immediately afterwards, he was never invited to the Driffield home again, and Sydney's friendship with him was discouraged.

They went up to the university together and their friendship was continued in spite of everything. One day Sydney was called to the dean's office in the middle of a lecture. His father, he was told, was seriously ill. He had had a heart attack and was partially paralysed. The young man took the first train home and greeted the weeping women, white-faced. It had happened suddenly. At first he was given no explanation but later his mother confessed that there had been some sort of trouble in the factory.

It was shortly before the war and a big rebuilding scheme had been under way in the plant to cope with a government contract. His father had recently acquired some new partners with whom he appeared to have had serious difficulties. It was all rather vague; his mother understood none of the details; the old man had told her very little. For the first time in his life since the boyhood episode when he had realised the responsibility he had assumed on the day of his birth, he was faced with the stark reality of his burden.

"Who are these men, Mother? Why did Father take them into the firm?"

"I don't know, they are terrible men, Sydney. Your father has not slept for weeks. He was fighting them incessantly, to all hours of the night the meetings went on. . . . They used to come here and I could hear shouting in the library. It was frightful."

The doctor, an old family doctor, came out just then and

told Sydney his father wanted to see him. "Don't stay long. He needs rest above all things. And on no account must he be allowed to have anything to do with business matters. His life depends on it."

His father was in bed, a fragile figure so shrunken and wasted as to be almost unrecognisable. He tried in vain to sit up when Sydney entered the room. He could only speak in whispers, after the most terrifying effort at muscular co-ordination. ". . . your mother . . . and sisters, Sydney . . . you must take care . . . now."

He sank back in a coma.

The young man was appalled by his inadequacy to deal with the situation. He had no training, no knowledge of commercial matters; he did not know even if he had the least aptitude for them; he knew only that his father's life depended on the successful outcome of his struggle with the interlopers.

His one asset however were his father's friends, the solicitors and accountants who understood the business thoroughly, the works manager, an old servant of the company, the chief engineer, men whose loyalty was beyond question.

He called a meeting with the accountant and the works manager, and it continued from five in the afternoon until four in the morning. The others went home to bed. Sydney began to study ledgers, company records, files, innumerable documents. Books about company practice and law were sent to him the next day, works on administration and the rules of banking, volumes and white papers on industrial matters concerning his own business, factory management, all matters relating to the theory and practice of a business such as his father had founded and built up to a large concern in some thirty-five years.

He worked incessantly, day and night, hardly stopping for meals, keeping going on black coffee and drugs, until his untrained mind learned to grasp not only essentials but points of the most subtle detail. The thirteen-year-old boy had risen at half-past five in the summer morning to go down alone into the gymnasium and for hours drive a ball with a squash racket against a blank wall until he had achieved mastery of muscular co-ordination and timing. The young man drove himself with a mature passion to achieve a similar mastery of affairs that are normally absorbed over years of training and experience.

One thought stuck in his mind like a thorn in the quick of his finger: *on the day of his birth* . . . It was with him in all his waking moments, in the brief spells of sleep that conquered him as a heavy sea plunges a fragile vessel into the depths.

Jagger, the old family solicitor, explained the position to the youth. "Your father, as you probably know, was the chairman of the firm from its inception. In fact, he founded it. Now these gentlemen are comparatively new directors. They have put a lot of money into the business for a large expansion policy of your father's, which has produced a considerable development of the firm's business and tangible assets. New machinery and installations alone amount to nearly £300,000."

"How much did they put in?"

"About £400,000."

"Why didn't Father borrow the money from the bank on mortgages? The government contract would have ensured that, surely?"

The solicitor regarded the youth with some surprise. "Indeed. That's a good question. Do you know anything about finance? I thought you were studying classics at the university."

"I was, but when Dad had that stroke . . ."

"You've made it your business to know? Good. Well, then, I'll try to explain the true position. You see, these gentlemen have really plotted to gain control of the business. They knew about the forthcoming government contract and offered to lend the money at a purely nominal rate of interest, three and a half per cent as against four per cent by the bank and not subject to recall at short notice like a bank loan. But they put in a trick

168

clause which your father, rather too trusting for a business man, overlooked."

"My father," said the youth, "is an honest man, a manufacturer. He is not a financier."

"I'm afraid you're right. You see, the clause said that if the firm's turnover fell below a certain figure in any quarter, they were entitled to recall their loan. He didn't think it could, and normally it wouldn't. And even if it did he thought they were only concerned about safeguarding their money in the event of a serious drop. At any rate they planned it that the factory's turn-over did fall."

"How did they do that?"

"By a clever stroke. They persuaded your father that the old building should be refitted and installed with fresh plant, up-to-date machinery. The change-over took about two months, during which time the actual productivity of the factory of course was considerably reduced temporarily. Now, of course, it's capable of far greater production than ever before, but in the meantime these wretched people have insisted on the terms of the loan agreement, and demanded shares to the value of the money which are held as collateral. The money isn't available, and the banks will not help to repay them because they have been persuaded by these same directors that the controlling power, your father, has been so inefficient that the turnover has fallen. The banks will only lend the money now if your father's control is vested with these new gentlemen."

"As I see it, then, if we can persuade the banks that the productivity is greater than ever, they will lend us the money to repay the loans."

"Oh, yes."

"How long will it take for the new plant to turn out enough production?"

"I understand about three or four weeks."

"And then we shall be able to present proof to the bank in the way of substantial turnover?"

"Yes. But these new directors refuse of course to allow us a day longer than next Friday, which is the end of the quarter, and their loans are liable to recall immediately."

"Any way of tying it up legally for three or four weeks?"

"No. There is a definite time limit, time is of the essence of the contract as we lawyers put it. Which means that we forfeit shares by Saturday which are collateral to the loans, and which they can demand in place of them."

"It looks pretty bad, then."

"It looks disastrous as far as your father's control of his own business is concerned. It's that which brought about the collapse."

"And my position is that of proxy? I can represent my father's interest as chairman?"

"Only till Friday. Then you can be voted out immediately."

The youth said: "And have you any suggestions?"

"I think the best you can do is to try to come to terms with them. Your loss of control is inevitable in my opinion. But you'll still be a very large shareholder."

"How many shares are held as collateral against the money loaned?"

"Fifty-one per cent. The control minimum."

"If we lose that, we have forty-nine left?"

"Yes."

"The problem then is to repay them by Friday."

"Yes."

"And of course there is no hope of borrowing the money privately in the time left?"

"Not a sum like that. Two days . . . no."

The youngster went to see the bank manager, bringing the works manager, an old employee of the firm—but not the general manager, a recently appointed staff member with an understanding with the new directors. He brought the firm's accountant, and certified reports of assets, works progress and a planned estimate of the capacity of the new plant. The manager was a comparatively old man but a recent administrator of the branch.

"Old Mr. Feathers," said the youngster, referring to the old manager, "would not hesitate to recommend the loan to Head Office. The facts are plain enough. We are quite capable of producing the turnover with the new plant and installations, and exceeding our normal production by almost two thirds, according to the estimate."

"When you have done so, it will remove the element of speculation from the proposition. The bank will then be quite willing to consider a loan against the collateral of buildings and machinery, but don't you see, the head of the firm is no longer active in the direction? I deeply regret his incapacity—but the facts remain that whilst we may be quite willing to agree with you as individuals that the risk is not a serious one at present, we cannot as bankers pay any attention to anything but the last quarter's production report, which, as you know, clearly shows a very large fall, and we must officially take into account the explanation of the new directors that the management was at fault."

The works manager shook his head. "They argued for new installations. The works department—that's me—pointed out at the time that a fall in production must result temporarily, and they understood that."

"Unfortunately they do not agree with that. They argue that the controlling director was at fault, and commitments with regards to the government contract are in arrears."

"The ministry agreed to wait when we explained about the refitting of capital installation. We'll be able to catch up and exceed our quota by the end of next quarter."

"That is still in the realms of speculation. When you can show us your certified figures in the next three months the bank will be able to act. Banking is a trust; we have to account for depositors' money, and security must be gilt-edged. Come and see us in three months' time with your production figures and we shall act promptly. Even one month's figures would convince us that you are operating satisfactorily."

"You know that this is a plan to gain control of the company, a company founded and run by my father for nearly thirty-five years. Are you prepared to see him lose the business after breaking his back over it?"

"Believe me, what I feel about this personally has nothing to do with my official view. You may be right; Mr. Jagger may be right; your works manager may be right; and your accountant. But the bank must sit on the fence and wait until the Board has agreed about policy and speak with one voice in connection with such matters as the cause of the fall of production. Either you or they must be proved wrong, and such proof must be in the form of hard production figures. We cannot support a divided house. We are well aware of your father's former capacities, but these new gentlemen are also figures of considerable repute in the city, with control of far bigger businesses than your father and yourself."

"They are adventurers in finance, and you must know it, Mr. Clynes." The manager shook his head. "These are hard words, young man. You must realise that a bank can only judge by results, and these gentlemen are very large customers of our bank and Head Office holds them in great esteem. Their methods are legitimate ones, whatever the ethical merits may be. A bank does not judge by what means you become an important client. A customer who holds a million-pound account with us is precisely ten times as important as one who is worth a hundred thousand. Our ledgers, not our personal sympathies, must dictate our policy. We are not dealing with our own money."

Jagger was about to make an appeal, but the young man stopped him. "We shall come to you within a month with record production figures, Mr. Clynes."

He rose politely. At the door the manager put a tentative

hand on his shoulder, an avuncular hand: "Mr. Sydney, please believe me when I tell you that my sympathies are with you in this matter. In fact when your father declined the bank offer for renewal of plant and told me that he had private offers of assistance at a lower rate of interest and for only a small share of dividend-earning shares, I told him at the time that I had no doubt that the intentions of the new associates must be suspect. It seemed too good a proposition at the time. Unfortunately, neither of us fully understood how these gentlemen operate to absorb competitors into their combine. He decided to proceed. I'm afraid it was a lonely and difficult path that he chose to follow. I deeply regret the effect it has had on his health. His doctor warned him about his heart, but he's a man of great determination; the will is stronger than the flesh. A sad business.

"However, be reassured. You will still own forty-nine per cent of the ordinary shares and the majority of the B, or dividend-earning, shares. Both you and your father have a most important rôle to play in the firm's progress; you will still be wealthy in your own right. Take the advice of an older man, the sort of advice your father declined to accept from me when I offered the bank's assistance. Settle this matter with the new directors amicably. They have no personal animosity against your father or yourself. They are extremely powerful and subtle men of affairs. I admire your spirit of resistance, but I feel that your best course is not to antagonise them in a lost cause. Capitulation is a hard word, but you are still astonishingly young, you have your whole life before you. Your father can retire, a wealthy man, and you will have all the money you'll ever need."

Sydney said: "I have to see this thing through for my father's sake. He would not have me give up without a fight to save a business for which he sacrificed his health. And we have old employees of great loyalty and devotion to our company who will lose their jobs if these city slickers move in. I have to think of them. And as you know, Mr. Clynes, our firm has been jealous of its reputation for standards of craftsmanship famous all over the world. This will be lost in the standardised mediocrity of the combine's production in the new directors' quest for higher profits. I must fight them. What success I'll have, I don't know. But to resist them is essential."

The manager said, after a long pause: "A young man like yourself torn from your studies at the university, torn from the playing fields, how can you fight such men?"

"I don't know, but I must."

"You are taking too great a burden. Your father, with all his experience, could not resist them; he was broken in the struggle."

"They were fighting a sick man. Thank heaven his son is able to stand the racket."

"I didn't know you had any interest in business," said the manager, shaking his head. "You were devoted to a different career. It was always one of your father's chief regrets that you showed no interest in the firm. What has brought about this change?"

Sydney smiled. "I still have not the slightest interest in business, Mr. Clynes. But my father needs me now. Surely, that must make all the difference in the world?"

Sydney went into the board room to take on the opposition, which consisted of three gentlemen with a retinue of assistants, experts, and consultants on aspects of finance and factory management. There were more than a dozen of them in all, and the chiefs, the three directors, sat with Sydney at an impressive mahogany table. Any point that had to be referred for information was attended to by a male secretary who pranced agilely from board room to annexe, returning with the nimbleness of a terrier retrieving a stick.

The only thought in the minds of the directors was the new control which was to take place on the Saturday. Sydney was ignored, treated as a nonentity; his presence at the meeting was required by law, but the other directors paid no attention to him. Discussions about the new management proceeded without reference to him, and when the others reached their decisions in spite of any comment or opposition on his part, they passed papers for him to register his vote in their favour. When he refused they shrugged their shoulders. "It can wait till after Friday. It won't be necessary then."

Having settled the affairs of the new management they proceeded to the question of the holdings that were not subject to collateral security of their loans. They made it clear to Sydney that there was no hope of the company earning dividends for some years to come, as all earnings would be devoted to expansion. "You may have to wait for a long time before you see a penny piece, young man. You and your father. All cash earned by this company will be set aside for development."

"For how long?"

"Years, if need be. Ten. Fifteen. Who knows?"

"And," said the most dynamic of the high-powered personalities, "not a penny in salary or other remuneration. No guinea-pig directors in our combine, eh, gentlemen? No doubt you know something about Euclid or Virgil or how to row a boat, but these aren't the qualifications required by our Board."

Sydney said nothing. He doodled.

The offer came sooner than he expected. "You will still own some shares in the business, some ordinary and some preference dividend-earning shares. They're worth nothing to you the way things will work out. In a private company, as your solicitor probably explained to you, control can wipe out any share value. We could vote ourselves fees and expense accounts that would eat up any profits in excess of the money set aside for expansion. As far as you're concerned the shares are worthless."

"I see."

"However, we don't want to be too hard on you. Nor on your father. We didn't get on in business, but we don't bear any grudge. (How is he, by the way?) What we suggest is that we pay the original value of the shares. That's quite a large sum of money, nearly forty thousand pounds. That should see your family quite comfortably settled."

"That's the capital my father started the business with thirty-five years ago, isn't it?"

Their faces were expressionless.

Sydney nodded. "What is he to get for thirty-five years' work? Building up the business until it's worth about a million pounds—once you gentlemen stop obstructing its administration?"

Dexter, the North Country man of the set-up, who made up in bluntness what he lacked in plausibility, said, "We don't want any lip from overgrown schoolboys. We're men of affairs. Your dad—well, it's hard luck for him—but he's lived well these thirty-five years on the firm, so that's his reward. Forty thousand or nothing. That's the short of it. No need for a youngster like you to worry about any thirty-five years' work. You haven't spent thirty-five minutes in this plant."

There was silence.

"Well, out with it? You must have some ideas besides how to make a rugby tackle?"

Sydney said: "I don't think forty thousand is enough."

"More than enough, son. More than enough!"

Brabant, a smooth, sleek-headed gentleman with an air of brooding profundity, said, "We're wasting time, gentlemen. Give him nothing. He understands nothing. He's worth nothing. He gets nothing. I told you we'd be wasting our time."

Jenkyns, a fat, sinister, silk-voiced creature, said with a soft mockery of geniality, "Hear, hear, I agree. Nothing."

Still no response from Sydney, who sat, wooden-faced, drawing designs on his pad.

They pretended they had lost interest in the subject and started to discuss other things. As this had no effect, Dexter suddenly said: "Well, I've got to get my train. There's nothing more, is there?"

"No, nothing," said Jenkyns. "You got anything to say before we close the meeting, Master Sydney?"

The others laughed.

"Nothing," said Sydney. "As you pointed out, I don't understand much about it."

Dexter said irritably, "Don't be totally daft, man. You must have something to say. You're not throwing forty thousand down the drain."

"I told you I don't think it enough."

"And we told you the shares are worthless to you. To us, too, for that matter." He realised the latter remark was a mistake even before the young man replied.

"Of course, you wouldn't be offering me forty thousand for worthless shares."

"All right, maybe they're worth something to us, but nothing to you. We told you you'll earn nothing from them."

"Well, then, nobody gets anything from them."

"You'd rather get nothing than forty thousand? We've got the resources to hold up dividends for ten or twenty years. You must know that."

"My family aren't destitute. And I always expected I'd have to earn my living. We can wait ten or twenty years, too."

Dexter was about to say something when Brabant waved him to silence. "Very well, then," he said, and for the first time a note other than mockery or irony was in his voice. "You've told us it's worth more than forty thousand. We don't agree with you. But we admit you can have a nuisance value to us. We want those shares. How much do you think they're worth?"

"To you, gentlemen, it's quite plain they must be worth four hundred thousand pounds and more. That's what you thought it was worth to secure half the ordinary shares. The other half is no smaller, gentlemen. Even my university teaches us that. According to the accountants' valuation the business is worth nearly a million at present. With the new plant just going into production it will double its value in about three years. You can then go to the public and get rid of these same shares for one million five hundred thousand pounds, a profit of about three hundred and eighty per cent. You know, gentlemen, the tactics of commerce are not very different from those of the rugby field which Mr. Dexter holds in such low esteem. There is the feinting move, when one player pretends that he has the ball when he has in fact passed it to somebody else; there are tackles, which are assaults in the open, and there is the scrum, gentlemen, which is a bit of in-fighting, not exactly illegal, but not visible to the referee, either, so the odd kick below the belt is often overlooked. And then, of course, it's rather a dirty game. So you see, my education hasn't been entirely wasted." He looked round, appreciating the silence. "I am just as anxious to end this association as you, gentlemen, but don't be persuaded that my family will not fight to the end for a fair return for thirty-five years' work building up this business and destroying my father's health. We have the means to hold out till the end of our lives." He added sharply, "'And if we hadn't a penny piece behind us, if I had to go out to dig ditches for a living—you won't see these shares for a penny less than four hundred thousand pounds."

Dexter started his explosive and abusive tactics but Brabant once more urged him to silence. "I think," he said slowly, "that Mr. Jenkyns might have something to explain to you . . . about the state of the business as your father left it."

Jenkyns said, "We didn't want to tell you this before—we hoped there would be no need. We know your father has suffered. But please don't think that we're responsible for his collapse . . . only indirectly. It's what we uncovered . . . tax matters, evasions . . . technical, of course. Many a business man who only has to account to himself—men without a partner like your father—they think they can do what they like with their own firm. Well, they can often get away with it, until new partners take over and get a sight of the books."

Sydney rose, and amidst tense silence went round the table to fix Jenkyns's eye. Jenkyns's glance wavered. By his side was a telephone, and the young man picked up the receiver and rang a number.

"Who are you phoning? What are you doing?"

"Is Mr. Jagger there? Please put him on. It's most urgent. Yes, it is—but it's Mr. Arnold Jenkyns who wishes to speak to him."

He handed the receiver to Jenkyns. "I want you to say to Mr. Jagger what you've just said to me. I want you to repeat your slander so that we can take appropriate action, Mr. Jenkyns. You say what you've just told me, and say it loud and plain and in the open, that my father is a crook. I'll be pleased to institute criminal proceedings for slander and attempted extortion against you or any of these gentlemen here who support you."

Jenkyns's moon face, white as whey, glistened with gathering moisture. He replaced the receiver. Sydney slapped him across the face.

"The price is four hundred thousand pounds. I want a certified cheque here tomorrow, gentlemen. And I shall sign an undertaking to take no further interest of any kind in this business."

Brabant rose and the others with him, Jenkyns tottering to his feet on quaking legs.

"Young man," said Brabant, lighting a cigar and waving his cronies out of the room, "I want a private word with you."

"What is it?"

"You have more in you than we first thought. There's a streak of devil in you which I like."

"Cut that out. It's inappropriate."

Brabant motioned him to sit down. He pushed his cigar case across the table. Sydney shook his head.

Brabant leaned forward confidentially. "Those are your father's shares you're proxy for, aren't they?"

"Yes, you know that. I'm his nominee."

"A nominee usually earns ten per cent on a deal. Do you know what I'd like to suggest to you?"

Sydney remained silent.

Brabant said, with a laugh: "I'm not Jenkyns, you know. I don't want to stick my neck out."

"What have you to say to me?"

"You're doing a good job here representing your father's interests. You've played your cards well and you seem to know what they're worth, up to a point."

"Go on."

"We can close the deal at a hundred thousand pounds. Officially forty thousand. That's all they expect to get out of this. Forty thousand. Believe me Jagger, your accountant fellow, all of them. That's all they hope for." He paused. "*Officially* forty; *in fact,* a hundred."

"And the other sixty thousand—for me?"

"Now, you said that. Not me. Remember that."

Sydney was silent, shaking his head. "Mr. Brabant, you leave me speechless."

The subtlety and tenacity of his antagonists was a revelation to the young man.

"You won't take it?"

Sydney shook his head.

"And any time you're ready you can have a job with me starting at three thousand a year. Any time."

"Remember, Mr. Brabant, I'm just an overgrown schoolboy."

Brabant said: "My God, I like a good fighter. So does the chief."

"The chief?"

"Oh, yes, didn't you know? This isn't my money. Elias Gunther is the boss; I'm only a fiscal agent."

"So you're not your own master, Mr. Brabant. You disappoint me."

Brabant shrugged. "You'll have to have dinner with us, after this is over."

"Mr. Brabant," said Sydney suddenly. "I'll make a deal with you. I'll tell the chief, Mr. Gunther, that I was holding out for seven hundred thousand and that you beat me down to four. How's that?"

Brabant grinned. "All right, Sydney, there's something else you ought to know. You're not a great student of company law. You must realise that with one stroke of the pen we can transform *all* these shares to bits of paper."

"How?"

"We can sell the assets for a nominal sum to a new company, owned by Mr. Gunther. As soon as we get control on Friday we propose to do that—if you're still obstinate."

Sydney said, "Fraud."

"What did you say?"

"I said it would be fraud. A fraud on the shareholders. And I shall be pleased to give evidence at the Old Bailey when Mr. Gunther is indicted together with you and the rest of your criminal gang."

"Don't be absurd."

"Mr. Gunther is over eighty. He wouldn't like it in gaol, Mr. Brabant. Nor would you. They don't supply Havana cigars." He added: "If I don't get a fair price for those shares by Friday morning I shall go to Scotland Yard and tell them exactly what you've said to me. I called Jenkyns's bluff and, by God, I'll call yours."

"You're being silly. You don't understand company law. You know nothing about it."

"I don't have to. But I can tell the difference between honesty and dishonesty. And I'll let the judge and the jury decide the rest."

There was another heavy, stony silence.

Sydney said sombrely, "Mr. Elias Gunther is an old man. Old men are in a hurry. That makes you in a hurry, too. You want to capitalise on those shares quickly. Capital appreciation in a sale to the public. That makes it free of tax, doesn't it? Think it over, Mr. Brabant."

Brabant called in his partners and the wrangling continued. They had used up the big shot, and now they settled down to attrition. They would work on him in turn like interlocutors in a police investigation. Dexter had left fairly early, but the others stayed on till the office closed; they continued late without a break, arguing, disputing, threatening; Jenkyns would try to browbeat, Brabant to tempt. The young man fought them on every issue, the threat to sack the old employees, to cheapen the old and honoured trade mark, to reveal to the tax authority that certain fixed assets had been 'written down' in value by Sydney's father, to urge the authorities to re-assess his tax liability—the other innuendo of tax evasion and the slur on the old man's honesty having been dropped—and finally to use all their powers in the city to undermine Sydney's father's investments in other smaller concerns.

He fought them back, this youth, fought back the unscrupulous, experienced financiers across the board room table hour by hour. He remained unyielding in his demands. At last, faint from fatigue, hoarse from speech and shouting, the meeting broke up in sullen, bitter animosity, neither side having given way an inch.

Sydney had the parting shot: when they demanded a meeting at nine in the morning, he said: "Fetch your master. I won't waste my time any more. I should have known better than to deal with subordinates."

He left them shaking with rage.

A week previously the youth had been an innocent spectator of life; he was transformed in a few days to an iron maturity. Goaded by the picture of the broken man who was his father, he attacked and fought back with the smooth ferocity of a young tiger.

He went back from the meeting straight to the offices and

private homes of production men, accountants, solicitors, investors, moneylenders, stockbrokers, government officials, Board of Trade experts, anyone who could help him with advice, instruction, influence or money. Till the small hours he studied documents, industrial charts, blue prints, contracts, conveyances, deeds; he could quote pages of company law by heart; as though overnight he acquired a grasp of subtleties of accountancy and legal matters that was astounding.

And all the time he planned a desperate crushing counterstroke.

They met, the five—for Elias Gunther did attend next morning, which was fought out with all the mounting bitterness of the previous day, on Friday, the day of the take over, Gunther was wheeled into the board room in a chair: a cadaver, a death's head, a frail, shaking, fiendish creature wrapped stiflingly in blankets, an ebony stick rattling against the wheel of the chair in his palsied grasp. They faced each other at opposite ends of the table.

Gunther waved his stick and Jenkyns promptly produced a legal document. "Give it to him."

Sydney absorbed the brief lines in a moment's frenzied concentration. All rights, all interest, all powers to assign . . . everything . . . control, equity, preference shares, debentures . . . every stick and stone . . . thirty-five years' of struggle, creative struggle . . . everything . . . and the figure Four Hundred Thousand Pounds, bold as you please, every penny he had demanded.

"Show him." The stick waved.

Jenkyns produced the certified cheque.

They called in witnesses, their men and his. The loyal works manager, Sanders, who stared with dumb reproach at the young serene man who returned his look gravely.

"Sign it, and get." The stick rapped.

Sydney was about to sign the transfer when Jenkyns said, "By the way, how old are you?"

183

"I had my twenty-first birthday a couple of months ago."

"How can be we sure of that?"

"I'll put it above my signature. I don't carry a birth certificate."

"Write it in, then. Your own handwriting and initial it."

Sydney write: 'I covenant that I had my twenty-first birthday two months before the date of this contract.' He initialled it and signed the contract. The cheque was handed to him.

He departed through the silent ranks of men like a robber baron with his ransom.

At an hour before noon—that is, two hours after the completion of the transfer of his remaining shares—he re-entered the office of the board room, interrupting a Ways and Means Committee of the new management, presided over by Brabant.

Brabant rose to his feet; a silence fell on a speaker. All present felt the extraordinary forcefulness of his calm. Brabant, in spite of himself, and with a curious sense of foreboding, began to stutter.

"What are you doing here? What do you want? You have been paid off. You have no business to come in like this."

Sydney felt a curious faintness coming over him, as at the end of a long journey, when the destination is well in sight.

"Do you mind if I sit down a moment?" he muttered, and went to a side table to drink a glass of water from the carafe.

"I must disturb you gentlemen," he said at length. "I have repaid the loan, Mr. Brabant, that you and your colleagues have advanced to the company. The money has been paid into your accounts by banker's draft this morning."

"You're trifling," said Brabant, stiffly. "The money will be returned to you. No doubt you have paid over the purchase money for the remainder of your shares, which we advanced to you this morning."

"That is correct."

"You must be a little addled, my young friend. The strain of these meetings must have proved too much for you. Don't you

184

remember that you signed a contract this morning which not only bought out the remainder of your holdings but secured your undertaking that both you and your father for whom you act as proxy relinquish all your interests in the company?"

"I remember signing the contract, and I must advise you that it is valueless. I am a minor. It is not a legal document."

"If I'm not mistaken that point was well taken by Mr. Jenkyns, who insisted that you declare your age in writing. Do you wish to plead ignorance of your age?"

Sydney suddenly broke down. His dry sobbing was of such a curious hysterical mixture of laughter and heartbreak that Brabant became convinced that he was witnessing a mental collapse, and he was so uncomfortably reminded of Sydney's father in similar circumstances that he felt a moment of genuine remorse; the brittle armour began to crack.

At last Sydney got control of himself and said coldly: "Mr. Brabant, I shall acquaint you with the precise situation. I am a minor. I am twenty years of age. I wrote into the contract that I have had my twenty-first birthday two months ago. That is correct. I don't know why this idiom is used incorrectly, but it is. When you say you have had a first birthday one assumes that you're a year old. That is not accurate. You are a day old on your first birthday. On your second birthday you are a year and a day, on your twenty-first birthday, you are twenty years and a day old. You work it out."

Brabant did.

"You'll never get away with it, you know. We can prove trickery."

"It's arguable. You have two alternatives. One is to request the return of the purchase money, which is an eminently reasonable request. It will be repaid to you within three months, possibly within one month, when the production figures will clearly convince the bank that there was never any mismanagement by my father. Your other alternative. . . ."

But Brabant was no longer listening. He began to shout, to wave his arms; red in the face, he was totally inarticulate, until the startled staff members quickly began to stumble out of the room. Jenkyns and Dexter hurried in.

"Lock the door!" roared Brabant.

Jenkyns dithered. "Haven't a key."

Brabant forgot his request as soon as he made it. He whirled on Jenkyns, seized him by the collar and shook him as a dog shakes a rat. "You blithering imbecile. . . ."

The two men tussled on the carpet, Jenkyns fighting for breath with Brabant's grip on his collar; Dexter tried to separate them and got kicked on the shins for his pains. Brabant ceased wrestling with Jenkyns as suddenly as he had attacked him.

"Get the law!" he shouted. "Get the police! That contract. . . . That man!" He pointed a denunciatory finger at Sydney. "That man. . . . He's a minor!"

In gasping interludes he explained the trick that had been played on them. The state they were in made it impossible for Jenkyns and Dexter to grasp the subtlety of the wording in the contract.

"He says he's *had* his twenty-first birthday. That means he says he's twenty-one. If he's not we can gaol him for false pretences. Absolutely cut and dried. Absolutely."

Brabant snarled: "He didn't say he was twenty-one. He said he's had his twenty-first birthday. He had his first birthday when he was a *day* old, not a *year* old. That makes him *twenty* on his twenty-first birthday!"

"No . . . no. . . . Don't be an idiot . . . everyone knows it means he's twenty-one years old . . . if you say you've had your twenty-first birthday you mean . . ."

". . . It's wrong. It's wrong to say that, if you mean you're twenty-one. You've had twenty-two birthdays . . . the first one doesn't count . . . you're only a *day* old. . . ."

"A day old on your first birthday? How can that be? What

are you saying? It's obvious . . . everybody knows it means . . ."

"Shut up!"

". . . means you're twenty-one if you say . . ."

"Shut up, man. *Shut up!*"

Brabant turned to Dexter, who was now silent. "You get it, don't you? You explain it to him. But not now."

Jenkyns suddenly saw it, too; he collapsed in a chair.

Brabant lit a cigarette with a hand trembling with rage. He stared at Sydney, deep consternation in his eyes. "Who put you up to this? You think you can get away with it? You're greatly mistaken. You've never been more mistaken in anything in all your born days. No, sir. No. No, no, no. Absolutely no. Positively no. Finally, absolutely and positively *no!* It's cold-blooded systematic fraud."

"It's arguable," said Sydney.

"No buts about it. It's calculated. You knew you were sup posed to be twenty-one to sign a contract and get money."

"You'll have to prove that I knew that. In any case, you'll get your money back. I keep the shares, you get your money back within a month when the production figures convince the bank. That's all you need to bother about. What alternative have you?"

"Rest assured. We shall call in the Yard over this. In spite of your ingenuity over that wording, when the facts are examined intent to defraud is plain."

Sydney had thought of that, too.

"You won't. You'll never get your four hundred thousand if you make a criminal issue of it. Get me prosecuted and you forfeit all rights to the return of the money. You ought to know that." He indicated Jenkyns and Dexter. "Get them out of here . . . and as for you, Mr. Brabant, you're occupying my chair."

It had not finished there.

For months afterwards the Gunther syndicate tried every means in their power to smash the firm. By the most ferocious

187

cut-throat competition, by exerting pressure with their customers, by a dozen well known methods of trade practice and malpractice they tried to force Driffield and Son into bankruptcy. Sydney's father was recovering very slowly; month by month he was gradually finding the strength and will to return to the fight. Sydney told him that all had gone well and that all would be well by the time he was back in harness.

Eight months of unremitting struggle continued before the syndicate at last admitted defeat to the twenty-year-old youngster, but for Sydney it was an experience of a foulness that left a permanent stain on his soul. He felt himself corrupted, unclean; he had evil dreams that his blood, his sputum, was polluted. When his father finally returned to the business he took the first opportunity to retire. He studied medicine—the war had started and he wished to join the services in the R.A.M.C. He had studied day and night hoping to take his exams in record time and believing that the courses would be shortened by the emergency. Finally he saw service in Italy and Burma.

When he returned to civilian life he had had six years of grim responsibility behind him, had known every form of bitter struggle, had been lacerated by every form of mental anguish. Death and destruction, agony and waste, had been his constant daily encounter.

A sky-blue life. . . .

After his first week home following his discharge from the Army Noel had arranged for him to play in a cricket match. The sight of the green fields, the white-flannelled figures of his team-mates, the gentle contest of skill with bat and ball, the ladies in their deck-chairs, had had a mesmeric effect on him. It was like a form of crystal-gazing. The world was lost . . . the world of evil and violence that he had known all these years . . . melted in the magic of these green and golden hours.

Yes, it had been an escape. Noel was right. An escape . . . or a quest for the childhood he had never known, for the universal

188

birthright that had been denied him with the responsibility he had assumed on the day he had been born.

Driffield felt someone touch his shoulder; he awoke with a start. "Didn't want to worry you, skipper. Noel's been hurt."

Driffield shook off the past with an impatient movement.

"Noel. . . ?"

"Yes, play was resumed a few minutes ago. It's a real sticky dog out there," said Harry Halliday. "Greasy surface, and underneath like iron."

"One of Ryder's bumpers?"

Driffield was already out on the veranda; they were bringing Noel in on a stretcher. He heard the full details later: a ball had shot up viciously off the hard slippery pitch, struck Noel on the forehead as he played on top of it. Driffield examined the prone figure, feeling the moist skull; it was impossible without an X-ray photograph to estimate whether or not there was any damage to the head. An ambulance was already on the way.

Sam Halliday went on the field to join Stavenden. In the pavilion they were silently grouped around the inert figure, anxiously watching Driffield's expression. Driffield's agitation was inexplicable. As a medical man he felt he should be able to examine the injured man with professional coolness; he could hardly keep his hands from trembling.

"It can't be that bad. . . . He's not . . ."

"No, no, it's not grave. I don't think so. Where the hell's that ambulance?"

It arrived almost immediately; Driffield would have liked to have gone with him, but his presence was obviously required until the last minutes of the Test.

Dick Sinclair volunteered, and they began to take the limp form away. Harry Halliday noticed Noel's lips moving, and bent down.

"I think he's trying to say something, skipper. . . ."

Driffield heard some slurred words, incomprehensible to him. "Something about a clock," said Harry. "He's saying something about a clock."

Townsend said: "No, he thinks he's back in the R.A.F. Talking about bandits at three o'clock." He bent down; he grinned: "He reckons it's the wrong way to tickle Mary. . . ."

The words were clear at last. There was a throw-back to his flying days, some association with an injury received in the Battle of Britain. They were silent as the man on the stretcher was carried off.

"What lousy luck. He was going like thunder, too."

"Those damned bumpers . . ." began Harry Halliday, when Driffield cut him short.

"Enough of that. No one's to blame."

Then they thought of Harkness.

The little band of men dispersed. Driffield began to pace the veranda; he knew it was foolish to try to anticipate the medical report, but his head was full of terrifying possibilities. When Harry asked if it was at all possible for Noel to recover sufficiently to play that day he almost jumped down his throat: "Let's think of something else for a moment other than cricket, Harry."

"Yes, skipper, sorry." Harry looked crestfallen. It was not an unnatural question in the circumstances, with the game moving to a grand climax. There were two and a half hours or so left in which to score a hundred and sixty-six runs. Noel's hectic twenty-two minutes, during which he had scored thirty-five runs, had revitalised the spectators at a time when Stavenden was tiring with the hours of effort and tension in the scorching sun. Even with Noel out of the game there was still Stavenden, the Hallidays, Jeffers and Townsend, five men apart from the tail-enders, who could score such a total in the time necessary.

Driffield looked at the score board. For a fourth innings it was exceptional; here was a real chance of victory, a chance to equal the record of Bradman's men in 1947, the only time in four hundred Tests that it had been done.

"We've got a real chance," he muttered, at last. "You're right, Harry. It's tremendous."

The feeling of excitement gripped the whole of the cricket world that afternoon, from Melbourne to Johannesburg, from Calcutta to Manchester. In Pakistan, the West Indies, and in Kent and Surrey, the millions listened to the radio sets, discussed and argued, interrupted their work and their sport, to hear bulletins of the latest progress of the match as though it were a momentous battle raging for the survival of civilisation.

"Steve might do it solo," said Harry. "He's not given a chance so far. What can stop him now? He looks as comfortable as when he started."

It was true. Even the shooting ball seemed to make no difference to the iron control of the man's reactions. He had just played a slashing stroke to the boundary, beautifully fielded by Reynolds, who sprinted like a track athlete to intercept it.

Sam Halliday, facing the bowler now for the first time, was caution personified as he played the first one with a dead straight bat. The Twins were not stroke players in the same sense as their predecessors; they were played for their spin bowling almost as much as their batting, but, without Stavenden's or Sinclair's range of strokes, they were first-class batsmen in the Lancashire tradition of solid defence and forcing play. At the end of the over, Goodger began to bowl to Stavenden, who had mastered the little man as he had done all the other bowlers. Goodger's intellectual grasp of the game, however, matched any man's on the field, and he had been, for some overs, putting into operation his plan to lure Stavenden out of his crease. By pitching just a little short of a length and making the ball hang a little, he had sometimes put Stavenden into two minds momentarily, to play forward or to wait and play it off the back foot through the slips. Stavenden had seen the ball easily enough, and usually played forward, driving or pulling as the case may be, but now, after nearly three and a half hours in the blazing sun, the impulse to play forward was slackening. It required a special exertion to jump out to a ball and Stavenden, although he had a pretty shrewd suspicion of Goodger's intention, was beginning to yield to the temptation of relaxing and playing the more comfortable and less aggressive stroke.

This was all that Goodger hoped for: the hesitation, the change of mind at the last fraction of time. Three times in this new over he had made Stavenden play forward, driving twice and then playing the ball back to the bowler. Down it went a fourth time, just a little shorter-pitched; another effort; another forward surge required here . . . or let it come to him and cut it. Stavenden hesitated, suddenly lunged forward, the ball, viciously spinning, curled over the shoulder of his bat, his foot dragged. He spun in a flash, but Fallon had pounced, whipped off the bails and the whole field were shouting their appeal in unison.

Stavenden did not look at the umpire. He put his hat under his arm and strolled over to Goodger. He had to get close to the man for him to hear the words: "Foxed me, Cy. A real good 'un."

The century-spinner took off his cap. He was cheered all the way to the pavilion.

"Great knock, Steve!"

"Terrific, Steve!"

The crowd continued to cheer as he mounted the steps of the pavilion; their appreciation was tinged with thankfulness and relief.

The Aussie skipper now began to pursue a novel policy of mixing fast with slow bowling; the wicket favoured fast bowling but spin was doing unpredictable things with the ball on the sticky turf. When the Halliday Twins got together, a little before tea, they struggled harder for runs than at any time in their lives. Ryder was sending down balls that shot, Sterndale made them slither, Goodger made them hang or bump, and

Carmichael turn quickly. Ryder was the most dangerous bowler at the moment, but also the most expensive in the fighting mood of the English batsmen. It only required an accurate touch through the slips or the leg field for the ball to travel to the boundary. And there was a complication: it was so wet that the field could hardly hold it.

Driffield, who had just phoned the hospital, to be informed that Noel was not seriously hurt—although a fractured skull was suspected—they were waiting for X-ray photographs to develop—discussed the situation with Stavenden and Jeffers.

"Noel's out for the day. Not as badly hurt as I feared, but still in a semi-conscious state with a pretty high temperature."

"Definitely won't be able to play, then?"

"No. There are six stitches in his head right now."

"What do you think, Bob?" said Driffield. "With this wicket, dare we play for runs?"

"Well, we've still got five wickets standing."

"A run a minute on this pitch?"

Stavenden shook his head. "I don't see it. A thousand to one shot. I hate to say it, but with Noel gone I can't see much hope of runs being scored in that time. Bob won't have anyone to keep pace with him. Bill's batting . . . well, if he doesn't play his normal defensive game the opposition will slaughter him."

Jeffers refused to make a comment.

The Hallidays—the telepathic twins, as they were called—were about the best run-stealers in the game. Their method of signalling was a complete enigma to the field. When Driffield once asked them what methods they used Harry said, "We don't." "You don't signal?" "Not that you'd notice. We just naturally know when the other one's decided to run." That was all he could get out of them. It was as though a single heart beat in the two bodies, a single mind motivated their actions.

The rate of scoring had slowed down from the Stavenden-controlled clockwork pace and the Erskine power-dive to a slow jog trot; anything else, with the advantages the bowlers enjoyed, was courting suicide. Only four runs were added to the total by tea time and the players adjourned to the lounge with two hours of play left, and a hundred and fifty-two runs to make for victory. A little before the close of the tea interval Jeffers strolled out on to the pitch and examined it closely. When he was returning Stavenden joined him.

"What do you think?" he asked the veteran player.

"Reckon it will improve."

"Think so?"

Jeffers nodded. "It was a sharp shower, but it's drying off at a terrific rate in this heat. And the moisture that's penetrated is going to do what. . . ?" He suddenly stopped and looked at Stavenden closely; the young man's heart quickened as he understood immediately the older player's reasoning.

"Bind it up?"

"Yes. By about five-fifteen, five-thirty, it will be better than it's been all day. It will be playing true."

"Almost."

"That's good enough," said Jeffers sharply He breathed deeply. He said to Stavenden: "Don't tell them. Don't tell anyone."

Stavenden was about to say something when Jeffers seized his arm. His face was puckered with suffering: "Let the— skipper work it for them himself."

"Bob!"

The older man suddenly looked tired. "You're right. I'll tell Sam and Harry and young Townsend." He nodded. "Guess I would have done anyway."

Suddenly a broad grin broke over his face; he slapped his thigh hard. "Steve, son, don't you know what I can do with the stuff now?"

"You'll go all out. I know."

"I can slaughter it." He spoke rapidly, tense, his mouth trembling.

194

Stavenden gripped his arm, "Steady, Bob . . ."

"No, you don't understand." It was the old Bob Jeffers speaking to the youngster playing in his first great international game, the Bob Jeffers at the height of his greatness. "It's like this. . . . These bowlers are going to face me at the tail end of a five-day clash; five days of grilling heat. (And they're used to dealing with tail enders by number eight or nine, so even their mental outlook is different.) Five hours in this perishing heat and they've just about bowled their hearts out, shot their bolt. And me . . . I'm used to dealing with them when they're fresh and on the rampage; it's always been my job as opener to take the first blast, meet the first shock of the assault, so that the white-headed boys, chaps like you and Dick Sinclair and Noel, can get going. What do you think, Steve? Will I slaughter them?"

Stavenden thrilled. It was a privilege to be the confidant of this great old-timer at this moment.

He nodded; his voice shook a little: "You'll slaughter them."

The stab of the needle in his arm was a little voltage spark of life. Noel opened his eyes, stared at the surgical instrument in the nurse's hand, and groaned. He tried to speak once or twice. The nurse, anticipating his request, gave him a drink through a tube; consciousness began to slip away as he realised that his head was encased in bandages; he tried to raise his hand to stop them pounding on his skull. The ball had shot up suddenly in his face off the turf that hadn't looked so green all day. The ball was new, and red against it, a touch of flame, a pinpoint of fire against the bright green; so good. He was wild with the excitement of it, as he had not known excitement since the old days, since it meant something; it had got tame lately, there wasn't much edge to it. Of course the applause was still there, but the tameness of the matches, the tameness and the sameness of them, the sameness and the tameness of them. And Sydney, dear old Sydney, who could never

195

really forgive him for having picked the flower first, and tried so hard to love him like a brother. Of course, he did love him; lay down his life for Noel. It was almost too easy, to make them lay down their lives for you; they insisted on it; a bore at times, particularly with the women. Prove to me you love me, prove to you you love you; love.

Somewhere it had all gone wrong.

The tameness and the sameness. That was the trouble.

A sky-blue life, he had told Sydney. By God, it was that in the old days: the mile-long trailers of white smoke, the smell of cordite, the timing of it as you passed in the dancing flash of a second, with the little black cross in your gunsights, and the way it quivered as the guns spoke. You were wielding a blade, a scythe in the sky, and your timing and judgment had to be true-blue Erskine and no nonsense.

Nothing like that now. Well, just a little this afternoon after that downpour which was the sky-blue life tearing itself to strips. It had meant something. Answered him back probably. Anyway, a bit like the old days with the bright green shining danger of the turf, and the red bullet whistling, *Duck, Noel!* It had only lasted a few minutes, rocket-shooting stuff travelling fairly slow by comparison, only a hundred miles an hour off, admitted not like the scythe in the sky, but you were on the ruddy floor now, wing-commander winkle, and had to make the best of what you got. Silly though, after he had warded off the rockets to be dropped by that cloud hopper coming up at him from six o'clock.

Well, the red and the green had been good colours that day, not as good as some, as the ones in Monte last year when he had had that run on the tables, and then chucked the lot away on number thirty-five, of all damned silly things betting on his age, should have known never to bet on himself.

Thirty-five, why, that's half your life, I told Sydney. Half a life better than none and what have I made of it? Where did it begin to go wrong? Noel with all his natural advantages,

Aunt Clarissa said, Noel is full of virtuosity (that's what she called it): born two days before Christmas (why couldn't Mother have held out a bit?), and Father insisting on sainting me for good measure, Noel St. John; starting me off with all the advantages plus my natural ones. So it was all right then at the beginning, and family and fortune right, plus all my virtuosity, so where did it go wrong?

It's all in the numbers, the stars and the horoscopes. Think of a number, your number will come up, if your number's on it it's no good ducking. For instance, it had been bad luck about his brother Mark who had been killed when he was only eleven. How did it happen? He couldn't remember. Oh, no, he'd forgotten; he hadn't thought of Mark for donkey's years; but eleven of course was *his* lucky number. That last fling in the early hours of the morning; he should have followed his first impulse, instead of betting on nine, on himself, when it happened. What happened when he was nine? He'd forgotten . . . yes, he'd forgotten . . . something happened when he was nine. . . . It didn't matter, he should have bet on eleven, on Mark, Mark's bad luck was his good fortune. He'd known that all the time; his instincts had told him that when he wanted to back eleven.

When he was only nine his mother had taught him to play cricket ("The only game fit for a gentleman," she said). Her father had played for Hampshire, and had been *pretty good.* Maybe that's why he'd bet on nine, forgetting he must never bet on himself. And also because nine was his mother's number, the mystical number that united him with her, the nine months of procreation. He should have bet on Mark's bad luck, that's when it really happened, when it went wrong, but no, he'd forgotten the thing, hadn't thought about Mark for more than twenty years, Mark never mentioned at home. He'd never lived at all, really. It wasn't true about Mark. No, he couldn't bear to think it was true.

Numbers. That gloomy magnificent airman, Murray, the

chap who led their first squadron, he'd known about them. He and Murray were the only two left out of the original lot. It had taken less than three months. Eleven little nigger boys and then there were two. (How were they getting on out there on that strip of fading green, green for danger? How many were left of the eleven nigger boys?) Murray had said to young Rayner, who was sweating a bit after his sixth sortie, "What are you worried about? You're dead now. Five is the average life. After that you've borrowed time. Don't hope to come out of this alive, son. You're written off. Once you know you're already dead, there's nothing to worry about, is there?"

Borrowed time.

The cold night between the stars—our little spark of life was only a billionth part of that night, was two hundred and sixty-seven degrees below freezing point, and dark as the back of your skull. That's where Mark had gone. Somewhere in that Night he was waiting for him. (*Brother, it's cold outside.*)

Yes, that was where Noel had sent him.

It was a terrible thing that he had done, when Mark was eleven years old. He knew Mark could not ride properly, let alone sit an animal like Tiffin. He knew that all along.

But he wouldn't leave it alone. He would taunt and argue with Mark until the boy had become desperate.

Just the way Mark looked at Tiffin brought out the devil in Noel. Noel could sit him, Noel could ride him. He only wanted a chance to show them all he could.

The boys watched Hawkins, the stable man, take him out, that big black brute with the star-blaze on his forehead; watched the half-broken animal mincing, tossing his small murderous head, tensing and quivering under the rein of Hawkins's authoritative grip. Noel had exulted in schemes to get Tiffin out of the stable without their knowing about it. He had suggested ways it could be done.

198

Noel would show them all he could ride the animal. He could, too. He could do anything better than Mark. He would prove it to them.

Mark.

"Don't you know that a gentleman can do anything better than a pro?" he had said to Mark. Mark was forced to agree with him. "If you do, you won't be such a scary cat about riding. I'm going out on Tiffin today." *"Noel!* You *know* no one's allowed to go out on Tiffin." "Pater rides him. So does Hawkins. I'm not afraid of cutting an arser." "But Father says we mustn't. He's not properly broken." "The way Hawkins handles him you wouldn't think so." "But Hawkins' a pro." "But a gentleman can do anything a pro can do, and better."

Funny how he should remember every word of that conversation after so many years. Mark was the quiet sort, but game. "He hasn't Noel's natural advantages," he heard Aunt Clarissa say to mother. No, he didn't have Noel's virtuosity. But he was game. A bit like Sydney. Maybe, that's why he had chosen Sydney later, looked after him, coached him a bit. Sydney and Mark. Sydney was his brother, too. He'd never let Sydney down. He'd pluck the flower first, of course; he had to do that—*les droits de seigneur,* dammit, Sydney's father was no more than a glorified tradesman, after all . . . but he'd never let Sydney down. He'd let him keep his precious Cynthia, although she tempted him more than any other woman. Even on that occasion she'd come to him so fed up with Sydney running off to play at the end of the world when she needed him, he wouldn't touch her. He wouldn't let Mark down. Sydney. Mark.

He never did ride Tiffin; that is, Noel didn't. Never got a chance. Father had the stallion shot. Noel's mother came to him and put her arms round him and told him they would never see Mark again. "Your brother's had an accident, darling. He tried to ride Tiffin and got thrown. We must all face things

199

like this in life, be brave about them, my darling, *my only son!*"
And she had put her face on his breast and wept as he had
never seen his young lovely mother weep in her life. He had
cried too, sobbed out his heart. For days he was inconsolable,
and even after the funeral, when he should have started to
forget, he had screaming nightmares about Mark and Tiffin and
God, until they began to get concerned about him. They never
thought he loved Mark so dearly, they said. They didn't know
about the conversation he had with Mark, nor that he had
prayed deep in his heart for years that Mark should go away
from them, and now that it had happened he knew that it was
he who'd made him. *Pitch dark and two hundred and sixty-
seven degrees below zero.*

Only old Hawkins had been able to penetrate the stark misery
and guilt in the boy. "Don't take on so, Master Noel. Young
Mark ought never have done it, gone and taken out Tiffin, but
that's the way it goes. There was nothing he or anyone could
have done about it, really. When your number's on it, there
ain't nothing no one can do." "What number?"

There was singing in the mess that night, and the drink was
flowing, and the Mad Pole Kravicz was showing them how to
play Russian roulette. He spun the chamber of the revolver
with the one loaded shell, put the barrel to his temple and
pulled the trigger. There was a dull click as the hammer struck
an empty compartment. "You see, my friends, I just can't go
that way. A hundred and six sorties without a scratch. I tell
you the good Lord is saving me up for something terrible."
Noel took the revolver from his hand and spun the chamber
of the well-oiled mechanism. "You're loading the dice, Paul,"
he said. He put the barrel in his mouth and pulled the trigger.
A dreadful silence followed; the drunks sobered up; the singing had stopped. "The weight of the shell drops the live compartment down to six o'clock. There's nothing in this, nothing
in it at all. I can do it without a drink inside me." He spun
the chamber and pulled the trigger again with the revolver

pointing at his heart. Someone went outside to be violently sick.

Sticky dog.

Bob Jeffers sat down beside Driffield. He was padded up and looked restless. The players crowded the veranda, a little dejected. Stavenden had changed already. The score board was standing still and the clock was racing ahead; the precious minutes that had been lost during the storm had broken the back of their advantage; the wet steaming wicket, or the 'sticky dog', the most dreaded pitch for a batsman, had almost forced a standstill of scoring.

England struggling. England behind the clock. Every run fought for desperately. A ceaseless attack of fast bowling mixed with slow on a bowler's paradise of a pitch, the ball shooting along the ground like a scarlet serpent. Ryder and Sterndale back in business, then Goodger and Sterndale alternating to add confusion to the chaos. The best batsmen gone and still over a hundred runs to get. No chance of a fighting finish for any batsman on the treacherous surface. The shift of fortune back with the Australians with a vengeance.

"Foul luck about that rain, I must say. We would have made it. . . ."

"We aren't through yet," said Driffield.

Jeffers gave him a sidelong look.

"Yes," said Driffield. "We've still got the best batsman on a sticky dog in the world, I reckon, here with us. That's the way they breed them in Yorkshire. Let the Southerners play the fancy strokes, but when it's fight that's needed, give me Yorkshire."

The others looked at Bob Jeffers, who was staring at the skipper with a sort of surly good humour.

"Talking of me?" said Bob.

"What," said Driffield in pretended astonishment, "you from Yorkshire?"

Sam Halliday made a roundhouse swing at a ball that suddenly rose instead of shooting. Driffield got up. He couldn't stand watching it any longer. Sam and Harry, for all their experience and skill, were almost helpless as novices on this pitch. Sam, particularly, seemed unable to do anything in the way of run-making in spite of the most desperate efforts.

He went back to the pavilion for a drink; Jeffers came in a moment later. He looked a trifle embarrassed.

"Anything on your mind, Bob?"

"It was nice of you to say that, skipper."

"Nonsense. It's perfectly true. I believe it."

"It's nice of you . . . because you don't."

Driffield said briefly, "You're knocking your head against a wall, Bob, if you think that."

It was on the tip of Driffield's tongue to reassure him about his place in the team for the last Test; wasn't he aware that there was no danger of his losing his place at this juncture in the series? Far too late to break a youngster in at opening position (the experiment with Wilson had been successful, but could not be repeated unless in special circumstances). Jeffers's place was therefore a fixture. Had they planned a change it would have had to come not later than the fourth Test; but Jeffers had had Driffield supporting his place in the team at that stage.

A dozen words would have reassured Jeffers, a word of explanation about his—Driffield's—support of the old-timer at the last selection would have restored the player's devotion and friendliness towards him.

But Driffield would not have revealed the confidential policy and secret discussion of the selection committee under torture; such a breach appeared unthinkable to him; and he hated to see an England player putting his own interest before the team, as Jeffers was doing.

Jeffers was struggling for words. "Skipper . . . I want to apologise the way I spoke to you . . . last time."

It was on the tip of Driffield's tongue to retaliate harshly. He was deeply embarrassed by Jeffers's manner. He wanted to tell him roundly what he thought of such an 'apology', and the motives that prompted it. He had had a world of respect for the fighting stand Jeffers made for his beliefs even if they went counter to his captain's views; he had swallowed Jeffers's observations about 'amateurism' without any sense of resentment. For the man to come back now and start kow-towing, because he thought that might increase his chances of re-appointment in the team for the final Test, was insupportable in an England player.

He said shortly, "Don't let yourself down, Bob."

He walked past him with a face of thunder.

Jeffers looked at his back, startled; his hands shook a little as he picked up his bat. Suddenly his figure stiffened.

A shout from the field and then a vast roar from the crowd. Another wicket down.

Sam Halliday returning, despondent; Jeffers quickly stepping out into the sun. No time to waste.

"It's murder," he muttered as he passed Jeffers at mid-field.

"It's all in the mind," retorted Jeffers. He was examining the surface of the grass.

"What is?" Sam Halliday stood and stared after Jeffers's departing figure.

Jeffers ran his hand on the surface of the pitch. The moisture had been drying off so rapidly that his original calculation was even a few minutes to the good. The heavy rainfall had soaked through quickly and was softening the soil whilst the surface was almost dried off in the intense heat; not a feather-bed, of course, never that, but a good resilient pitch. Five or ten minutes more of this grilling sun and the sticky dog would have his tail between his legs. Ten minutes, say. Enough to get your eye in, get the hang of it . . . and then . . .

Goodger was bowling. Spin stuff. Nothing much to worry

about. He knew every movement of Goodger's fingers and wrist of old. No surprises there. Ryder would be the danger spot, for a couple of overs maybe, Sterndale more manageable. And when the wicket was dried off on the surface he would show them what an opening player did with tired bowlers.

Skipper quite right. Don't let yourself down, Bob. (Bit of a shock, that.) Quite right. He had no need for anyone to intercede for him. If he was good, he was good. If not, he was out of the team. They all had to go sometime. This pussyfooting around with Noel putting in a word for him, so that the skipper should put in a word with the committee, a word in your ear, a word at the right time, a word here, a word there. . . . (Don't let yourself down, Bob. Quite right.)

Fallon greeted him ironically, friendly. "Can't say I'm glad to see you at this time of day, Bob. What's the idea? It's time for the bunny rabbits."

"I'm a secret weapon, the skipper reckons."

"Well, as long as you don't stay too long, you're welcome."

"Okay, cut it out now, let's get down to the meat and potatoes. Middle and leg, please, Mr. Toley. And look sharpish."

Driffield had a sense of relief to see Jeffers play the first over with the assurance of a man determined to succeed. Usually his view of the batsman was in close-up, playing opposite him; he could regard him somewhat more objectively from the veranda. Jeffers's style was restrained, economical of gesture, canny through long experience; he was particularly strong in front of the wicket. He got the fourth ball of the over away with a hard chop, obviously finding no great problem with the pitch. Driffield's deep satisfaction in Jeffers's apparent confidence surprised himself; it was a clue to the anxiety he had felt about the old player, an anxiety that had nothing to do with the result of the match itself. Although he had refused to be swayed by Noel's plea on behalf of Jeffers he had nevertheless taken his problem to heart, more than he himself realised.

The problem of the veteran player on the verge of retirement was a very serious one and it had been brought to his attention more through his relationship with Jeffers on this tour than ever before. Finished at forty! Sinclair's words. Jeffers, of course, was comparatively fortunate. A great record in cricket must have its effect on his future, but that so much should depend on retirement in an aura of success—and how few professionals enjoyed such a fate—seemed hard in the extreme. Most of them, of course, had some sort of job to go to, usually coaching or umpiring; others, who had preserved a bit of money earned in benefit matches, could buy a small business, a sports shop, tobacconist's or the like, but the problem was in the sudden decline of earning power at an age when most men were beginning to enjoy the harvest of a chosen profession. There was not much one could do for people without any specialised training at the age of forty. Some small proportion could continue to earn handsomely from the aftermath of an exceptional career, but the majority, who had been the daily concern of millions at the peak of their success, were forgotten as soon as the new heroes pushed them out of the picture.

Driffield had seen it happen too frequently in his cricket career. He could imagine no worse fate than to have to depend on the impeccable fitness and resilience of the human body for his livelihood. That the frailties, the temperamental vagaries, of muscle and nerve and sinew should determine a man's success or failure in life seemed to be a sad relic of barbarism. Who made money in sport? Surely, only the manufacturers and suppliers of equipment, of special apparatus and clothing. Here was big business indeed. Thousands of shops and stores daily served customers to the tune of thousands of pounds. Even the greatest names in sport considered themselves fortunate to be employed by these concerns to publicise their wares. The clubs did not make money, the Test tours were big commercial successes, but most of the profits earned went back to help maintain the sport. The problem remained as to what happened to the men whose talent had served as a guide and inspiration to millions of youngsters in their physical education. Time and again Driffield found himself faced with this, and each time it had become more depressing. It seemed to him sheer ostrichism to continue as though it didn't exist. The Jeffers episode had brought it to a head.

Ben Wilson, coming out on the veranda from the pavilion, dropped down beside him. "Seems a little brighter. Bob's getting on top now. The bowling should be getting slack."

Ben Wilson looked a happy man. He had climaxed his career as wicket-keeper with his best score as a batsman in a Test. And he was not much younger than Jeffers.

Driffield wondered what the old war horse's reaction would be to Jeffers's problem.

"Reckon Bob will be retiring soon . . . probably his last Test series. It would be nice if he went out on the crest of the wave," said Driffield.

"I reckon."

"Has he got any money, do you know?"

"Bob's got a large family. Four youngsters. He's not too well off."

"Enough to buy a business?"

"Maybe a shop. I don't think he's got a lot. He lost quite a large part of his 'benefit' in some wildcat investment that promised double his money back in a couple of years. Bob's not much of a business man."

"That's the problem. When you haven't much capital you get tempted by these get-rich-quick schemes."

"What *can* you invest in? I've got a bit saved. Too young for an annuity. Gilt-edged stuff doesn't give you a worthwhile return. Finish up as a small shopkeeper. It's quite a problem, skipper. Running a shop isn't much after a life like this. I lost a bit in some restaurant scheme. You don't know what to do quite. You're a business man—maybe you could give me some advice when the time comes."

206

"Be happy to, Ben."

Wilson hesitated. "Look, Mr. Driffield. I don't know what the others will say, but I would like to have your advice about an idea that Bob and Mac put up to me. It's Mac's scheme."

"I'd be glad to discuss it with you."

Wilson nodded and went off to the pavilion; he returned with Macready. Both men looked a trifle embarrassed.

"What is it?"

Wilson sat down. After a pause, he said:

"You know what we have to face when we have to give up the game. With Bob it might be fairly soon. Mac and I haven't more than a few years left. Well, rather than wait till we're faced with it we wondered if there was a way of safeguarding the future. We thought that if we pooled our savings we stood a better chance in launching some business. Well, Mac can tell you. It's his scheme."

"I don't think we should bother you with it, skipper. Right now, anyway."

"Oh, that's all right. Pull up a chair. We can watch the game and chat about it."

Mac came to a decision. He sat down beside Driffield. Mac collected his thoughts. They watched the game in silence for a moment or two. Driffield felt the uncertainty and anxiety of the man beside him; Mac was thirty-five, a sobering age in the life of a cricketer, and Jeffers's problem was far more acute.

Finally Mac said, "Well, what Ben says is quite right. When you first start in this everything looks rosy, retirement a long way off. It might never happen. Once you're in the thirties the years just speed by. You begin to think you're slipping even if you're not. You begin to sweat about the final benefit match. Will it peter out in a quick win in a couple of days? Will it be a wash-out through a downpour? A shower of rain, and there goes your nest egg. It's quite a problem."

"I can imagine. Tell me about your scheme, Mac."

"Well, neither of us have much money to start a business. Bob has some—he's made plenty in his time, but he's got four children at school, two at boarding-school. Ben had a bit, but he lost some of that. I never quite made it, you know. Top earnings in my best season wasn't much more than fifteen hundred. On our own we could buy a small tobacconist's in some out of the way place. Not much of a life, and we're not so sure it would be a success commercially. You never can be sure what you're getting."

"I understand."

"Well, I thought about this for some time now. I've discussed it with Ben and Bob Jeffers. Talked about precious little else this trip. You see, if we combine all our money we've got about eleven or twelve thousand pounds. I thought that might be enough to have a real go, launch a proper business. It's been done. What are big businesses today sometimes weren't founded with much less."

"Name some."

This was a little difficult, so Mac carried on a little hastily, a little uncertainly, "My idea was a sports goods workshop, a small factory say, with about a dozen or so workpeople. Put a good bloke in charge, and then the three of us go out and sell the stuff—using our goodwill as old Test pros to rake in the business. We all know lots of people. In the press, for instance, the buyers at some of the department stores where we used to autograph cricket bats, and in our home towns where we're still celebrities. That sort of thing. What do you think of the idea, skipper?"

"No," said Driffield.

Wilson was startled by this reaction, Mac flushed. "Well, I thought it wasn't much good asking you, Mr. Driffield. I told Ben it wouldn't be."

"What's wrong with the idea?" asked Ben Wilson.

Driffield lit his pipe. "Know what a preference share is, Ben?"

"No."

"A debenture? Know how to draw up a bill of exchange? Ever worked out a production schedule? Estimated a margin of error? Can you read a balance sheet? Do you know what breaches or nullifies a contract? Ever borrowed money against collateral?"

Ben was silent.

"Well," said Driffield, "even that's not the important thing. You could learn all about that. Mind you, it's fatal to launch a factory until you have. The important thing, however, is that you'll just break your heads against competition. Sports goods production is big business these days. You need mass-production plant, a planned technique. Any established concern could cut you out of the picture by adjusting their prices for a few months. With mass-production methods even that might not be necessary. You simply could not face up to them. They would out-price and out-sell you within a few months.

"And you say, 'We'll put a bloke in charge of the workshop and go out to sell.' And who's to decide who this bloke is going to be? To pick your technical expert you have to be one yourself."

He stared at the glum faces and suddenly grinned. "I don't know this particular line of business. I'm only talking from first principles, generally. Maybe I'm wrong. But I don't think so." He added, "There's the glimmer of an idea there." He tapped Ben's knee with the stemp of his pipe. "You boys have all, one time or another, sponsored sports goods advertisements? Well, that proves something."

The others stared at him.

"Proves what, skip?" asked Ben.

"Proves you've got something they need. Can't do without, perhaps. Who knows? It's an asset, anyway." He rubbed his chin. "You'd need capital backing of between fifty to a hundred thousand pounds for the premises and plant. It's light industry; maybe you could get away with fifty thousand. Have to go into that. Can't promise anything, mind you. Can't commit myself till I've gone into figures. That's of course impossible till we get back to England."

Ben Wilson and Macready exchanged startled glances.

"The way I see it is this," said Driffield, thinking aloud, and watching appreciatively Bob Jeffers slipping a ball mathematically between first and second slip for two runs. "You boys have been casual employees of big business in their advertising. You're a business asset. But although any one of you has done more for the game than all the shareholders of Lozenger's, they make the money. No harm in trying to even it up a bit. Don't know much about light industry. Heavy industry is Driffields' speciality. Still, it can't be more difficult to make a cricket bat than a railway locomotive, can it? Selling. That's where we might score. You see, we'll have *you*. And *you* represent all this." He indicated the vast crowd. "Publicity. Any one of us has a hundred thousand pounds' worth of free publicity a year through the press, radio and television. A combine. A players' co-operative. Behind the firm. Why not? The players' own company to produce sports goods and equipment—yes, and including sports tailoring if it can be adapted to the same premises. We'll have to have training courses in management, salesmanship, administration, publicity, every department of the executive and technical departments. A man shouldn't be finished at forty! Enough of that!" His face darkened, recalling Sinclair's words, Jeffers's expression when he came to apologise and eat humble pie. "Enough of that," he muttered. "Finished at forty be damned. We must do something about that."

Mac and Wilson, listening in rapt attention, were not there any more. Driffield was back in the board room facing Brabant across the shining mahogany table. "We'll be up against competition, of course. There'll be the established concerns. It might be a tussle." An expression came into his eyes that Wilson and Mac had never seen before. "Well, let it be.

"I don't know. We'll see. I'll have to go into figures," he added a few moments later, catching Wilson's eyes. "Something to think about. Just an idea. Still, that's the way they all began."

Yes, this was better than saving a man's future through nepotism, better than intriguing and wire-pulling in selection committees. This was the honest way, the proper way. Driffield's way. Let the old men know when they were finished in sport, let the youngsters have the chances they earned. But let the old ones have an opportunity to continue to make a living, utilising the goodwill they had earned through their superlative skill and rigorous self-discipline over the years. Not that Driffield failed to anticipate the objections that the average business man would raise to such a scheme. Nothing but philanthropy! A business was not a charitable institution—an assault on basic principles, the old man would argue. How do you know what latent ability these men have? Batsmen and bowlers and wicket-keepers— excellent. But manual workers, administrators, organisers, publicists and salesmen—who knows? And the apprenticeship period from the age of forty or so—ridiculous! Still, Driffield was prepared to back his faith in men he had known intimately for years, men of intelligence well above average, of character, of great skill, above all, with the will to perfectionism. That was the crux of it: this tremendous personal drive to achieve supremacy in a chosen profession. It mattered little whether this will to success was in games or business, any enterprise, he would back that quality against any opposing argument of the orthodox business school; he would back such a quality against youth or any other factor in determining a man's fitness for a job of work.

Once again memory took him back to the days when torn from the lecture rooms and playing fields he was tossed into the maelstrom of big business and told to sink or swim. He could do it; their course would not be a tenth as difficult, he would see to that.

The constitution of such a company . . . the financial structure . . . a loan of fifty thousand by Driffields', redeemable over twenty-five years say, at five per cent, with fifty thousand more in a suspense account, on call when required, should see the thing through. Two general managers of experience to run the thing jointly, a business man and a technical man—somebody like Evans, head of the industrial research department at Driffields', would be a good choice as business administrator. The equity? Only ex-cricketers would be eligible to hold stock: that was important. The boys must feel it was *their* team they were playing for. And the operative factor for success was the goodwill of the press and the public earned on the playing fields. The B.B.C. would have to help, too. He would see about that, have the Governor to dinner. There wasn't a leading personality in business or politics he wasn't on terms of acquaintance with, and if he didn't know him Stavenden would, Noel would, the chairman of the selectors would.

Like an engine with its gears engaged his mind raced on; power and knowledge that had remained dormant these many years following his semi-retirement from Driffields' woke to life. It would be something worth planning and doing. A little of the excitement and tension of his conflict of former days reached out to him over the years. He would have to do a lot of serious thinking, get the thing in motion, write to Evans and the old man. By the time he got back to England some sort of rough plan would be ready for examination. Driffields' could spare the money, many times over—thanks to him. The old man would know that.

He thought of Cynthia. He would tell her all about it to-night. After all, more than Jeffers or Noel, it was she who was really responsible for the scheme, sparked it off in his mind. That parting shot of hers that rankled so much . . . and now . . . well, here was a real job of work to be done and he would do it. It wouldn't be all play from now on.

There was a great roar from the stands. Jeffers had walked into a long-hop and pulled it, long-handle style, for four; off the very next ball he had scored another two runs. Now he was halfway down the pitch to a loose one which he had driven for yet another boundary.

The vast crowd was electrified. The grandstand fight to the finish had begun.

Driffield turned to Macready. "Where's Bill? He should be out here. And get your pads on, Mac. We must be ready to move fast. Every second is precious. Bob looks as though he might pull it off. Hurry, man."

Driffield went into the pavilion for a moment or two. He wanted a word with Sam Halliday and young Gogarty; Sam, because whichever twin preceded the other in the trek back from the wicket found it necessary for a little reassurance that he was still just as good as his brother; Gogarty, because he was in a blue funk. Sam Halliday, however, was in the process of reassuring Gogarty; he appeared to have forgotten his own minor misfortune. He was explaining the dangers of hooking to the young bowler, who was too confused to understand.

"If you haven't learned to hook by now, now isn't the time to catch up on your studies, Dan."

"Yes, skipper." He burst out, "It might all depend on me." He dropped his voice in the realisation that this might not be quite the most modest attitude to adopt. "Sorry."

"What are you sorry about? And what's wrong with it all depending on you?"

Gogarty found this unanswerable.

"You say that because you reckon you're a bowler. Well, for your information, you're a batsman now. Go in there and bat!"

"Yes, skipper."

Gogarty retired to the dressing-rooms to make ready for his anticipated ordeal.

"Bowlers! They're *cricketers*!" Driffield shrugged; the humorous expression in his eyes found its reflection in Sam Halliday's.

213

"Everything okay, Sam?"

Sam ceased grinning; he suddenly remembered his grievance. "I was put off," he announced after some careful thought.

"Were you?"

"*That* end of the field's tougher, skip. The pavilion end." This was his alibi; he wouldn't say so, of course, but the implication was designed to be crystal-clear: it was necessary to him to explain why he had made fewer runs this time than Harry.

"Too bad." Driffield tried to adopt a consolatory tone, with difficulty, because the twin's necessity to excuse his lower score was too preposterous to be taken with any seriousness.

Sam continued, encouraged by the captain's manner. "Yes, and there was a proper balls-up over that signalling."

"Signalling?"

"Surely, you saw it, skip? It was when I wondered about taking that third run and Harry——"

"Yes?"

"Oh, nothing."

"Oh, get it off your chest about Harry," said Driffield.

"Well . . . Harry signalled 'don't'. So I started to run and . . ."

"Harry signals 'don't' so you start to run? That doesn't make sense, Sam."

Sam said patiently, "When he *actually* signals it's for the benefit of the field, skipper; a feint. It means the *opposite.*"

"Oh."

"When we intend to run we never signal each other so that anyone would notice."

"I get it. Carry on, genius."

"As I was saying, Harry signals 'don't', so naturally I come on. When I start to run he sits on the ground. He *means* it. Well, I ask you! Enough to put anyone off."

Driffield tried to control the corners of his mouth. "I see. Too bad." He clicked his tongue.

"Yes . . . and that end—the pavilion end where I was—much

more wear on the pitch. That's where Ryder dragged his foot."

"Yes, I remember."

"Bad business about that signalling," Sam repeated. "If it wasn't for that I'd have felt right for the rest of the innings, somehow."

Driffield paused for his effect; when the words were spoken he made them sound light, like a throw-away line in a play. It sounded as though he might be thinking aloud. "Sometimes I wonder whether it wouldn't be better if I separated you two boys. Put one of you in a bit earlier."

This one always had the same reaction. A startled look appeared on Sam's face, almost an expression of panic. "Oh, *no,* skip! That won't be at all necessary."

"Ah. Well, don't worry. I won't if that's how you feel about it." There was only one other thing to say, and that almost in the delicate tone of a doctor's bedside manner. "You don't want me to mention that bit about the signalling to Harry, do you?"

"No. Oh, no. He *knows.*"

Driffield returned to the veranda with an encouraging word about Sam's play: the routine was concluded.

"Hallo, there. And how's the breathless hush in the close tonight?"

They stared at Noel blankly. Driffield got to his feet hastily. "What the hell do you think you're doing?"

"It is . . . Noel," said Stavenden. Noel's head was almost swathed in bandages."

"Yes, I got six stitches up there," boasted Noel proudly. "Want to examine my scars, Sydney? Maybe you've got an interesting appendix, too."

Sinclair said apologetically, "He got away. The nurse came looking for him, so I grabbed a cab. I guessed he'd make for the ground."

Driffield cut short Sinclair's chatter. He was examining Noel's pulse. "I'll have to get you back to the hospital. You're running a fever."

"How can you tell without a thermometer?"

"If I had one it'd crack. Back to bed with you. I don't know how you manage to keep on your feet. Your temperature's sky-high."

"Nonsense. My feet are like ice."

Driffield helped him into the pavilion lounge and he suddenly sank into an armchair, his face strained with the pains in his head.

"How's it going?" he said, a little later, when speech was possible.

"As far as you're concerned the match is over. All you have to do now is to sleep. With all that surgery you'll do yourself permanent injury if you don't go back to the hospital right away." He watched Noel's struggle with the next wave, a glimmer in his eye. "It comes and goes, doesn't it? It's the blood pumping through the arteries. Wave on wave, a never ending tide, like the lines of grey in the first unpleasantness."

"How's it going?"

"Sam made eighteen. Harry thirty-one. And Bob Jeffers has gone berserk. He's made sixty-two in twenty-eight minutes. He's doing just what he wants to out there. I've only seen it done twice before. Bradman at Leeds and Wally Hammond in that New Zealand match. If only we can get someone to stay with him till close of play. . . ."

"Good old Bob. Who's with him?"

"Bill Townsend. He's scored five. They've closed him up like a trap. I don't think he can hold out."

There was a tremendous shout as he spoke; he looked out and nodded. "Afraid of that. Bill's gone. Still . . . two more to go. We might make it."

"Three," said Noel. "Don't look like that. I've got a thick skull."

Driffield sighed. "It's thick for a purpose, Noel. It houses the

most delicate and complex network of nerve cells in the body."
He had taken a cigarette from a box on the table. "Here . . .
catch!"

Noel started, a spasm of excruciating pain crossed his face at
the sudden exertion.

"What did you feel just now?" asked Driffield. "Furnace
here." He touched Noel's head. "Ice-cold there." He touched
his stomach. "And violent trembling as though you're suffering
from ague. Do you think you would have felt that before your
injury if I tossed you a cigarette? It's shock. You're in no state
to face a puff-ball, let alone one of Ryder's bumpers. They've
been saving him up for the last minutes. There's no telling
what might happen if you go out there this afternoon."

He lit a cigarette.

"When did you start smoking cigarettes, Sydney?"

Driffield said, "I'll phone for an ambulance right away. How
on earth did you manage to get out?"

"Got the nurse to phone up for me to find out the score
and whilst she was out of the room, bob's your uncle. Which
reminds me, I must certainly watch this."

"I'll tell you the score. Don't move."

The English team required thirty-one runs to win; they had
fourteen minutes in which to do it.

"I'm staying," said Noel. "Light me a cigarette, there's a
good chap. I don't want to move if I can help it."

They smoked in silence for a moment, then Driffield went to
the telephone and rang the hospital.

"This is tiresome, Sydney. I'm not going."

"Orders, my boy. Doctor's orders."

"I'm not your patient, Doctor."

Driffield said, grinning, "It's only a *game,* Noel."

"Stop trying to quote me or I'll brain you."

"Why do you want to go out there? Another shock—any
shock which wouldn't affect a normal man—in your condition
could produce anything from raving lunacy to paralysis. Don't

you realise that? It's murder out there. They're after blood. Ryder will go crazy with that ball."

Noel puckered up his eyes from the smoke of the cigarette; he said, "Cynthia will be proud of the medical man emerging in you."

"What makes you say that?"

Neither of them spoke for a moment.

Driffield felt an extraordinary sense of relief at the words; then he said, in surprise, "Did you really think I put the game first?"

"No. I didn't, Sydney. I know you. But women and children must be taught. Stop being such a monument and speak to her. You should also have told Bob Jeffers that you had given him your support at the last selection of players; there wouldn't have been this feeling between you if you had."

"I don't owe him an explanation."

"That's what I mean," said Noel. He frowned; the smoke was hurting his eyes and he put out his cigarette. He waited for the wave of pain to recede; it was sickening the way it beat up regularly, like a furnace pump blowing through the multiple arteries; he could picture his head like some metal whitening under heat and pressure. He waited, his fists clenched till the pain receded.

Driffield was studying his expression with compassion.

"Why do you want to take such a risk out there?"

Noel began to grin as the vice-like pressure on his head relaxed. "Maybe," he said, "this is the chance I've been waiting for for Uncle Frank the banker—bless his morocco-bound double-entry ledgers—to get me out of the hole, pay my creditors in style, twenty bob to the pound. This is just up my street. Erskine rushes to England's aid from hospital bed. It's tailor-made for Noel."

"If I thought that that was why you were doing it I'd hit you harder than Ryder."

"Then why am I doing it?"

218

Driffield said, "Does this mean anything to you? 'Bandits coming up at three o'clock'?"

"Not a thing."

"Sure?"

"Quite sure. You must have dreamed it."

Jeffers felt the pulse of the crowd stirring as he faced the bowling once more; felt the giant heart throb quicker, with excitement, exultation, and with fear! Yes, there was fear in that crowd. The restlessness, the shuffling, the sudden hoarse shouting and raucous laughter with a touch of hysteria about it over the least trifle was fear; there was fear in the sudden impenetrable gloom that settled on them as he sent that ball away with truculent force. Oh, they had cheered and applauded Jeffers, they had shouted their delight and appreciation when he opened out after the first few minutes of his innings and began to show them that there was going to be a fight after all; but now it was different. Now he had subdued that field to his will as no man had done since the match began; he had done more, he had demoralised it. The sudden crushing onslaught he had launched on the bowling was maintained with unremitting fury; he had not merely beaten the field, he had whipped it. He was doing just as he liked with the bowling, placing the ball where he wanted, scoring at will. It was humiliating, demoralising.

It had taken him four or five overs to judge the strength of the opposition and the state of the wicket. He had good luck; Ryder was being rested for the last overs of the game, Sterndale had been so exhausted by the afternoon spell that he was finished for the day; Goodger—and here was some real luck—Goodger, the only bowler who could get any real venom off this new green wicket, had split the skin of his spinning-finger, blistered with the friction of the dry and then the wet ball, and was retired to the boundary. That left Foreman and Carmichael, medium-pace men, with no real devil in their spin, bowling on a new wicket that was firm and resilient, with just enough gloss on it to dull the turn of the ball. It came up knee-high whatever their efforts. And finally, they were tired men; tired of the endless toil in the sun, deadened by the heat and concentration of five days' effort.

And here was a new Jeffers, a man inspired by his test, the supreme test of his career, a veteran who knew every turn and twist of the game, who had lore and wisdom in the marrow of his bones, an opponent with the fruits of a lifetime's service at stake. He was remorseless. He had promised Stavenden slaughter; he had produced massacre. He had slashed and hacked Carmichael and Foreman all round the wicket, punished the nerve-racked helpless 'change' bowlers who had, in desperation, been pushed on to bowl for the first time in a Test match. The thrashing he had given them wrought such mental havoc in them that they could not even keep a length. Raeburn, the captain, took the ball for one disastrous over, Reynolds, who hadn't bowled a ball for his State team, was tried. When Fallon, the wicket-keeper, began to take off his pads—they were even going to try him out for an over—Jeffers complained to the umpires about time-wasting tactics, and Raeburn was compelled to drop the idea.

The Halliday Twins had put on some useful runs, but the wicket was still drying when they were batting, and the rate of scoring had been slow. When Jeffers came in there were ninety-five runs to be scored in a little under fifty minutes. It seemed an almost impossible task.

And now, after a complete break-through, if he could get someone to stay in with him, victory was inevitable. Harry had gone, clean bowled by Goodger in his last over; Townsend had gone after a most unfortunate miscalculation, playing too far back to a ball. He had been told to hold the fort and let Jeffers make the runs, and in a bout of over-zealousness had stepped back a little too far, knocking down his own wicket. Mac had come in and survived the rest of the over.

After him, there was only young Gogarty, a complete rabbit. Jeffers faced Carmichael, who had real anxiety in his eyes. The murmur of the crowd was angry and disturbing at the slashing he had received the last time he had bowled to Jeffers; it would become really hostile if he allowed himself to be knocked all over the field. He took his run and sent a quick one, fast for him, and Jeffers, shaping mechanically, had time to make up his mind where to send it. It came up knee-high exactly as Jeffers had estimated by the state of the wicket; Jeffers drove it for a couple of runs through mid-field; there were two men on the boundary in that part of the field alone, otherwise it would have been a boundary. With Jeffers their only hope was to keep the runs down.

The Aussies were backing each other up in the field, two men chasing the ball, one tossing it backwards or back-heeling to the other to let him take the throw-in from a better vantage point or stance. Fours were frequently cut down to three or even two runs, three to two; singles were almost out of the question.

But in spite of their desperate efforts, sheer physical exhaustion after so many hours affected their alertness and agility, disrupted the accuracy of their returns, took the snap out of Fallon's speed behind the stumps.

Jeffers did not miss a point. He slashed two more to the boundary which were intercepted and converted to couples, and then glided one past second slip, far beyond reach of gully; two more runs where normally a slip fielder would have prevented a run. He was playing on the nerves of the fieldsmen with his placing of the ball. Hysterical clapping from the pavilion; sullen silence from the mammoth crowd.

He played back a couple of balls to rest—he was watching the danger of tiring just before the ordeal with Ryder in the last overs—and then forced a single off the last ball.

There were three, possibly four, overs of play left. Twenty runs to win; twelve minutes of play.

They would put on Ryder. It was inevitable.

The sudden silence that greeted the choice of bowler, the new tension in the crowd, the tightening of Jeffers's attention—here was a foe worthy of his steel at last—the rapid regrouping of the field on the leg side, and Ryder was marking out the run for his flat-out effort: thirty yards. Jeffers, through some elaborate pantomime, tried to register his disapproval of this time-wasting run. The umpires were unresponsive.

Then Jeffers suddenly trotted down the field, signalling Macready, his partner, to approach. There was a quick word from Jeffers, a look of incredulity on Mac's face, a reassuring vigorous nod from Jeffers, who turned a dark look at Ryder with almost melodramatic menace and then a hurried return to the wicket as Ryder turned to commence his run. It was completely baffling to everyone of the fifty-three thousand spectators. What was that old fox Jeffers up to? What else did he have to pull out of his hat? Not a single player, not a veteran sports expert sitting up in the press box, not a team-mate, not a single member of that huge audience could guess. Ryder appeared to have scorned, prima-donna-like, the menace of Jeffers's look.

They watched in their tens of thousands, and wondered.

Ryder bowling to Jeffers; four men in the leg trap, and two men at silly mid-on.

Jeffers had been anticipating this final and supreme tussle and had given it a lot of thought. The wicket was playing fairly true now but the ball would still bump or shoot up with the impetus of the tremendous propulsion; he had devised a method of dealing with the dangerous outswinging and rising ball; a method made possible only when he had his eye in and was well settled. As now.

The first ball, pitched on the leg stump, did not rise much, and Jeffers played it back with a dead bat. The second and the third balls were fast yorkers on the middle stump; too dangerous to play a forcing stroke, Jeffers stabbed them into the ground.

A wave of relief passed through the crowd, a surging forward, a mounting of tension. Jeffers was being forced to a standstill.

And now there was the ball they were all waiting for, the Ryder special, the high kicking outswinger, chest-high, and still rising. The ball had struck the pitch with the thud of a mallet and shot up, inches off the leg stump, straight into the leg trap; the glide or glance would have required the peak skill of a Stavenden. Jeffers dropped on one knee, his bat sunny side up and flipped the ball, tossing it over his shoulder for a six, clean into the stands.

Reluctantly the vast crowd shouted their appreciation. Ryder stood at the wicket, his head downcast, gloomy. He shook his head.

Mac called out, "How are you going to face your Maker on Founder's Day with a stroke like that, Bob?" He was grinning from ear to ear.

Fourteen runs, nine minutes to play, two wickets to fall.

Ryder had learned his lesson. No more of this unorthodox stuff; God, it wasn't even cricket. Where did he cook up a stroke like that? Jeffers could have told him: on any village green.

Jeffers dead-batted the short-pitched dead-on bumpers.

One more ball of Ryder's over. He would have to force a single to collar that bowling.

Ryder went back for the thirty-yard run slowly, thoughtfully. Another yorker perhaps; anything to keep the runs down. Practically no turn on this pitch, no shine on the ball, no polish on that surface. He turned for his elaborate run up, heedless of Jeffers's early pantomime reproof that it wasted valuable time.

But where was the Joker? What had Jeffers brought Mac up to confer at mid-field earlier in the over? An impenetrable enigma.

Then, as Ryder began to run, so did Mac, so did Jeffers, all three of them, running like madmen! Before Ryder had completed a dozen yards of his preliminary approach to the bowling crease Mac was at the crease opposite. They had run a single before the ball had been delivered!

Consternation!

Ryder stopped and started haranguing Jeffers, the umpire approaching. The other umpire was crossing over to join them. Raeburn joined them. The argument proceeded: Ryder furious, Raeburn indignant, Jeffers arguing. At length the umpire turned and signalled a bye! The ball, he ruled, was in play from the moment Ryder began his run up.

A great roar, and then a guffaw, rose in a vast exhalation of breath. The old fox had holed, outwitted the whole pack. He had paid back Ryder for his mammoth run and collared the bowling.

And now what? Carmichael? Foreman? Who?

Sterndale.

Sterndale recalled for a final effort. The last over of the day from the pavilion end. Two more overs, Sterndale and Ryder.

Ryder and Sterndale, the original shock troops; first line of offence. That's how it began; this would be the grand final curtain.

Sterndale set a more defensive field than Ryder, five men on the leg side, two in the outfield, a mid-on, a mid-off.

A difficult field to penetrate.

Thirteen runs to make. Two wickets standing.

The first two balls, turning a little, and very accurate and fast, Jeffers left alone. He stopped a scorcher dead on target, then cracked a short-pitched one for four runs, a perfect drive along the carpet. The next ball was flighted, tossed up; Jeffers watched it with suspicion then stepped forward and swept it to leg. Mac was already running; Jeffers took an easy single, turned . . . and shook his head. The leg field had been off the mark like greyhounds; another run could have been chased; Jeffers wanted to conserve strength. There was not much left of the over. Mac would have to pull his weight a bit.

Sterndale to Macready, a tremendous ball, a thundering express. Mac played forward; there was a snick. Fallon's gloves closed on the ball like a trap.

He made no appeal.

But Sterndale was shouting, and the umpire's hand went up.

The rest of the field was mystified by Fallon's failure to appeal. Jeffers strolled over to Mac, who was shaking his head, moving away from the wicket.

"A padstrap. A ruddy loose padstrap. That's what he heard. I swear I didn't touch the ball."

Jeffers nodded: "Hard luck, Mac."

"Hard luck nothing. I ought to be whipped. Hard luck, England. I shouldn't have been so ruddy slipshod leaving a padstrap unfastened."

He walked off the field, his eyes on the ground.

All the cogitations of Driffield, the tenacity of Wilson, the skill of Stavenden, the brilliance of Erskine and the inspired craft and passion of Jeffers . . . all this for what? When the issue was balanced on the razor's edge of decision, a loose pad-strap could reduce it to nothing. Well, that's the way it goes, thought Jeffers, watching the forlorn back of the batsman retiring into the oblivion of a lost opportunity. So it is with a cricket match, or a clash of arms, or any mortal conflict. A loose padstrap. (The next day the sports writers eulogised about the brilliant ball of Sterndale that had found the edge of Macready's bat; it was unanimously considered to have been unplayable.)

And now the last man in.

Eight runs to make, one wicket standing.

And the last man, Gogarty, the rabbit. So scared, so jittery that his hands were slipping with moisture and the handle of his bat floated from his grasp.

('So you're a bowler, are you?' Driffield had said. 'Well, that's the biggest mistake you've made in your life. You're a batsman now. Go in and stay in.')

It was the shortest walk Gogarty ever took in his young life, his walk from the pavilion to the wicket, and when, a moment later, Sterndale, bowling like an inspired demon, shot his middle stump eight feet in the air, it was the longest walk back.

Noel was standing on the steps of the pavilion, padded and gloved, his bat under his arm. Driffield had passed a message that he might play in an emergency, so that the field remained motionless in expectation, the eyes of the fielders on him, the umpires rooted like white trees on the green; he stepped forward, using his bat as a walking-stick.

The blow that the sun struck him as he stepped out of the shelter of the pavilion took his breath away; it was so agonising that he stopped with the shock of it. He moved forward slowly, a slightly stooping figure. Sinclair, who was going to run for him, followed on his heels. He made his way forward cursing under his labouring breath. He had stepped out too quickly, misjudged the wave that was beating up steadily into his head. A woman in labour pains went through something of the same sort, the steady mounting anguish that rises to a climax until you are a mere instrument, a vehicle of it; no stoicism can repress the scream that has its roots in the entrails, in the nerve centre, shatters the feeble censorship of will and transforms you into an animal on the rack.

Noel's head was drenched with moisture, moisture ran down into his eyes. He walked like an automaton, stiff-legged. The small shadow he threw was his focal point of concentrated attention. He was practising a form of self-hypnosis: the shadow is me, I am the shadow; if it's steady I am all right, if it wavers I've had it.

Had it.

Just one of Sterndale's flyers or Ryder's bumpers to touch off the straining thread of equilibrium and he would be a raving lunatic, or, dreadful alternative, a paralytic. Sydney had described it to him, passionately, in authentic detail. A warn-

226

ing. ('Why do you want to go out there? . . . Does this mean anything to you. . . . ? Bandits at three o'clock. Bandits at three o'clock. Bandits at three o'clock.' Dear Sydney . . . that's what he thought. Tell England! 'One of Ryder's bumpers and you'll be a raving lunatic in an asylum . . . a paralytic. . . .' *Don't you see, Sydney? That's what makes it so interesting.*)

Sterndale and his whizz-bang flyers, mechanical rockets, a pair of animated scissors stalking him, the ball a bullet. No shaping up for a stroke. Too late. *How's that?* Out. *Out!* Out on a stretcher. Bandit coming up at six o'clock, whistling, 'Duck, Noel!'

"Noel. . . ." said the voice.

". . . . . . Noel. . . ."

". . . . . Noel. . . ."

"Are you all right, son?"

"Yes, I can make it. . . ."

Sinclair's hand for a moment on his arm, the shadow in focus again. "Okay, Dick. I'll be all right."

He jerked up the sleeve of his shirt, soaked up the moisture on his face. The crease. The white battered line. Greying now, wearing. But home. It would only take a fraction of a second, the whole of this sortie. One ball. Between the stirrup and the ground. No time even for a prayer. Well, here goes. (Here I come, Mark.)

Dick Sinclair dropped down beside him, pulled a blade of grass, and started to chew it.

There was a general feeling of relaxation about him. He looked behind him. Where was Fallon? Where was the wicket-keeper? He looked askance at Dick.

"It's the end of the over. Ryder's going to bowl the last one to Bob. Relax."

Bill Townsend looked about him on the veranda. Apart from the skipper, sitting rapt in concentration, brooding over his acceptance of Noel's responsibility to go out in the heat of the sun and into the fury of the last minutes of the grand-stand finish of this relentlessly fought battle for honours, there was no one.

"Where have they all gone, skip?"

Driffield looked around in surprise. All the other players had disappeared into the pavilion.

"Couldn't stand it any longer, I suppose," said Bill.

Driffield nodded. Before Ryder began his run Bill got up, a little groggy.

"Bill. . . ."

"I can't take it, either."

"If I can take it so can you. Sit down."

They were long-winded about changing field, in retaliation for Jeffers's more than unorthodox stolen run.

"Great innings of Bob's. About his best." Townsend looked at Driffield questioningly; he knew all about the tug-of-war between Jeffers and the skipper.

It was one of Driffield's proudest moments. He could have told Townsend about the final decision he had to take in the face of Noel's urgent requests to favour the old cricketer for the sake of sentiment. Driffield's instinct to let the veteran resolve his own problem, stand on his own feet, had been richly rewarded. Both men had scored their own victory over themselves; both men had refused, in the final count, to take the easy way out. Maybe Jeffers would hate the skipper till the end of his days for it, but Driffield, never a man to bother about cheap popularity, was happy in his decision to force Jeffers to take his test as he should, without fear or favour. Jeffers would retire from international cricket with genuine pride in his own unaided triumph, sharing his knowledge of its true worth with only one other man.

Thus it went: failure with Sinclair, possible failure with Stavenden, but success with Jeffers. The profit and loss account was not such a bad one, after all. Cynthia would have cast her vote for sentiment, for 'humanity', with Noel. Both would have been wrong. The 'overgrown schoolboy' had moments of maturity that surpassed their worldliness and scepticism. It was Driffield's final resolution of his own problem, and the balance sheet was quite a healthy one.

He said, "Bob still had it in him. I guess it's all a question of confidence."

Raeburn and Ryder still in consultation, the field being modified at Ryder's insistence. Noel was leaning heavily on his bat.

"Thank heavens it's still Bob. Do you reckon Noel could face that stuff?"

Driffield shrugged. Noel's special relationship with the skipper and the team put him beyond the bounds of control; here was a man who must make his own decisions.

"He looked a pretty sick man, skipper. Should he have been allowed to go on?"

"I told him not to, as a doctor. But as skipper, if he feels he can make it, I can't prevent him."

Townsend said, "I reckon it's not that important."

Driffield was startled. "You would not have allowed him to go in with the game in the balance like that?"

"I don't think I would have done. It's all wrong. For the sake of a crowd, because of vanity. No."

Driffield was impressed, in spite of himself. Townsend went on speaking as though to himself. "A man shouldn't put his life in jeopardy for things like that."

Driffield said nothing. Bill Townsend gave him a sharp glance. He began to speak and the words, held back for so many months, came out with a rush. "Do you know where I first learned to play cricket, Mr. Driffield? I learned it in a ward of the London Hospital. At the age of nine I was with a crowd of kids, all suffering in varying degrees from polio." He paused, lost in thought. Driffield felt an extraordinary force in his voice, and the words, startling in themselves, made him turn in astonishment.

229

"You've seen them, Doctor," said Bill Townsend, the last word uttered with perfect naturalness as if that was the image in the young man's mind. "You've seen them. The little ones. Every day would begin with a strange sound.—You know the noise a lot of kids make when they wake up. They look out at the sun, hop out of bed, and with the first breath they draw they're practically crowing. Well, our mornings started with noise, all right. It was like a lot of little old men at a funeral. We just couldn't understand what it was all about, *waking up* to find you couldn't move your limbs. A nightmare in reverse. And every morning it was the same, the nightmare was going on month after month.

"Well, one day we had a visitor, a famous cricket pro—" Bill mentioned an illustrious name—"he came into our ward, a giant of a chap, with a dark tan, immense shoulders, moving like a lion. We'd all heard of him, of course. We were wildly excited. And he sat down with us and began to tell us a strange and tremendous story. He said that he was going to prove to us we could all walk again, all run and jump and do everything any normal boy could do. He told us that when *he* was a kid of five, *he* had infantile paralysis. He had believed he could walk and run again and began to learn and try and use all his will, until his muscles began to come to life again. It was the most wonderful and inspiring thing I had ever heard. Well, he came every week during the whole of that winter, teaching, encouraging, and every time I knew I would one day be all right. I was going to be like him. Just like him. Run faster, jump farther, play a better game of cricket than any man in the world, if I could. Yes, I reckon cricket has its point. But risking your life to thrill a crowd or prove that you're top man, that's not it."

Driffield was moved, amused, baffled; the words kicked up from the depths of an experience fixed at a childhood level, when all images are clear, all feeling reduced to simplicity, when the heart is a pure vessel, uncomplicated by doubt, scepticism. Here were the children waking from sleep and moaning and feebly crying, greeting the day with a dirge, a litany of frustration; and here was the great man, the famous athlete, bursting into their sick dormitory and dispelling the fœtid atmosphere with the cold bracing wind of the great out-doors, an heroic figure, leaving the applause and adulation of the world to succour them and to teach them.

Driffield knew all about these visits to hospitals made by so many of his colleagues from time to time as calls of conscience. He himself was a frequent visitor of children's hospitals on certain holidays. An hour or so in the sick wards, playing with the children in the garden, having tea with the older youngsters, autographing balls or cricket bats: really, it was part of the price one expected to pay for the applause, the hero-worshipping. He thought nothing of it. It was an experience forgotten as soon as he left the sick rooms and with relief tasted the air untainted by hospital smells. But Bill Townsend's experience retained all the purity of the childhood impression at which it had been arrested. To him it was the motivating force and the ultimate meaning. Driffield wondered whether the pro who had visited them indeed had suffered from infantile paralysis as a child. Not that it mattered. The purpose of the story had been served, particularly in the miracle that was Bill Townsend.

He stared at Bill, recalling for the first time a story that he had either heard or read somewhere about the bowler's triumph over a childhood illness. When he had met Bill it had been unaccountably dismissed from his mind; it was possible that he could not reconcile this powerful specimen—when Bill hurled his sixteen stone of bone and muscle at the bowling crease, every ounce of it was fulfilling a single purpose as efficiently as a mechanism—no, he could not reconcile him with the image of a seriously ailing child. He had thought that the story he had heard might be publicity.

"It really happened, then. . . ." he said. "I just couldn't believe it when I saw you."

231

Bill Townsend nodded. "At the age of ten I was learning to crawl, dragging my legs like a fox caught in a trap."

Driffield said, after a moment or two, "Well, I suppose that entitles you to see things a bit differently from the rest of us." And once again he thought of Townsend's new vocation.

"As I said," said Bill Townsend, "I can't help the way I feel about things, skipper. When the chaps try and argue with me about it they don't understand that my way is a question of *feeling,* and there's no argument to that.' '

He got up. The team's general exodus into the pavilion had made him restive.

"Don't go, Bill. You're the philosopher. Stay and philosophise. Stay and explain to me that all this is part of a daily adventure, that there is nothing final about any Test, that, win or lose, what is it but a little urn of ashes that none of us have ever seen, that it's a handful of dust. Tell me all about it, Bill."

"What's that?"

It was a wireless speaker coming from the pavilion, with a commentary of the last minutes of the game, of course. With some sort of Irish logic the players, who could not bear to stay and watch the finish, were glued to the receiver, listening to it at second hand, as though in some way the reality of the ordeal would be minimised. Both Driffield and Townsend understood simultaneously. They laughed uproariously.

Driffield was touched. When all is said there is something blessed about the eternal child in the heart of every man. And in spite of her sweet exasperation, her chiding, even, at times her anger, it was the child in him, the child that he had never had a chance to be and was always seeking, that was the mainspring of Cynthia's love for him, without her slightest conscious comprehension of it in herself. Perhaps.

Raeburn and Ryder's problem was a knotty one: one over left, one wicket to fall, eight runs to save. Raeburn reasoned

232

that with Jeffers in real fighting mood and top form the chances of his beating the clock were with him; Raeburn wanted a defensive field, four men on the boundary in the leg and on-field, one at deep mid-off. He reasoned that Jeffers would go all out for the runs, it would be a batsman's finish. Let him go for the sixes and there was a possibility of a mis-hit; otherwise convert boundaries to twos, or allow three runs to get Erskine down at the receiving end (he looked pretty groggy, and seemed to be able only to prop up the wicket as a sleeping partner). In other words, to play for a draw as first-line policy, and if possible to tempt Jeffers into error with big scoring strokes to beat the defensive field.

Ryder wanted to attack. He had it in him, he felt, for a last effort. Like Jeffers he had played himself into devastating form; he could place the ball on a half-crown, hit any stump at will; he could get the swing off the pitch, and the demon of pure pace that was in possession of him in this last over would make him the most dangerous bowler in the world. On the other hand Jeffers would be nerve-strained to breaking point in this last over, the climax of his ordeal; he would have that to contend with as well as fatigue—he had carried the burden of the batting for an hour at an intensive rate. Ryder argued that eight runs was no mean score to make in an over and under such conditions it might well prove an insupportable burden. He would not make the ball rise high on that leg field, thus obviating the danger of Jeffers tossing it over his shoulder for six as in his previous over; he could keep it low, rendering a repetition of that stroke impossible. Finally, if he had to, he could keep the runs down by sending down those dead-on shooting short-pitched ones on the leg stump against which a forcing stroke was almost out of the question—most batsmen would even be discouraged to raise their bat waist-high to counter them. Ryder's enthusiasm finally persuaded Raeburn to make a real fight of it.

Ryder placed his field accordingly: six men in the leg trap, including two at silly mid-on, one man at deep fine leg, with Fallon keeping at thirty yards behind the wicket. The barrier of fielders could almost touch each other's shoulders by stretching their arms. They stood like centurions; when the ball was played they crouched like sprinters tensed for the gunshot.

Ryder's policy was to immobilise the batsman until the last three balls of the over, when he would be forced to try to make runs . . . and then, those fast low outswingers into the leg trap

Jeffers studied the field quickly; the off side, almost denuded was a terrible temptation, but it would be impossible to turn a ball there if Ryder maintained the same accuracy he had shown in the previous over. He would have to break through the leg field.

The first ball—from a greatly reduced run—like the fast accurate yorkers of the last of Ryder's overs, had to be dead-batted into the ground. Jeffers hammered it down and both silly mid-on dived headlong; there was no chance there at all and they only got a grazed elbow for their efforts. The second ball was a replica of the preceding one and instantly Jeffers grasped Ryder's tactics. He was being forced to defend until the last three or four balls, when hitting became imperative, and then Ryder would use the leg trap.

The instant knowledge touched off instant reaction in Jeffers; instead of dead-batting he straight-drove with all his strength back to Ryder—the only forcing shot possible with any safety in the circumstances. Although his bat had not been raised more than inches from the ground in the back lift he got real venom into the drive. Ryder, conscious that there was no man covering the field behind him, had to stop the scorcher himself. He got his right hand to it—his left would not be accurate enough—and the ball smashed into the palm of it like a whip. The flesh swelled up immediately. A couple more like that and Ryder's bowling hand would be out of commission. Jeffers was countering threat with threat.

Jeffers stood, poker-faced; Ryder glowered. His glance

mingled hatred, affection, respect in almost equal proportions. As he walked back to the commencement of his run, he nursed the tingling palm thoughtfully. He had no way of meeting Jeffers's retort now. His field was set, his tactics assured; everything was in the melting-pot. There was no way back. Somehow or other he would have to get both hands to that ball next time.

Dick Sinclair, the most unremarked player on the field at this juncture, had his own view of the game: Noel Erskine. It had not taken him more than a few seconds to assess his fitness at this time of crisis. He realised that Noel could barely stand. The pains in his head had driven the colour from his face and eyes; his mouth was quivering with his efforts to suppress the agony. He leaned on his bat, swaying a little. Jeffers was not to know the state Noel was in, and Jeffers, being what he was, was obviously basing his calculation on Noel's fitness. Noel was no rabbit; he was just as capable as Jeffers of making a winning hit off the last ball of the game. Jeffers would snatch every run possible, regardless of which batsman had to face the bowler in the last crucial phase. Sinclair was worried.

Ryder bowling to Jeffers again. The same ball as last time, even a trifle shorter-pitched, almost a yorker, on the leg stump and shooting low. Jeffers, using the same retort, straight-drove with all his strength, yards wide of the bowler this time. The ball sped along the ground to deep mid-on, who was bound to intercept at the boundary. Jeffers was racing for runs. He crossed with Dick Sinclair, the fastest player on the field. Before his bat touched the crease at Noel's end he had time to mutter, "Come in, Noel . . ." and as he turned ". . . the water's lovely." He was half-way down the pitch for the third run, to leave Noel facing Ryder. Dick raced to meet him and shouted as he passed, "Run *four*!"

The throw-in would be to Ryder's end, Dick Sinclair's end on his return trip. Dick sprinted down the pitch and was in mid-stride returning before Jeffers had touched down. Jeffers had a moment's panic when he heard Sinclair's shout. He threw a glance at Noel as he raced home for the third run and turned to take the fourth: he understood. He was far slower than Dick, but home for him was the safe end, the far end from the boundary where Reynolds had fielded the ball. Dick would have to make that run during the ball's flight from fielder to bowler, who was crouching behind the stumps doing Fallon's work. Thank heavens, it wasn't Fallon behind that wicket, crouching, waiting for the ball to drop from that eighty-five-yard return hurtling out of the dazzling sun. Dick's feet hardly touched the ground. Whilst the ball was in flight he was sprinting on his toes; as it bounced in front of the wicket he sprang some twenty feet short of the crease, diving headlong, his bat outstretched. The bat crossed the crease a clear fifth of a second before Ryder tore the middle stump out of the ground, before the whole fifty thousand crowd were roaring their appeal to the umpire.

"By a neck," said Noel.

The Australian broadcast commentator was saying, ". . . and two more balls to the end of the over, with the English team requiring three runs to draw. One wicket standing . . . one wicket. . . . A supreme effort on Ryder's part, and the game will be won. Only ten minutes ago, when Sterndale broke through the English defence and scattered the wickets of Macready and Gogarty, it seemed that the game was ours, but Erskine, who had been found fit enough to stand and hold a bat, came in to put up a token resistance, the chief menace remaining Jeffers. And now only two more balls for Ryder to smash home and seal our victory. If the game goes against us we shall never forget the last minutes of supreme effort by Stern dale. Not many of us knew that at the time he was bowling his heart out in the sun, pin-pointing those deadly deliveries that turned the battle in our favour during the thrilling minutes of final testing, his wife had been undergoing a dangerous

236

operation. His fortitude, his single-mindedness during this ordeal will never be forgotten when the story of this game comes to be recounted in years to come wherever cricket lovers meet. That and the fighting heart of Ryder who in the last minutes slowed down and drove to a stop the threat of Jeffers; Jeffers, the nigger in the woodpile, the non-stop, unstoppable danger who almost forced the match from our grasp. But then came Ryder, and with him a wave of relief over the tens of thousands met on this most memorable day, for with his first ball Jeffers's onslaught broke down; his juggernaut tactics were broken. Ryder's bowling in the last two overs has been something inspired; the rate of runs has been reduced from an express rush to a mere trickle. And his work in the field has been superb. He intercepted a tremendous straight drive of Jeffers from close range, and if Reynolds's throw-in had only pitched an ace closer he would have scattered Erskine's wicket. . . . And here he comes for the tremendous all-out effort, a heroic effort in the last——"

"Well," said Wilson, cutting off the speaker with a savage twist of the knob, "I've just about had enough of Mr. Ryder's heroism. Don't they understand who the real heroes of this match are?"

"Yes, it's odd, isn't it?" said young Gogarty. "Funny the way they're on the wrong side."

Driffield was saying, ". . . thirteen men on this field and every one of them straining for the last test. The throw-in, the catch at the last minute, the unplayable ball, the slash to the boundary—every one of them has his test, hasn't he, Bill? Well, tell me this: if He really knows everything, why so many test-tubes?"

"Skipper . . . please! Not now."

A sky-blue life.
Noel leaned on his bat, his head clearing as the wave receded,

237

leaving him free for a moment to breathe, to be conscious of the sweat, the smell of the hot soil, the grass. The umpire had restored the wicket scattered by Ryder. Dick Sinclair, the side of his face bruised, grimy and a little bloody from his head-long assault on the crease, was sitting astride his bat, happily grinning at Ryder's back as the bowler walked the long trek to his bowling mark. Noel winked at Dick, who winked back.

"Five to one we make it. Good odds, Dick."

"No takers." Dick's grin widened. "I'm not breaking my neck to earn money for you."

"Shh!" said the umpire, frowning severely, as Ryder turned to bowl. Noel shielded his face conspiratorially. He mouthed the words, "Eight to one." Then the shadow of the bowler loomed up and Jeffers—no-nerves Jeffers, as fresh as ever, strain-ing like a champion at the leash, his bat raised for the final assault, shuffling forward, head forward, a hunter stalking, a boxer setting up for the kill—advanced to sweep the inswinger through the leg trap. Noel knew the stroke with a happy exult-ing knowledge; so did Dick; expert to expert, connoisseur to connoisseur. It would have been the one they would have chosen for this ball. Automatically, they tensed, mentally shaped for it, sighed with envy and affection for Jeffers in this moment of his glory. The clear music of it, the ice-fresh draught of pure achievement. How perfectly phrased was the sweep of the stroke, the bat, blade down, like an oar feather-ing the waters at Henley, cutting across the flight of the ball as the falcon swoops on its prey.

All over bar the shouting.

Driffield, in the pavilion, watching through binoculars the last stroke of the match, taking stock, profit and loss, as he did from so many years past; the pros and the cons, the lessons learned, this player and that, this surprise, that disappointment . . . *now, next time. . . .*

"Somebody must get the *ball*!"

"We've *got* it. Reynolds picked it up from the boundary and
. . . yes, I think . . . yes . . . that's friendly of him. He's
given it to Bob Jeffers."

"Yes, that's fair."

("All over . . . and not a bandit in sight, Mark. They didn't
mean it this time. Tell England! Tell England nothing. A
sleeping partner, pure and simple. Might as well have stayed
in that hospital bed. Not a smell, not a sight of it. Not even
a sitter from Foreman. Funny. I thought this time my number
was on it. *'You see, my friends, I just can't go that way. The
good Lord is saving me up for something terrible.'*)

". . . but, Noel, eight to one was ridiculous. . . ."

"Nonsense. Jeffers could have gone on all night."

"But the *clock*! Off the last ball but one of the final over!"

"How do you know it was the final over? The last one went
pretty quickly. There was all of two minutes and fifty seconds
of play left. We would have had time for another. We
walked it."